Everything That Rises Must Converge

by the same author

WISE BLOOD
THE VIOLENT BEAR IT AWAY
MYSTERY AND MANNERS: Occasional Prose
THE HABIT OF BEING: Letters

A GOOD MAN IS HARD TO FIND
(Published by The Women's Press Limited)

Everything That Rises Must Converge

Flannery O'Connor

With an Introduction by
HERMIONE LEE

FABER AND FABER
London and Boston

First published in England in 1966
by Faber and Faber Limited
3 Queen Square London WC1
First published in Faber Paperbacks 1980
Printed in Great Britain by
Whitstable Litho Ltd Whitstable

Acknowledgement is made to the editors of the following publications in whose pages some of these stories first appeared: *The Kenyon Review*, *The Sewanee Review*, *New World Writing*, *Partisan Review*, *Esquire*, and *Harper's Bazaar*.

British Library Cataloguing in Publication Data

O'Connor, Flannery
Everything that rises must converge.
I. Title
823' .9'1FS PS3565.C57E/

ISBN 0-571-11614-0

Contents

INTRODUCTION

Since Flannery O'Connor's death in 1964 at the age of thirty-nine, and the posthumous publication of these stories in the following year, her reputation has grown only slowly in England, though she has been highly regarded in America since the fifties. This neglect is understandable. It is a modest opus: two novels, *Wise Blood* (1952) and *The Violent Bear It Away* (1960); two volumes of stories, this one and *A Good Man is Hard to Find* (1955); a collection of essays and prose pieces, *Mystery and Manners*, edited by her friends Robert and Sally Fitzgerald in 1969, and the magnificent letters, selected by Sally Fitzgerald in 1979 under the title *The Habit of Being*. English readers may have been put off by her recondite titles, or even by her name, which, as with other under-valued writers of the Deep South—Eudora Welty, Walker Percy—has a bizarre ring to our ears. And there may have been a tendency to bracket her with Carson McCullers (whose work she "disliked intensely") as an imitator of Faulkner (whom she avoided reading), one of the "Southern School". The term, she says, "conjures up an image of Gothic monstrosities and the idea of a preoccupation with everything deformed and grotesque. Most of us are considered, I believe, to be unhappy combinations of Poe and Erskine Caldwell." The truck driver in *The Violent Bear It Away* might be O'Connor's average reader:

> "You belong in the booby hatch," the driver muttered. "You ride through these states and you see they all belong in it. I won't see nobody sane again until I get back to Detroit."

Even where her achievement has been recognized, it has also been misunderstood. Flannery O'Connor writes from the standpoint of Catholic orthodoxy: her novels describe the torments of the reluctant saint or prophet, her stories enact the descent of the Holy Ghost ("The Enduring Chill"), visions of Purgatory ("Revelation"), and the mystery of the Incarnation ("Parker's Back"). She knows this means trouble:

> One of the awful things about writing when you are a Christian is that for you the ultimate reality is the Incarnation, the present reality is the Incarnation, and nobody believes in the Incarnation; that is, nobody in your audience. My audience are the people who think God is dead.

The very cause of her neglect here—the conjunction of a particular geographical and spiritual locale—is what makes Flannery O'Connor a remarkable figure. As a Catholic Southerner, she is "bound through the senses to a particular society and a particular history" in which she is "both native and alien". She finds herself infinitely more in sympathy with the religious enthusiasm and scripture-ridden language of the Protestant, fundamentalist, rural South than with the liberal humanism, the secular urban materialism of the more "advanced" states. "Technology without Christianity is, I think, barbarism quite simply." In fact the phrase is Allen Tate's (from "The New Provincialism", 1945). O'Connor's affinity with Agrarianism has been noticed: the Fugitive symposium *I'll Take My Stand* (1930) similarly sets a Southern, rural, conservative, Christian ethos against the encroachments of Northern, homogenizing industrialism. John Crowe Ransom published some of O'Connor's stories in the *Kenyon Review*, and Allen Tate's wife Caroline Gordon was a close friend and literary advisor.

But though O'Connor has a strange feeling of "kinship" with her environment, at the same time she finds the "do-it-yourself" religion of the South "painful and touching and grimly comic". "Wise blood has to be these people's means of grace—they have no sacraments." The grotesqueness and violence which characterize her stories arise directly out of the peculiar yet fruitful clash between her belief and her materials. Ultimately her plot is always the same: characters who are "freaks" because "they have no sacraments"—but whose cast of mind makes them particularly susceptible to ideas of salvation and damnation—are violently introduced to the possibility of grace. The violence is a factor both of the region's primitive, dramatic religious imagination, lacking dogma and formality, and of the writer's need to spell things out to a secular audience: "You have to make your vision apparent by shock—to the hard of hearing you shout, and for the almost blind you draw large and startling figures."

Though, like Faulkner, Flannery O'Connor spent most of her life in the same part of the Deep South, this confinement was not, in the first instance, voluntary. She lived with her mother on a dairy farm near Milledgeville, Georgia, where, in between writing and going on lecture tours, she raised peacocks, Muscovy ducks and Chinese geese. But between the ages of twenty and twenty-five she went away. She took an M.A. in writing at Iowa, worked at the writers' colony, Yaddo (with Robert Lowell and Elizabeth Hardwick, among others), and lived for two years in Connecticut with the Fitzgeralds. Nor did she become an unworldly recluse. She kept keenly abreast of new fiction and criticism, and her letters, especially to her agent Elizabeth McKee, are very sharp about contracts and options, and stand no nonsense from publishers asking her to write more "conventional" novels.

But in 1951 she developed disseminated lupus erythematosus ("or as we litterary [*sic*] people prefer to call it, Red Wolf"), an incurable disease of metabolic origin from which her father had died when she was fifteen. Lupus could be controlled by steroids, but necessitated a life of extreme restrictions: a totally salt-free diet, no exposure to sunlight, daily treatment, and very short working hours: "It takes seven years to write a novel. The four-hour week." The mental effects of the disease are incalculable, and the treatments also took their toll. By 1955 she was on crutches—the steroids caused bone disintegration—and in 1963, when the lupus was dormant, she developed anaemia from a fibroid tumour. The operation for its removal reactivated the lupus, and she died soon after.

The restrictions of her life make themselves felt in the stories in the powerful treatment of intractable hostilities within families (especially in "A View from the Woods" and "Greenleaf") and in the enraged frustration of those characters—Asbury in "The Enduring Chill", Julian in the title story, Mary Grace in "Revelation"—who feel themselves, as O'Connor did when she first had to come back to the South, to be "roped and tied and resigned the way it is necessary to be resigned to death". Quoting Braque in the letters, she says, "I like the rule that corrects the emotions": and correction, resignation, are the key to her life and work. Both are shaped by what Teilhard de Chardin, in *The Divine Milieu*, calls "passive diminishments": "those afflictions that you can't get rid of and have to bear." There is a manifest parallel between the restrictions of her own life, the disciplines which she imposes on the characters in her stories, and the rigorous, exacting "corrections" which she made to her writing—finding it hard to part with the stories, and frequently coming to dislike them after they were published.

O'Connor's admiration for Père Teilhard, a palaeontologist, a Jesuit and a mystic, is expressed in the title of this volume, which is taken from his theory in *The Phenomenon of Man* that the universe is in a continuous process of upward, anti-entropic convergence towards "point Omega", the ultimate, mysterious, central "Great Presence". Love is the agent of convergence; egoism, élitism, racism and ignorance are retrograde, dragging the world "backwards towards plurality and into matter".

> The outcome of the world, the gates of the future, the entry into the super-human—these are not thrown open to a few of the privileged nor to one chosen people

to the exclusion of all others. They will open to an advance of *all together*, in a direction in which *all together* can join and find completion in a spiritual renovation of the earth.

Evidently, Julian, in the title story, despising his mother's absurd family pride, pleased with his own rational liberalism, looking out at the South from "the inner compartment of his mind where he spent most of his time," is a long way from "point Omega". The principle of convergence seems to be satirized by Julian's mother's insensitive comments on her "coloured friends" ("They should rise, yes, but on their own side of the fence") and by the ridiculous coincidence of the identical hats worn by the white and the black mother on the integrated bus. O'Connor casts a bleak, caustic eye on race relations in the South, and is not interested in voicing outrage or sympathy: "I say a plague on everybody's houses as far as the race business goes." Nevertheless, the story does effect an unexpected and alarming "spiritual renovation". Julian is catapulted into the purgatorial world "of guilt and sorrow", and Teilhard de Chardin's proposition is proved by the action of grace upon distorted, negative, retrograde materials.

That is the characteristic programme of an O'Connor story (and, indeed, the same stories recur: "Judgement Day" reworks an early piece called "The Geranium", and "The Lame Shall Enter First" is another version of *The Violent Bear It Away*). Smug, hard-working women like Mrs. May in "Greenleaf" and Mrs. Turpin in "Revelation", who consider themselves good Christians, are granted "an abysmal life-giving knowledge": that they have no "insurance", that their very virtues will have to be "burned away". Liberal intellectuals, sceptics, rationalists—of whom the ironically-named social worker Mr. Sheppard, in "The Lame Shall Enter First", is the most pitiful example—are found painfully wanting. The most grotesque figures—Sheppard's club-footed delinquent boy protégé, the hideous Mary Grace in "Revelation"—prove to be prophets and agents of grace; the most unlikely characters—the coarse priest in "The Enduring Chill", the white-trash faith-healer in "Greenleaf"—are vessels of truth. The very landscapes which the characters inhabit ominously display the waiting presence of Christ: again and again the sun looms threateningly on the horizon, like "someone wounded behind the woods", or like "a strange potentate", or as though about to "burst through the tree line". The stories drive on relentlessly to the point at which grace is offered: "I can't allow any of my characters . . . to stop in some half-way position. This doubtless comes of a Catholic education and a Catholic sense of history—everything works toward its true end or away from it, everything is ultimately saved or lost."

Not all the stories end as explicitly as "The Enduring Chill", but all move towards this pentecostal arrest:

> The boy fell back on his pillow and stared at the ceiling. His limbs that had been racked for so many weeks by fever and chill were numb now. The old life in him was exhausted. He awaited the coming of new. It was then that he felt the beginning of a chill, a chill so peculiar, so light that it was like a warm ripple across a deeper sea of cold. His breath came short. The fierce bird which throughout the years of his childhood and the days of his illness had been poised over his head,

> waiting mysteriously, appeared all at once to be in motion. Asbury blanched and the last film of illusion was torn as if by a whirlwind from his eyes. He saw that for the rest of his days, frail, racked, but enduring, he would live in the face of a purifying terror. A feeble cry, a last impossible protest escaped him. But the Holy Ghost, emblazoned in ice instead of fire, continued, implacable, to descend.

This stark vision takes its strength from the lucid, passionate, exact prose in which it is couched, and from the unerring authenticity of the comedy which leads up to it: it is important that Asbury should be suffering from undulant fever after having drunk unpasteurized milk while showing off to his mother's Negro farm-hands. That comic level is superbly established in all the stories: Mrs. May's visit to the Greenleaf boys' milking parlour, the conversation in the doctor's waiting room in "Revelation", and the behaviour of the sheriff in "The Comforts of Home" are fine examples. The power of the stories lies in the suppression of their severely orthodox subject beneath a brilliantly sustained commonplace surface, or what O'Connor calls the convergence of a sense of "mystery" with a sense of "manners". Her term for this marriage of the moral and the dramatic faculty, drawn, characteristically, from medieval Scriptural commentaries, is "anagogical vision . . . the kind of vision that is able to see different levels of reality in one image or one situation . . . an enlarged view of the human scene."

HERMIONE LEE, 1980

Quotations from Flannery O'Connor are taken from *The Habit of Being: Letters* by Flannery O'Connor, selected and edited by Sally Fitzgerald, Farrar, Straus and Giroux, Faber, 1979; and from *Mystery and Manners: Occasional Prose*, selected and edited by Sally and Robert Fitzgerald, Farrar, Straus and Giroux, 1969. Accounts of O'Connor's relation to Agrarianism can be found in *The Added Dimension: The Art and Mind of Flannery O'Connor*, edited by Melvin Friedman and Lewis Lawson, Fordham University Press, New York, 1966. The quotation from Teilhard de Chardin is taken from *The Phenomenon of Man*, translated by Bernard Wall, with an introduction by Julian Huxley, Collins, 1961.

Everything That Rises Must Converge

Everything That Rises Must Converge

Her doctor had told Julian's mother that she must lose twenty pounds on account of her blood pressure, so on Wednesday nights Julian had to take her downtown on the bus for a reducing class at the Y. The reducing class was designed for working girls over fifty, who weighed from 165 to 200 pounds. His mother was one of the slimmer ones, but she said ladies did not tell their age or weight. She would not ride the buses by herself at night since they had been integrated, and because the reducing class was one of her few pleasures, necessary for her health, and *free*, she said Julian could at least put himself out to take her, considering all she did for him. Julian did not like to consider all she did for him, but every Wednesday night he braced himself and took her.

She was almost ready to go, standing before the hall mirror, putting on her hat, while he, his hands behind him, appeared pinned to the door frame, waiting like Saint

Sebastian for the arrows to begin piercing him. The hat was new and had cost her seven dollars and a half. She kept saying, "Maybe I shouldn't have paid that for it. No, I shouldn't have. I'll take it off and return it tomorrow. I shouldn't have bought it."

Julian raised his eyes to heaven. "Yes, you should have bought it," he said. "Put it on and let's go." It was a hideous hat. A purple velvet flap came down on one side of it and stood up on the other; the rest of it was green and looked like a cushion with the stuffing out. He decided it was less comical than jaunty and pathetic. Everything that gave her pleasure was small and depressed him.

She lifted the hat one more time and set it down slowly on top of her head. Two wings of gray hair protruded on either side of her florid face, but her eyes, sky-blue, were as innocent and untouched by experience as they must have been when she was ten. Were it not that she was a widow who had struggled fiercely to feed and clothe and put him through school and who was supporting him still, "until he got on his feet," she might have been a little girl that he had to take to town.

"It's all right, it's all right," he said. "Let's go." He opened the door himself and started down the walk to get her going. The sky was a dying violet and the houses stood out darkly against it, bulbous liver-colored monstrosities of a uniform ugliness though no two were alike. Since this had been a fashionable neighborhood forty years ago, his mother persisted in thinking they did well to have an apartment in it. Each house had a narrow collar of dirt around it in which sat, usually, a grubby child. Julian walked with his hands in his pockets, his head down and thrust forward and his eyes glazed with the determination to make himself completely numb during the time he would be sacrificed to her pleasure.

The door closed and he turned to find the dumpy figure, surmounted by the atrocious hat, coming toward him. "Well," she said, "you only live once and paying a little more for it, I at least won't meet myself coming and going."

"Some day I'll start making money," Julian said gloomily —he knew he never would—"and you can have one of those jokes whenever you take the fit." But first they would move. He visualized a place where the nearest neighbors would be three miles away on either side.

"I think you're doing fine," she said, drawing on her gloves. "You've only been out of school a year. Rome wasn't built in a day."

She was one of the few members of the Y reducing class who arrived in hat and gloves and who had a son who had been to college. "It takes time," she said, "and the world is in such a mess. This hat looked better on me than any of the others, though when she brought it out I said, 'Take that thing back. I wouldn't have it on my head,' and she said, 'Now wait till you see it on,' and when she put it on me, I said, 'We-ull,' and she said, 'If you ask me, that hat does something for you and you do something for the hat, and besides,' she said, 'with that hat, you won't meet yourself coming and going.' "

Julian thought he could have stood his lot better if she had been selfish, if she had been an old hag who drank and screamed at him. He walked along, saturated in depression, as if in the midst of his martyrdom he had lost his faith. Catching sight of his long, hopeless, irritated face, she stopped suddenly with a grief-stricken look, and pulled back on his arm. "Wait on me," she said. "I'm going back to the house and take this thing off and tomorrow I'm going to return it. I was out of my head. I can pay the gas bill with that seven-fifty."

He caught her arm in a vicious grip. "You are not going to take it back," he said. "I like it."

"Well," she said, "I don't think I ought . . ."

"Shut up and enjoy it," he muttered, more depressed than ever.

"With the world in the mess it's in," she said, "it's a wonder we can enjoy anything. I tell you, the bottom rail is on the top."

Julian sighed.

"Of course," she said, "if you know who you are, you can go anywhere." She said this every time he took her to the reducing class. "Most of them in it are not our kind of people," she said, "but I can be gracious to anybody. I know who I am."

"They don't give a damn for your graciousness," Julian said savagely. "Knowing who you are is good for one generation only. You haven't the foggiest idea where you stand now or who you are."

She stopped and allowed her eyes to flash at him. "I most certainly do know who I am," she said, "and if you don't know who you are, I'm ashamed of you."

"Oh hell," Julian said.

"Your great-grandfather was a former governor of this state," she said. "Your grandfather was a prosperous landowner. Your grandmother was a Godhigh."

"Will you look around you," he said tensely, "and see where you are now?" and he swept his arm jerkily out to indicate the neighborhood, which the growing darkness at least made less dingy.

"You remain what you are," she said. "Your great-grandfather had a plantation and two hundred slaves."

"There are no more slaves," he said irritably.

"They were better off when they were," she said. He

groaned to see that she was off on that topic. She rolled onto it every few days like a train on an open track. He knew every stop, every junction, every swamp along the way, and knew the exact point at which her conclusion would roll majestically into the station: "It's ridiculous. It's simply not realistic. They should rise, yes, but on their own side of the fence."

"Let's skip it," Julian said.

"The ones I feel sorry for," she said, "are the ones that are half white. They're tragic."

"Will you skip it?"

"Suppose we were half white. We would certainly have mixed feelings."

"I have mixed feelings now," he groaned.

"Well let's talk about something pleasant," she said. "I remember going to Grandpa's when I was a little girl. Then the house had double stairways that went up to what was really the second floor—all the cooking was done on the first. I used to like to stay down in the kitchen on account of the way the walls smelled. I would sit with my nose pressed against the plaster and take deep breaths. Actually the place belonged to the Godhighs but your grandfather Chestny paid the mortgage and saved it for them. They were in reduced circumstances," she said, "but reduced or not, they never forgot who they were."

"Doubtless that decayed mansion reminded them," Julian muttered. He never spoke of it without contempt or thought of it without longing. He had seen it once when he was a child before it had been sold. The double stairways had rotted and been torn down. Negroes were living it it. But it remained in his mind as his mother had known it. It appeared in his dreams regularly. He would stand on the wide porch, listening to the rustle of oak leaves, then wander through the high-ceilinged hall into the parlor that opened onto it and gaze at the worn rugs and faded draperies. It occurred to him that it was he, not she, who could have appreciated it. He preferred its threadbare elegance to anything he could name and it was because of it that all the neighborhoods they had lived in had been a torment to him—whereas she had hardly known the difference. She called her insensitivity "being adjustable."

"And I remember the old darky who was my nurse, Caroline. There was no better person in the world. I've always had a great respect for my colored friends," she said. "I'd do anything in the world for them and they'd . . ."

"Will you for God's sake get off that subject?" Julian said. When he got on a bus by himself, he made it a point to sit down beside a Negro, in reparation as it were for his mother's sins.

"You're mighty touchy tonight," she said. "Do you feel all right?"

"Yes I feel all right," he said. "Now lay off."

She pursed her lips. "Well, you certainly are in a vile humor," she observed. "I just won't speak to you at all."

They had reached the bus stop. There was no bus in sight and Julian, his hands still jammed in his pockets and his head thrust forward, scowled down the empty street. The frustration of having to wait on the bus as well as ride on it began to creep up his neck like a hot hand. The presence of his mother was borne in upon him as she gave a pained sigh. He looked at her bleakly. She was holding herself very erect under the preposterous hat, wearing it like a banner of her imaginary dignity. There was in him an evil urge to break her spirit. He suddenly unloosened his tie and pulled it off and put it in his pocket.

She stiffened. "Why must you look like *that* when you

take me to town?" she said. "Why must you deliberately embarrass me?"

"If you'll never learn where you are," he said, "you can at least learn where I am."

"You look like a—thug," she said.

"Then I must be one," he murmured.

"I'll just go home," she said. "I will not bother you. If you can't do a little thing like that for me . . ."

Rolling his eyes upward, he put his tie back on. "Restored to my class," he muttered. He thrust his face toward her and hissed, "True culture is in the mind, the *mind,*" he said, and tapped his head, "the mind."

"It's in the heart," she said, "and in how you do things and how you do things is because of who you *are.*"

"Nobody in the damn bus cares who you are."

"I care who I am," she said icily.

The lighted bus appeared on top of the next hill and as it approached, they moved out into the street to meet it. He put his hand under her elbow and hoisted her up on the creaking step. She entered with a little smile, as if she were going into a drawing room where everyone had been waiting for her. While he put in the tokens, she sat down on one of the broad front seats for three which faced the aisle. A thin woman with protruding teeth and long yellow hair was sitting on the end of it. His mother moved up beside her and left room for Julian beside herself. He sat down and looked at the floor across the aisle where a pair of thin feet in red and white canvas sandals were planted.

His mother immediately began a general conversation meant to attract anyone who felt like talking. "Can it get any hotter?" she said and removed from her purse a folding fan, black with a Japanese scene on it, which she began to flutter before her.

"I reckon it might could," the woman with the protruding teeth said, "but I know for a fact my apartment couldn't get no hotter."

"It must get the afternoon sun," his mother said. She sat forward and looked up and down the bus. It was half filled. Everybody was white. "I see we have the bus to ourselves," she said. Julian cringed.

"For a change," said the woman across the aisle, the owner of the red and white canvas sandals. "I come on one the other day and they were thick as fleas—up front and all through."

"The world is in a mess everywhere," his mother said. "I don't know how we've let it get in this fix."

"What gets my goat is all those boys from good families stealing automobile tires," the woman with the protruding teeth said. "I told my boy, I said you may not be rich but you been raised right and if I ever catch you in any such mess, they can send you on to the reformatory. Be exactly where you belong."

"Training tells," his mother said. "Is your boy in high school?"

"Ninth grade," the woman said.

"My son just finished college last year. He wants to write but he's selling typewriters until he gets started," his mother said.

The woman leaned forward and peered at Julian. He threw her such a malevolent look that she subsided against the seat. On the floor across the aisle there was an abandoned newspaper. He got up and got it and opened it out in front of him. His mother discreetly continued the conversation in a lower tone but the woman across the aisle said in a loud voice, "Well that's nice. Selling typewriters is close to writing. He can go right from one to the other."

"I tell him," his mother said, "that Rome wasn't built in a day."

Behind the newspaper Julian was withdrawing into the inner compartment of his mind where he spent most of his time. This was a kind of mental bubble in which he established himself when he could not bear to be a part of what was going on around him. From it he could see out and judge but in it he was safe from any kind of penetration from without. It was the only place where he felt free of the general idiocy of his fellows. His mother had never entered it but from it he could see her with absolute clarity.

The old lady was clever enough and he thought that if she had started from any of the right premises, more might have been expected of her. She lived according to the laws of her own fantasy world, outside of which he had never seen her set foot. The law of it was to sacrifice herself for him after she had first created the necessity to do so by making a mess of things. If he had permitted her sacrifices, it was only because her lack of foresight had made them necessary. All of her life had been a struggle to act like a Chestny without the Chestny goods, and to give him everything she thought a Chestny ought to have; but since, said she, it was fun to struggle, why complain? And when you had won, as she had won, what fun to look back on the hard times! He could not forgive her that she had enjoyed the struggle and that she thought *she* had won.

What she meant when she said she had won was that she had brought him up successfully and had sent him to college and that he had turned out so well—good looking (her teeth had gone unfilled so that his could be straightened), intelligent (he realized he was too intelligent to be a success), and with a future ahead of him (there was of course no future ahead of him). She excused his gloominess on the grounds that he was still growing up and his radical ideas on his lack of practical experience. She said he didn't yet know a thing about "life," that he hadn't even entered the real world—when already he was as disenchanted with it as a man of fifty.

The further irony of all this was that in spite of her, he had turned out so well. In spite of going to only a third-rate college, he had, on his own initiative, come out with a first-rate education; in spite of growing up dominated by a small mind, he had ended up with a large one; in spite of all her foolish views, he was free of prejudice and unafraid to face facts. Most miraculous of all, instead of being blinded by love for her as she was for him, he had cut himself emotionally free of her and could see her with complete objectivity. He was not dominated by his mother.

The bus stopped with a sudden jerk and shook him from his meditation. A woman from the back lurched forward with little steps and barely escaped falling in his newspaper as she righted herself. She got off and a large Negro got on. Julian kept his paper lowered to watch. It gave him a certain satisfaction to see injustice in daily operation. It confirmed his view that with a few exceptions there was no one worth knowing within a radius of three hundred miles. The Negro was well dressed and carried a briefcase. He looked around and then sat down on the other end of the seat where the woman with the red and white canvas sandals was sitting. He immediately unfolded a newspaper and obscured himself behind it. Julian's mother's elbow at once prodded insistently into his ribs. "Now you see why I won't ride on these buses by myself," she whispered.

The woman with the red and white canvas sandals had risen at the same time the Negro sat down and had gone further back in the bus and taken the seat of the woman who had got off. His mother leaned forward and cast her an approving look.

Julian rose, crossed the aisle, and sat down in the place of the woman with the canvas sandals. From this position, he looked serenely across at his mother. Her face had turned an angry red. He stared at her, making his eyes the eyes of a stranger. He felt his tension suddenly lift as if he had openly declared war on her.

He would have liked to get in conversation with the Negro and to talk with him about art or politics or any subject that would be above the comprehension of those around them, but the man remained entrenched behind his paper. He was either ignoring the change of seating or had never noticed it. There was no way for Julian to convey his sympathy.

His mother kept her eyes fixed reproachfully on his face. The woman with the protruding teeth was looking at him avidly as if he were a type of monster new to her.

"Do you have a light?" he asked the Negro.

Without looking away from his paper, the man reached in his pocket and handed him a packet of matches.

"Thanks," Julian said. For a moment he held the matches foolishly. A NO SMOKING sign looked down upon him from over the door. This alone would not have deterred him; he had no cigarettes. He had quit smoking some months before because he could not afford it. "Sorry," he muttered and handed back the matches. The Negro lowered the paper and gave him an annoyed look. He took the matches and raised the paper again.

His mother continued to gaze at him but she did not take advantage of his momentary discomfort. Her eyes retained their battered look. Her face seemed to be unnaturally red, as if her blood pressure had risen. Julian allowed no glimmer of sympathy to show on his face. Having got the advantage, he wanted desperately to keep it and carry it through. He would have liked to teach her a lesson that would last her a while, but there seemed no way to continue the point. The Negro refused to come out from behind his paper.

Julian folded his arms and looked stolidly before him, facing her but as if he did not see her, as if he had ceased to recognize her existence. He visualized a scene in which, the bus having reached their stop, he would remain in his seat and when she said, "Aren't you going to get off?" he would look at her as at a stranger who had rashly addressed him. The corner they got off on was usually deserted, but it was well lighted and it would not hurt her to walk by herself the four blocks to the Y. He decided to wait until the time came and then decide whether or not he would let her get off by herself. He would have to be at the Y at ten to bring her back, but he could leave her wondering if he was going to show up. There was no reason for her to think she could always depend on him.

He retired again into the high-ceilinged room sparsely settled with large pieces of antique furniture. His soul expanded momentarily but then he became aware of his mother across from him and the vision shriveled. He studied her coldly. Her feet in little pumps dangled like a child's and did not quite reach the floor. She was training on him an exaggerated look of reproach. He felt completely detached from her. At that moment he could with pleasure have slapped her as he would have slapped a particularly obnoxious child in his charge.

He began to imagine various unlikely ways by which he could teach her a lesson. He might make friends with some distinguished Negro professor or lawyer and bring him home to spend the evening. He would be entirely justified but her blood pressure would rise to 300. He could not push her to the extent of making her have a stroke, and moreover, he had never been successful at making any Negro friends. He had tried to strike up an acquaintance on the bus with some of the better types, with ones that looked like professors or ministers or lawyers. One morning he had sat down next to a distinguished-looking dark brown man who had answered his questions with a sonorous solemnity but who had turned out to be an undertaker. Another day he had sat down beside a cigar-smoking Negro with a diamond ring on his finger, but after a few stilted pleasantries, the Negro had rung the buzzer and risen, slipping two lottery tickets into Julian's hand as he climbed over him to leave.

He imagined his mother lying desperately ill and his being able to secure only a Negro doctor for her. He toyed with that idea for a few minutes and then dropped it for a momentary vision of himself participating as a sympathizer in a sit-in demonstration. This was possible but he did not linger with it. Instead, he approached the ultimate horror. He brought home a beautiful suspiciously Negroid woman. Prepare yourself, he said. There is nothing you can do about it. This is the woman I've chosen. She's intelligent, dignified, even good, and she's suffered and she hasn't thought it *fun*. Now persecute us, go ahead and persecute us. Drive her out of here, but remember, you're driving me too. His eyes were narrowed and through the indignation he had generated, he saw his mother across the aisle, purple-faced, shrunken to the dwarf-like proportions of her moral nature, sitting like a mummy beneath the ridiculous banner of her hat.

He was tilted out of his fantasy again as the bus stopped. The door opened with a sucking hiss and out of the dark a large, gaily dressed, sullen-looking colored woman got on with a little boy. The child, who might have been four, had on a short plaid suit and a Tyrolean hat with a blue feather in it. Julian hoped that he would sit down beside him and that the woman would push in beside his mother. He could think of no better arrangement.

As she waited for her tokens, the woman was surveying the seating possibilities—he hoped with the idea of sitting where she was least wanted. There was something familiar-looking about her but Julian could not place what it was. She was a giant of a woman. Her face was set not only to meet opposition but to seek it out. The downward tilt of her large lower lip was like a warning sign: DON'T TAMPER WITH ME. Her bulging figure was encased in a green crepe dress and her feet overflowed in red shoes. She had on a hideous hat. A purple velvet flap came down on one side of it and stood up on the other; the rest of it was green and looked like a cushion with the stuffing out. She carried a mammoth red pocketbook that bulged throughout as if it were stuffed with rocks.

To Julian's disappointment, the little boy climbed up on the empty seat beside his mother. His mother lumped all children, black and white, into the common category, "cute," and she thought little Negroes were on the whole cuter than little white children. She smiled at the little boy as he climbed on the seat.

Meanwhile the woman was bearing down upon the empty seat beside Julian. To his annoyance, she squeezed herself into it. He saw his mother's face change as the woman settled herself next to him and he realized with satisfaction that this was more objectionable to her than it was to him. Her face seemed almost gray and there was a look of dull recognition in her eyes, as if suddenly she had sickened at some awful confrontation. Julian saw that it was because she and the woman had, in a sense, swapped sons. Though his mother would not realize the symbolic significance of this, she would feel it. His amusement showed plainly on his face.

The woman next to him muttered something unintelligible to herself. He was conscious of a kind of bristling next to him, a muted growling like that of an angry cat. He could not see anything but the red pocketbook upright on the bulging green thighs. He visualized the woman as she had stood waiting for her tokens—the ponderous figure, rising from the red shoes upward over the solid hips, the mammoth bosom, the haughty face, to the green and purple hat.

His eyes widened.

The vision of the two hats, identical, broke upon him with the radiance of a brilliant sunrise. His face was suddenly lit with joy. He could not believe that Fate had thrust upon his mother such a lesson. He gave a loud chuckle so that she would look at him and see that he saw. She turned her eyes on him slowly. The blue in them seemed to have turned a bruised purple. For a moment he had an uncomfortable sense of her innocence, but it lasted only a second before principle rescued him. Justice entitled him to laugh. His grin hardened until it said to her as plainly as if he were saying aloud: Your punishment exactly fits your pettiness. This should teach you a permanent lesson.

Her eyes shifted to the woman. She seemed unable to bear looking at him and to find the woman preferable. He became conscious again of the bristling presence at his side. The woman was rumbling like a volcano about to become active. His mother's mouth began to twitch slightly at one corner. With a sinking heart, he saw incipient signs of recovery on her face and realized that this was going to strike her suddenly as funny and was going to be no lesson at all. She kept her eyes on the woman and an amused smile came over her face as if the woman were a monkey that had stolen her hat. The little Negro was looking up at her with large fascinated eyes. He had been trying to attract her attention for some time.

"Carver!" the woman said suddenly. "Come heah!"

When he saw that the spotlight was on him at last, Carver drew his feet up and turned himself toward Julian's mother and giggled.

"Carver!" the woman said. "You heah me? Come heah!"

Carver slid down from the seat but remained squatting with his back against the base of it, his head turned slyly around toward Julian's mother, who was smiling at him. The woman reached a hand across the aisle and snatched him to her. He righted himself and hung backwards on her knees, grinning at Julian's mother. "Isn't he cute?" Julian's mother said to the woman with the protruding teeth.

"I reckon he is," the woman said without conviction.

The Negress yanked him upright but he eased out of her grip and shot across the aisle and scrambled, giggling wildly, onto the seat beside his love.

"I think he likes me," Julian's mother said, and smiled at the woman. It was the smile she used when she was being particularly gracious to an inferior. Julian saw everything lost. The lesson had rolled off her like rain on a roof.

The woman stood up and yanked the little boy off the seat as if she were snatching him from contagion. Julian could feel the rage in her at having no weapon like his mother's smile. She gave the child a sharp slap across his leg. He howled once and then thrust his head into her stomach and kicked his feet against her shins. "Be-have," she said vehemently.

The bus stopped and the Negro who had been reading the newspaper got off. The woman moved over and set the little boy down with a thump between herself and Julian. She held him firmly by the knee. In a moment he put his hands in front of his face and peeped at Julian's mother through his fingers.

"I see yoooooooo!" she said and put her hand in front of her face and peeped at him.

The woman slapped his hand down. "Quit yo' foolishness," she said, "before I knock the living Jesus out of you!"

Julian was thankful that the next stop was theirs. He reached up and pulled the cord. The woman reached up and pulled it at the same time. Oh my God, he thought. He had the terrible intuition that when they got off the bus together, his mother would open her purse and give the little boy a nickel. The gesture would be as natural to her as breathing. The bus stopped and the woman got up and lunged to the front, dragging the child, who wished to stay on, after her. Julian and his mother got up and followed. As they neared the door, Julian tried to relieve her of her pocketbook.

"No," she murmured, "I want to give the little boy a nickel."

"No!" Julian hissed. "No!"

She smiled down at the child and opened her bag. The bus door opened and the woman picked him up by the arm and descended with him, hanging at her hip. Once in the street she set him down and shook him.

Julian's mother had to close her purse while she got down the bus step but as soon as her feet were on the ground, she opened it again and began to rummage inside. "I can't find but a penny," she whispered, "but it looks like a new one."

"Don't do it!" Julian said fiercely between his teeth. There was a streetlight on the corner and she hurried to get under it so that she could better see into her pocketbook. The woman was heading off rapidly down the street with the child still hanging backward on her hand.

"Oh little boy!" Julian's mother called and took a few quick steps and caught up with them just beyond the lamp-post. "Here's a bright new penny for you," and she held out the coin, which shone bronze in the dim light.

The huge woman turned and for a moment stood, her shoulders lifted and her face frozen with frustrated rage, and stared at Julian's mother. Then all at once she seemed to explode like a piece of machinery that had been given one ounce of pressure too much. Julian saw the black fist swing out with the red pocketbook. He shut his eyes and cringed as he heard the woman shout, "He don't take nobody's pennies!" When he opened his eyes, the woman was disappearing down the street with the little boy staring wide-eyed over her shoulder. Julian's mother was sitting on the sidewalk.

"I told you not to do that," Julian said angrily. "I told you not to do that!"

He stood over her for a minute, gritting his teeth. Her legs were stretched out in front of her and her hat was on her lap. He squatted down and looked her in the face. It was totally expressionless. "You got exactly what you deserved," he said. "Now get up."

He picked up her pocketbook and put what had fallen out back in it. He picked the hat up off her lap. The penny caught his eye on the sidewalk and he picked that up and let it drop before her eyes into the purse. Then he stood up and leaned over and held his hands out to pull her up. She remained immobile. He sighed. Rising above them on either side were black apartment buildings, marked with irregular rectangles of light. At the end of the block a man came out of a door and walked off in the opposite direction. "All right," he said, "suppose somebody happens by and wants to know why you're sitting on the sidewalk?"

She took the hand and, breathing hard, pulled heavily up on it and then stood for a moment, swaying slightly as if the spots of light in the darkness were circling around her. Her eyes, shadowed and confused, finally settled on his face. He did not try to conceal his irritation. "I hope this teaches you a lesson," he said. She leaned forward and her eyes raked his face. She seemed trying to determine his identity. Then, as if she found nothing familiar about him, she started off with a headlong movement in the wrong direction.

"Aren't you going on to the Y?" he asked.

"Home," she muttered.

"Well, are we walking?"

For answer she kept going. Julian followed along, his hands behind him. He saw no reason to let the lesson she had had go without backing it up with an explanation of its meaning. She might as well be made to understand what had happened to her. "Don't think that was just an uppity Negro woman," he said. "That was the whole colored race which will no longer take your condescending pennies. That was your black double. She can wear the same hat as you, and to be sure," he added gratuitously (because he thought it was funny), "it looked better on her than it did on you. What all this means," he said, "is that the old world is gone. The old manners are obsolete and your graciousness is not worth a damn." He thought bitterly of the house that had been lost for him. "You aren't who you think you are," he said.

She continued to plow ahead, paying no attention to him. Her hair had come undone on one side. She dropped her pocketbook and took no notice. He stooped and picked it up and handed it to her but she did not take it.

"You needn't act as if the world had come to an end," he said, "because it hasn't. From now on you've got to live in a new world and face a few realities for a change. Buck up," he said, "it won't kill you."

She was breathing fast.

"Let's wait on the bus," he said.

"Home," she said thickly.

"I hate to see you behave like this," he said. "Just like a child. I should be able to expect more of you." He decided to stop where he was and make her stop and wait for a bus. "I'm not going any farther," he said, stopping. "We're going on the bus."

She continued to go on as if she had not heard him. He took a few steps and caught her arm and stopped her. He looked into her face and caught his breath. He was looking into a face he had never seen before. "Tell Grandpa to come get me," she said.

He stared, stricken.

"Tell Caroline to come get me," she said.

Stunned, he let her go and she lurched forward again, walking as if one leg were shorter than the other. A tide of darkness seemed to be sweeping her from him. "Mother!" he cried. "Darling, sweetheart, wait!" Crumpling, she fell to the pavement. He dashed forward and fell at her side, crying, "Mamma, Mamma!" He turned her over. Her face was fiercely distorted. One eye, large and staring, moved slightly to the left as if it had become unmoored. The other remained fixed on him, raked his face again, found nothing and closed.

"Wait here, wait here!" he cried and jumped up and began to run for help toward a cluster of lights he saw in the distance ahead of him. "Help, help!" he shouted, but his voice was thin, scarcely a thread of sound. The lights drifted farther away the faster he ran and his feet moved numbly as if they carried him nowhere. The tide of darkness seemed to sweep him back to her, postponing from moment to moment his entry into the world of guilt and sorrow.

Greenleaf

Mrs. May's bedroom window was low and faced on the east and the bull, silvered in the moonlight, stood under it, his head raised as if he listened—like some patient god come down to woo her—for a stir inside the room. The window was dark and the sound of her breathing too light to be carried outside. Clouds crossing the moon blackened him and in the dark he began to tear at the hedge. Presently they passed and he appeared again in the same spot, chewing steadily, with a hedge-wreath that he had ripped loose for himself caught in the tips of his horns. When the moon drifted into retirement again, there was nothing to mark his place but the sound of steady chewing. Then abruptly a pink glow filled the window. Bars of light slid across him as the venetian blind was slit. He took a step backward and lowered his head as if to show the wreath across his horns.

For almost a minute there was no sound from inside,

then as he raised his crowned head again, a woman's voice, guttural as if addressed to a dog, said, "Get away from here, Sir!" and in a second muttered, "Some nigger's scrub bull."

The animal pawed the ground and Mrs. May, standing bent forward behind the blind, closed it quickly lest the light make him charge into the shrubbery. For a second she waited, still bent forward, her nightgown hanging loosely from her narrow shoulders. Green rubber curlers sprouted neatly over her forehead and her face beneath them was smooth as concrete with an egg-white paste that drew the wrinkles out while she slept.

She had been conscious in her sleep of a steady rhythmic chewing as if something were eating one wall of the house. She had been aware that whatever it was had been eating as long as she had had the place and had eaten everything from the beginning of her fence line up to the house and now was eating the house and calmly with the same steady rhythm would continue through the house, eating her and the boys, and then on, eating everything but the Greenleafs, on and on, eating everything until nothing was left but the Greenleafs on a little island all their own in the middle of what had been her place. When the munching reached her elbow, she jumped up and found herself, fully awake, standing in the middle of her room. She identified the sound at once: a cow was tearing at the shrubbery under her window. Mr. Greenleaf had left the lane gate open and she didn't doubt that the entire herd was on her lawn. She turned on the dim pink table lamp and then went to the window and slit the blind. The bull, gaunt and long-legged, was standing about four feet from her, chewing calmly like an uncouth country suitor.

For fifteen years, she thought as she squinted at him fiercely, she had been having shiftless people's hogs root up her oats, their mules wallow on her lawn, their scrub bulls breed her cows. If this one was not put up now, he would be over the fence, ruining her herd before morning—and Mr. Greenleaf was soundly sleeping a half mile down the road in the tenant house. There was no way to get him unless she dressed and got in her car and rode down there and woke him up. He would come but his expression, his whole figure, his every pause, would say: "Hit looks to me like one or both of them boys would not make their maw ride out in the middle of the night thisaway. If hit was my boys, they would have got thet bull up theirself."

The bull lowered his head and shook it and the wreath slipped down to the base of his horns where it looked like a menacing prickly crown. She had closed the blind then; in a few seconds she heard him move off heavily.

Mr. Greenleaf would say, "If hit was my boys they would never have allowed their maw to go after hired help in the middle of the night. They would have did it theirself."

Weighing it, she decided not to bother Mr. Greenleaf. She returned to bed thinking that if the Greenleaf boys had risen in the world it was because she had given their father employment when no one else would have him. She had had Mr. Greenleaf fifteen years but no one else would have had him five minutes. Just the way he approached an object was enough to tell anybody with eyes what kind of a worker he was. He walked with a high-shouldered creep and he never appeared to come directly forward. He walked on the perimeter of some invisible circle and if you wanted to look him in the face, you had to move and get in front of him. She had not fired him because she had always doubted she could do better. He was too shiftless to go out and look for another job; he didn't have the initiative to steal, and after she had told him three or four times to do a thing, he did it; but he never told her about a sick cow until it was too late to call the veterinarian and if her barn had caught on fire, he would have called his wife to see the flames before he began to put them out. And of the wife, she didn't even like to think. Beside the wife, Mr. Greenleaf was an aristocrat.

"If it had been my boys," he would have said, "they would have cut off their right arm before they would have allowed their maw to . . . ."

"If your boys had any pride, Mr. Greenleaf," she would like to say to him some day, "there are many things that they would not *allow* their mother to do."

The next morning as soon as Mr. Greenleaf came to the back door, she told him there was a stray bull on the place and that she wanted him penned up at once.

"Done already been here three days," he said, addressing his right foot which he held forward, turned slightly as if he were trying to look at the sole. He was standing at the bottom of the three back steps while she leaned out the kitchen door, a small woman with pale near-sighted eyes and grey hair that rose on top like the crest of some disturbed bird.

"Three days!" she said in the restrained screech that had become habitual with her.

Mr. Greenleaf, looking into the distance over the near pasture, removed a package of cigarets from his shirt pocket and let one fall into his hand. He put the package back and stood for a while looking at the cigaret. "I put him in the bull pen but he torn out of there," he said presently. "I didn't see him none after that." He bent over the cigaret and lit it and then turned his head briefly in her direction. The upper part of his face sloped gradually into the lower which was long and narrow, shaped like a rough chalice. He had deep-set fox-colored eyes shadowed under a grey felt hat that he wore slanted forward following the line of his nose. His build was insignificant.

"Mr. Greenleaf," she said, "get that bull up this morning before you do anything else. You know he'll ruin the breeding schedule. Get him up and keep him up and the next time there's a stray bull on this place, tell me at once. Do you understand?"

"Where you want him put at?" Mr. Greenleaf asked.

"I don't care where you put him," she said. "You are supposed to have some sense. Put him where he can't get out. Whose bull is he?"

For a moment Mr. Greenleaf seemed to hesitate between silence and speech. He studied the air to the left of him. "He must be somebody's bull," he said after a while.

"Yes, he must!" she said and shut the door with a precise little slam.

She went into the dining room where the two boys were eating breakfast and sat down on the edge of her chair at the head of the table. She never ate breakfast but she sat with them to see that they had what they wanted. "Honestly!" she said, and began to tell about the bull, aping Mr. Greenleaf saying, "It must be *somebody's* bull."

Wesley continued to read the newspaper folded beside his plate but Scofield interrupted his eating from time to time to look at her and laugh. The two boys never had the same reaction to anything. They were as different, she said, as night and day. The only thing they did have in common was that neither of them cared what happened on the place. Scofield was a business type and Wesley was an intellectual.

Wesley, the younger child, had had rheumatic fever when he was seven and Mrs. May thought that this was what had caused him to be an intellectual. Scofield, who had never had a day's sickness in his life, was an insurance salesman. She would not have minded his selling insurance if he had sold a nicer kind but he sold the kind that only Negroes buy. He was what Negroes call a "policy man." He said there was more money in nigger-insurance than any other kind, and before company, he was very loud about it. He would shout, "Mamma don't like to hear me say it but I'm the best nigger-insurance salesman in this county!"

Scofield was thirty-six and he had a broad pleasant smiling face but he was not married. "Yes," Mrs. May would say, "and if you sold decent insurance, some *nice* girl would be willing to marry you. What nice girl wants to marry a nigger-insurance man? You'll wake up some day and it'll be too late."

And at this Scofield would yodel and say, "Why Mamma, I'm not going to marry until you're dead and gone and then I'm going to marry me some nice fat farm girl that can take over this place!" And once he had added, "—some nice lady like Mrs. Greenleaf." When he had said this, Mrs. May had risen from her chair, her back stiff as a rake handle, and had gone to her room. There she had sat down on the edge of her bed for some time with her small face drawn. Finally she had whispered, "I work and slave, I struggle and sweat to keep this place for them and soon as I'm dead, they'll marry trash and bring it in here and ruin everything. They'll marry trash and ruin everything I've done," and she had made up her mind at that moment to change her will. The next day she had gone to her lawyer and had had the property entailed so that if they married, they could not leave it to their wives.

The idea that one of them might marry a woman even remotely like Mrs. Greenleaf was enough to make her ill.

She had put up with Mr. Greenleaf for fifteen years, but the only way she had endured his wife had been by keeping entirely out of her sight. Mrs. Greenleaf was large and loose. The yard around her house looked like a dump and her five girls were always filthy; even the youngest one dipped snuff. Instead of making a garden or washing their clothes, her preoccupation was what she called "prayer healing."

Every day she cut all the morbid stories out of the newspaper—the accounts of women who had been raped and criminals who had escaped and children who had been burned and of train wrecks and plane crashes and the divorces of movie stars. She took these to the woods and dug a hole and buried them and then she fell on the ground over them and mumbled and groaned for an hour or so, moving her huge arms back and forth under her and out again and finally just lying down flat and, Mrs. May suspected, going to sleep in the dirt.

She had not found out about this until the Greenleafs had been with her a few months. One morning she had been out to inspect a field that she had wanted planted in rye but that had come up in clover because Mr. Greenleaf had used the wrong seeds in the grain drill. She was returning through a wooded path that separated two pastures, muttering to herself and hitting the ground methodically with a long stick she carried in case she saw a snake. "Mr. Greenleaf," she was saying in a low voice, "I cannot afford to pay for your mistakes. I am a poor woman and this place is all I have. I have two boys to educate. I cannot . . . ."

Out of nowhere a guttural agonized voice groaned, "Jesus! Jesus!" In a second it came again with a terrible urgency. "Jesus! Jesus!"

Mrs. May stopped still, one hand lifted to her throat. The sound was so piercing that she felt as if some violent unleashed force had broken out of the ground and was charging toward her. Her second thought was more reasonable: somebody had been hurt on the place and would sue her for everything she had. She had no insurance. She rushed forward and turning a bend in the path, she saw Mrs. Greenleaf sprawled on her hands and knees off the side of the road, her head down.

"Mrs. Greenleaf!" she shrilled, "what's happened?"

Mrs. Greenleaf raised her head. Her face was a patchwork of dirt and tears and her small eyes, the color of two field peas, were red-rimmed and swollen, but her expression was as composed as a bulldog's. She swayed back and forth on her hands and knees and groaned, "Jesus, Jesus."

Mrs. May winced. She thought the word, Jesus, should be kept inside the church building like other words inside the bedroom. She was a good Christian woman with a large respect for religion, though she did not, of course, believe any of it was true. "What is the matter with you?" she asked sharply.

"You broken my healing," Mrs. Greenleaf said, waving her aside. "I can't talk to you until I finish."

Mrs. May stood, bent forward, her mouth open and her stick raised off the ground as if she were not sure what she wanted to strike with it.

"Oh Jesus, stab me in the heart!" Mrs. Greenleaf shrieked. "Jesus, stab me in the heart!" and she fell back flat in the dirt, a huge human mound, her legs and arms spread out as if she were trying to wrap them around the earth.

Mrs. May felt as furious and helpless as if she had been insulted by a child. "Jesus," she said, drawing herself back, "would be *ashamed* of you. He would tell you to get up from there this instant and go wash your children's clothes!" and she had turned and walked off as fast as she could.

Whenever she thought of how the Greenleaf boys had advanced in the world, she had only to think of Mrs. Greenleaf sprawled obscenely on the ground, and say to herself, "Well, no matter how far they *go*, they *came* from that."

She would like to have been able to put in her will that when she died, Wesley and Scofield were not to continue to employ Mr. Greenleaf. She was capable of handling Mr. Greenleaf; they were not. Mr. Greenleaf had pointed out to her once that her boys didn't know hay from silage. She had pointed out to him that they had other talents, that Scofield was a successful business man and Wesley a successful intellectual. Mr. Greenleaf did not comment, but he never lost an opportunity of letting her see, by his expression or some simple gesture, that he held the two of them in infinite contempt. As scrub-human as the Greenleafs were, he never hesitated to let her know that in any like circumstance in which his own boys might have been involved, they—O. T. and E. T. Greenleaf—would have acted to better advantage.

The Greenleaf boys were two or three years younger than the May boys. They were twins and you never knew when you spoke to one of them whether you were speaking to O. T. or E. T, and they never had the politeness to enlighten you. They were long-legged and raw-boned and red-skinned, with bright grasping fox-colored eyes like their father's. Mr. Greenleaf's pride in them began with the fact that they were twins. He acted, Mrs. May said, as if this were something smart they had thought of themselves. They were energetic and hard-working and she would admit to anyone that they had come a long way—and that the Second World War was responsible for it.

They had both joined the service and, disguised in their uniforms, they could not be told from other people's children. You could tell, of course, when they opened their mouths but they did that seldom. The smartest thing they had done was to get sent overseas and there to marry French wives. They hadn't married French trash either. They had married nice girls who naturally couldn't tell that they murdered the king's English or that the Greenleafs were who they were.

Wesley's heart condition had not permitted him to serve his country but Scofield had been in the army for two years. He had not cared for it and at the end of his military service, he was only a Private First Class. The Greenleaf boys were both some kind of sergeants, and Mr. Greenleaf, in those days, had never lost an opportunity of referring to them by their rank. They had both managed to get wounded and now they both had pensions. Further, as soon as they were released from the army, they took advantage of all the benefits and went to the school of agriculture at the university—the taxpayers meanwhile supporting their French wives. The two of them were living now about two miles down the highway on a piece of land that the government had helped them to buy and in a brick duplex bungalow that the government had helped to build and pay for. If the war had made anyone, Mrs. May said, it had made the Greenleaf boys. They each had three little children apiece, who spoke Greenleaf English and French, and who, on account of their mothers' background, would be sent to the convent school and brought up with manners. "And in twenty years," Mrs. May asked Scofield and Wesley, "do you know what those people will be?

"*Society*," she said blackly.

She had spent fifteen years coping with Mr. Greenleaf and, by now, handling him had become second nature with her. His disposition on any particular day was as much a factor in what she could and couldn't do as the weather was, and she had learned to read his face the way real country people read the sunrise and sunset.

She was a country woman only by persuasion. The late Mr. May, a business man, had bought the place when land was down, and when he died it was all he had to leave her. The boys had not been happy to move to the country to a broken-down farm, but there was nothing else for her to do. She had the timber on the place cut and with the proceeds had set herself up in the dairy business after Mr. Greenleaf had answered her ad. "i seen yor add and i will come have 2 boys," was all his letter said, but he arrived the next day in a pieced-together truck, his wife and five daughters sitting on the floor in back, himself and the two boys in the cab.

Over the years they had been on her place, Mr. and Mrs. Greenleaf had aged hardly at all. They had no worries, no responsibilities. They lived like the lilies of the field, off the fat that she struggled to put into the land. When she was dead and gone from overwork and worry, the Greenleafs, healthy and thriving, would be just ready to begin draining Scofield and Wesley.

Wesley said the reason Mrs. Greenleaf had not aged was because she released all her emotions in prayer healing. "You ought to start praying, Sweetheart," he had said in the voice that, poor boy, he could not help making deliberately nasty.

Scofield only exasperated her beyond endurance but Wesley caused her real anxiety. He was thin and nervous and bald and being an intellectual was a terrible strain on his disposition. She doubted if he would marry until she died but she was certain that then the wrong woman would get him. Nice girls didn't like Scofield but Wesley didn't like nice girls. He didn't like anything. He drove twenty miles every day to the university where he taught and twenty miles back every night, but he said he hated the twenty-mile drive and he hated the second-rate university and he hated the morons who attended it. He hated the country and he hated the life he lived; he hated living with his mother and his idiot brother and he hated hearing about the damn dairy and the damn help and the damn broken machinery. But in spite of all he said, he never made any move to leave. He talked about Paris and Rome but he never went even to Atlanta.

"You'd go to those places and you'd get sick," Mrs. May would say. "Who in Paris is going to see that you get a salt-free diet? And do you think if you married one of those odd numbers you take out that *she* would cook a salt-free diet for you? No indeed, she would not!" When she took this line, Wesley would turn himself roughly around in his chair and ignore her. Once when she had kept it up too long, he had snarled, "Well, why don't you do something practical, Woman? Why don't you pray for me like Mrs. Greenleaf would?"

"I don't like to hear you boys make jokes about religion," she had said. "If you would go to church, you would meet some nice girls."

But it was impossible to tell them anything. When she looked at the two of them now, sitting on either side of the table, neither one caring the least if a stray bull ruined her herd—which was their herd, their future—when she looked at the two of them, one hunched over a paper and the other teetering back in his chair, grinning at her like an idiot, she wanted to jump up and beat her fist on the table and shout, "You'll find out one of these days, you'll find out what *Reality* is when it's too late!"

"Mamma," Scofield said, "don't you get excited now but I'll tell you whose bull that is." He was looking at her wickedly. He let his chair drop forward and he got up. Then with his shoulders bent and his hands held up to cover his head, he tiptoed to the door. He backed into the hall and pulled the door almost to so that it hid all of him but his face. "You want to know, Sugarpie?" he asked.

Mrs. May sat looking at him coldly.

"That's O. T. and E. T.'s bull," he said. "I collected from their nigger yesterday and he told me they were missing it," and he showed her an exaggerated expanse of teeth and disappeared silently.

Wesley looked up and laughed.

Mrs. May turned her head forward again, her expression unaltered. "I am the only *adult* on this place," she said. She leaned across the table and pulled the paper from the side of his plate. "Do you see how it's going to be when I die and you boys have to handle him?" she began. "Do you see why he didn't know whose bull that was? Because it was theirs. Do you see what I have to put up with? Do you see that if I hadn't kept my foot on his neck all these years, you boys might be milking cows every morning at four o'clock?"

Wesley pulled the paper back toward his plate and staring at her full in the face, he murmured, "I wouldn't milk a cow to save your soul from hell."

"I know you wouldn't," she said in a brittle voice. She sat back and began rapidly turning her knife over at the side of her plate. "O. T. and E. T. are fine boys," she said. "They ought to have been my sons." The thought of this was so horrible that her vision of Wesley was blurred at once by a wall of tears. All she saw was his dark shape, rising quickly from the table. "And you two," she cried, "you two should have belonged to that woman!"

He was heading for the door.

"When I die," she said in a thin voice, "I don't know what's going to become of you."

"You're always yapping about when-you-die," he growled as he rushed out, "but you look pretty healthy to me."

For some time she sat where she was, looking straight ahead through the window across the room into a scene of indistinct greys and greens. She stretched her face and her neck muscles and drew in a long breath but the scene in front of her flowed together anyway into a watery grey mass. "They needn't think I'm going to die any time soon," she muttered, and some more defiant voice in her added: I'll die when I get good and ready.

She wiped her eyes with the table napkin and got up and went to the window and gazed at the scene in front of her. The cows were grazing on two pale green pastures across the road and behind them, fencing them in, was a black wall of trees with a sharp sawtooth edge that held off the indifferent sky. The pastures were enough to calm her. When she looked out any window in her house, she saw the reflection of her own character. Her city friends said she was the most remarkable woman they knew, to go, practically penniless and with no experience, out to a rundown farm and make a success of it. "Everything is against you," she would say, "the weather is against you and the dirt is against you and the help is against you. They're all in league against you. There's nothing for it but an iron hand!"

"Look at Mamma's iron hand!" Scofield would yell and grab her arm and hold it up so that her delicate blue-veined little hand would dangle from her wrist like the head of a broken lily. The company always laughed.

The sun, moving over the black and white grazing cows, was just a little brighter than the rest of the sky. Looking down, she saw a darker shape that might have been its shadow cast at an angle, moving among them. She uttered a sharp cry and turned and marched out of the house.

Mr. Greenleaf was in the trench silo, filling a wheelbarrow. She stood on the edge and looked down at him. "I told you to get up that bull. Now he's in with the milk herd."

"You can't do two thangs at oncet," Mr. Greenleaf remarked.

"I told you to do that first."

He wheeled the barrow out of the open end of the trench toward the barn and she followed close behind him. "And you needn't think, Mr. Greenleaf," she said, "that I don't know exactly whose bull that is or why you haven't been in any hurry to notify me he was here. I might as well feed O. T. and E. T.'s bull as long as I'm going to have him here ruining my herd."

Mr. Greenleaf paused with the wheelbarrow and looked behind him. "Is that them boys' bull?" he asked in an incredulous tone.

She did not say a word. She merely looked away with her mouth taut.

"They told me their bull was out but I never known that was him," he said.

"I want that bull put up now," she said, "and I'm going to drive over to O. T. and E. T.'s and tell them they'll have to come get him today. I ought to charge for the time he's been here—then it wouldn't happen again."

"They didn't pay but seventy-five dollars for him," Mr. Greenleaf offered.

"I wouldn't have had him as a gift," she said.

"They was just going to beef him," Mr. Greenleaf went on, "but he got loose and run his head into their pickup truck. He don't like cars and trucks. They had a time getting his horn out the fender and when they finally got him loose, he took off and they was too tired to run after him—but I never known that was him there."

"It wouldn't have paid you to know, Mr. Greenleaf," she said. "But you know now. Get a horse and get him."

In a half hour, from her front window she saw the bull, squirrel-colored, with jutting hips and long light horns, ambling down the dirt road that ran in front of the house. Mr. Greenleaf was behind him on the horse. "That's a Greenleaf bull if I ever saw one," she muttered. She went out on the porch and called, "Put him where he can't get out."

"He likes to bust loose," Mr. Greenleaf said, looking with approval at the bull's rump. "This gentleman is a sport."

"If those boys don't come for him, he's going to be a dead sport," she said. "I'm just warning you."

He heard her but he didn't answer.

"That's the awfullest looking bull I ever saw," she called but he was too far down the road to hear.

It was mid-morning when she turned into O. T. and E. T.'s driveway. The house, a new red-brick, low-to-the-ground building that looked like a warehouse with windows, was on top of a treeless hill. The sun was beating down directly on the white roof of it. It was the kind of house that everybody built now and nothing marked it as belonging to Greenleafs except three dogs, part hound and part spitz, that rushed out from behind it as soon as she stopped her car. She reminded herself that you could always tell the class of people by the class of dog, and honked her horn. While she sat waiting for someone to come, she continued to study the house. All the windows were down and she wondered if the government could have air-conditioned the thing. No one came and she honked again. Presently a door opened and several children appeared in it and stood looking at her, making no move to come forward. She recognized this as a true Greenleaf trait—they could hang in a door, looking at you for hours.

"Can't one of you children come here?" she called.

After a minute they all began to move forward, slowly. They had on overalls and were barefooted but they were not as dirty as she might have expected. There were two or three that looked distinctly like Greenleafs; the others not so much so. The smallest child was a girl with untidy black hair. They stopped about six feet from the automobile and stood looking at her.

"You're mighty pretty," Mrs. May said, addressing herself to the smallest girl.

There was no answer. They appeared to share one dispassionate expression between them.

"Where's your Mamma?" she asked.

There was no answer to this for some time. Then one of them said something in French. Mrs. May did not speak French.

"Where's your daddy?" she asked.

After a while, one of the boys said, "He ain't hyar neither."

"Ahhhh," Mrs. May said as if something had been proven. "Where's the colored man?"

She waited and decided no one was going to answer. "The cat has six little tongues," she said. "How would you like to come home with me and let me teach you how to talk?" She laughed and her laugh died on the silent air. She felt as if she were on trial for her life, facing a jury of Greenleafs. "I'll go down and see if I can find the colored man," she said.

"You can go if you want to," one of the boys said.

"Well, thank you," she murmured and drove off.

The barn was down the lane from the house. She had not seen it before but Mr. Greenleaf had described it in detail for it had been built according to the latest specifications. It was a milking parlor arrangement where the cows are milked from below. The milk ran in pipes from the machines to the milk house and was never carried in no bucket, Mr. Greenleaf said, by no human hand. "When you gonter get you one?" he had asked.

"Mr. Greenleaf," she had said, "I have to do for myself. I am not assisted hand and foot by the government. It would cost me $20,000 to install a milking parlor. I barely make ends meet as it is."

"My boys done it," Mr. Greenleaf had murmured, and then—"but all boys ain't alike."

"No indeed!" she had said. "I thank God for that!"

"I thank Gawd for ever-thang," Mr. Greenleaf had drawled.

You might as well, she had thought in the fierce silence that followed; you've never done anything for yourself.

She stopped by the side of the barn and honked but no one appeared. For several minutes she sat in the car, observing the various machines parked around, wondering how many of them were paid for. They had a forage harvester and a rotary hay baler. She had those too. She decided that since no one was here, she would get out and have a look at the milking parlor and see if they kept it clean.

She opened the milking room door and stuck her head in and for the first second she felt as if she were going to lose her breath. The spotless white concrete room was filled with sunlight that came from a row of windows head-high along both walls. The metal stanchions gleamed ferociously and she had to squint to be able to look at all. She drew her head out the room quickly and closed the door and leaned against it, frowning. The light outside was not so bright but she was conscious that the sun was directly on top of her head, like a silver bullet ready to drop into her brain.

A Negro carrying a yellow calf-feed bucket appeared from around the corner of the machine shed and came toward her. He was a light yellow boy dressed in the cast-off army clothes of the Greenleaf twins. He stopped at a respectable distance and set the bucket on the ground.

"Where's Mr. O. T. and Mr. E. T.?" she asked.

"Mist O. T. he in town, Mist E. T. he off yonder in the field," the Negro said, pointing first to the left and then to the right as if he were naming the position of two planets.

"Can you remember a message?" she asked, looking as if she thought this doubtful.

"I'll remember it if I don't forget it," he said with a touch of sullenness.

"Well, I'll write it down then," she said. She got in her car and took a stub of pencil from her pocket book and began to write on the back of an empty envelope. The Negro came and stood at the window. "I'm Mrs. May," she said as she wrote. "Their bull is on my place and I want him off *today*. You can tell them I'm furious about it."

"That bull lef here Sareday," the Negro said, "and none of us ain't seen him since. We ain't knowed where he was."

"Well, you know now," she said, "and you can tell Mr. O. T. and Mr. E. T. that if they don't come get him today, I'm going to have their daddy shoot him the first thing in the morning. I can't have that bull ruining my herd." She handed him the note.

"If I knows Mist O. T. and Mist E. T.," he said, taking it, "they goin to say you go ahead on and shoot him. He done busted up one of our trucks already and we be glad to see the last of him."

She pulled her head back and gave him a look from slightly bleared eyes. "Do they expect me to take my time and my worker to shoot their bull?" she asked. "They don't want him so they just let him loose and expect somebody else to kill him? He's eating my oats and ruining my herd and I'm expected to shoot him too?"

"I speck you is," he said softly. "He done busted up . . ."

She gave him a very sharp look and said, "Well, I'm not surprised. That's just the way some people are," and after a second she asked, "Which is boss, Mr. O. T. or Mr. E. T.?" She had always suspected that they fought between themselves secretly.

"They never quarls," the boy said. "They like one man in two skins."

"Hmp. I expect you just never heard them quarrel."

"Nor nobody else heard them neither," he said, looking away as if this insolence were addressed to some one else.

"Well," she said, "I haven't put up with their father for fifteen years not to know a few things about Greenleafs."

The Negro looked at her suddenly with a gleam of recognition. "Is you my policy man's mother?" he asked.

"I don't know who your policy man is," she said sharply. "You give them that note and tell them if they don't come for that bull today, they'll be making their father shoot it tomorrow," and she drove off.

She stayed at home all afternoon waiting for the Greenleaf twins to come for the bull. They did not come. I might as well be working for them, she thought furiously. They are simply going to use me to the limit. At the supper table, she went over it again for the boys' benefit because she wanted them to see exactly what O. T. and E. T. would do.

"They don't want that bull," she said, "—pass the butter— so they simply turn him loose and let somebody else worry about getting rid of him for them. How do you like that? I'm the victim. I've always been the victim."

"Pass the butter to the victim," Wesley said. He was in a worse humor than usual because he had had a flat tire on the way home from the university.

Scofield handed her the butter and said, "Why Mamma, ain't you ashamed to shoot an old bull that ain't done nothing but give you a little scrub strain in your herd? I declare," he said, "with the Mamma I got it's a wonder I turned out to be such a nice boy!"

"You ain't her boy, Son," Wesley said.

She eased back in her chair, her fingertips on the edge of the table.

"All I know is," Scofield said, "I done mighty well to be as nice as I am seeing what I come from."

When they teased her they spoke Greenleaf English but Wesley made his own particular tone come through it like a knife edge. "Well lemme tell you one thang, Brother," he said, leaning over the table, "that if you had half a mind you would already know."

"What's that, Brother?" Scofield asked, his broad face grinning into the thin constricted one across from him.

"That is," Wesley said, "that neither you nor me is her boy . . . ," but he stopped abruptly as she gave a kind of hoarse wheeze like an old horse lashed unexpectedly. She reared up and ran from the room.

"Oh, for God's sake," Wesley growled, "What did you start her off for?"

"I never started her off," Scofield said. "You started her off."

"Hah."

"She's not as young as she used to be and she can't take it."

"She can only give it out," Wesley said. "I'm the one that takes it."

His brother's pleasant face had changed so that an ugly family resemblance showed between them. "Nobody feels sorry for a lousy bastard like you," he said and grabbed across the table for the other's shirtfront.

From her room she heard a crash of dishes and she rushed back through the kitchen into the dining room. The hall door was open and Scofield was going out of it. Wesley was lying like a large bug on his back with the edge of the over-turned table cutting him across the middle and broken dishes scattered on top of him. She pulled the table off him and caught his arm to help him rise but he scrambled up and pushed her off with a furious charge of energy and flung himself out of the door after his brother.

She would have collapsed but a knock on the back door stiffened her and she swung around. Across the kitchen and back porch, she could see Mr. Greenleaf peering eagerly through the screenwire. All her resources returned in full strength as if she had only needed to be challenged by the devil himself to regain them. "I heard a thump," he called, "and I thought the plastering might have fell on you."

If he had been wanted someone would have had to go on a horse to find him. She crossed the kitchen and the porch and stood inside the screen and said, "No, nothing happened but the table turned over. One of the legs was weak," and without pausing, "the boys didn't come for the bull so tomorrow you'll have to shoot him."

The sky was crossed with thin red and purple bars and behind them the sun was moving down slowly as if it were descending a ladder. Mr. Greenleaf squatted down on the step, his back to her, the top of his hat on a level with her feet. "Tomorrow I'll drive him home for you," he said.

"Oh no, Mr. Greenleaf," she said in a mocking voice, "you drive him home tomorrow and next week he'll be back here. I know better than that." Then in a mournful tone, she said, "I'm surprised at O. T. and E. T. to treat me this way. I thought they'd have more gratitude. Those boys spent some mighty happy days on this place, didn't they, Mr. Greenleaf?"

Mr. Greenleaf didn't say anything.

"I think they did," she said. "I think they did. But they've forgotten all the nice little things I did for them now. If I recall, they wore my boys' old clothes and played with my boys' old toys and hunted with my boys' old guns. They swam in my pond and shot my birds and fished in my stream and I never forgot their birthday and Christmas seemed to roll around very often if I remember it right. And do they think of any of those things now?" she asked. "NOOOOO," she said.

For a few seconds she looked at the disappearing sun and Mr. Greenleaf examined the palms of his hands. Presently as if it had just occurred to her, she asked, "Do you know the real reason they didn't come for that bull?"

"Naw I don't," Mr. Greenleaf said in a surly voice.

"They didn't come because I'm a woman," she said. "You can get away with anything when you're dealing with a woman. If there were a man running this place . . ."

Quick as a snake striking Mr. Greenleaf said, "You got two boys. They know you got two men on the place."

The sun had disappeared behind the tree line. She looked down at the dark crafty face, upturned now, and at the wary eyes, bright under the shadow of the hatbrim. She waited long enough for him to see that she was hurt and then she said, "Some people learn gratitude too late, Mr. Greenleaf, and some never learn it at all," and she turned and left him sitting on the steps.

Half the night in her sleep she heard a sound as if some large stone were grinding a hole on the outside wall of her brain. She was walking on the inside, over a succession of beautiful rolling hills, planting her stick in front of each step. She became aware after a time that the noise was the sun trying to burn through the tree line and she stopped to watch, safe in the knowledge that it couldn't, that it had to sink the way it always did outside of her property. When she first stopped it was a swollen red ball, but as she stood watching it began to narrow and pale until it looked like a bullet. Then suddenly it burst through the tree line and raced down the hill toward her. She woke up with her hand over her mouth and the same noise, diminished but distinct, in her ear. It was the bull munching under her window. Mr. Greenleaf had let him out.

She got up and made her way to the window in the dark and looked out through the slit blind, but the bull had moved away from the hedge and at first she didn't see him. Then she saw a heavy form some distance away, paused as if observing her. This is the last night I am going to put up with this, she said, and watched until the iron shadow moved away in the darkness.

The next morning she waited until exactly eleven o'clock. Then she got in her car and drove to the barn. Mr. Greenleaf was cleaning milk cans. He had seven of them standing up outside the milk room to get the sun. She had been telling him to do this for two weeks. "All right, Mr. Greenleaf," she said, "go get your gun. We're going to shoot that bull."

"I thought you wanted theseyer cans . . ."

"Go get your gun, Mr. Greenleaf," she said. Her voice and face were expressionless.

"That gentleman torn out of there last night," he murmured in a tone of regret and bent again to the can he had his arm in.

"Go get your gun, Mr. Greenleaf," she said in the same triumphant toneless voice. "The bull is in the pasture with the dry cows. I saw him from my upstairs window. I'm going to drive you up to the field and you can run him into the empty pasture and shoot him there."

He detached himself from the can slowly. "Ain't nobody ever ast me to shoot my boys' own bull!" he said in a high rasping voice. He removed a rag from his back pocket and began to wipe his hands violently, then his nose.

She turned as if she had not heard this and said, "I'll wait for you in the car. Go get your gun."

She sat in the car and watched him stalk off toward the harness room where he kept a gun. After he had entered the room, there was a crash as if he had kicked something out of his way. Presently he emerged again with the gun, circled behind the car, opened the door violently and threw himself onto the seat beside her. He held the gun between his knees and looked straight ahead. He'd like to shoot me instead of the bull, she thought, and turned her face away so that he could not see her smile.

The morning was dry and clear. She drove through the woods for a quarter of a mile and then out into the open where there were fields on either side of the narrow road. The exhilaration of carrying her point had sharpened her senses. Birds were screaming everywhere, the grass was almost too bright to look at, the sky was an even piercing blue. "Spring is here!" she said gaily. Mr. Greenleaf lifted one muscle somewhere near his mouth as if he found this the most asinine remark ever made. When she stopped at the second pasture gate, he flung himself out of the car door and slammed it behind him. Then he opened the gate and she drove through. He closed it and flung himself back in, silently, and she drove around the rim of the pasture until she spotted the bull, almost in the center of it, grazing peacefully among the cows.

"The gentleman is waiting on you," she said and gave Mr. Greenleaf's furious profile a sly look. "Run him into that next pasture and when you get him in, I'll drive in behind you and shut the gate myself."

He flung himself out again, this time deliberately leaving the car door open so that she had to lean across the seat and close it. She sat smiling as she watched him make his way across the pasture toward the opposite gate. He seemed to throw himself forward at each step and then pull back as if he were calling on some power to witness that he was being forced. "Well," she said aloud as if he were still in the car, "it's your own boys who are making you do this, Mr. Greenleaf." O. T. and E. T. were probably splitting their sides laughing at him now. She could hear their identical nasal voices saying, "Made Daddy shoot our bull for us. Daddy don't know no better than to think that's a fine bull he's shooting. Gonna kill Daddy to shoot that bull!"

"If those boys cared a thing about you, Mr. Greenleaf," she said, "they would have come for that bull. I'm surprised at them."

He was circling around to open the gate first. The bull, dark among the spotted cows, had not moved. He kept his head down, eating constantly. Mr. Greenleaf opened the gate and then began circling back to approach him from the rear. When he was about ten feet behind him, he flapped his arms at his sides. The bull lifted his head indolently and then lowered it again and continued to eat. Mr. Greenleaf stooped again and picked up something and threw it at him with a vicious swing. She decided it was a sharp rock for the bull leapt and then began to gallop until he disappeared over the rim of the hill. Mr. Greenleaf followed at his leisure.

"You needn't think you're going to lose him!" she cried and started the car straight across the pasture. She had to drive slowly over the terraces and when she reached the gate, Mr. Greenleaf and the bull were nowhere in sight. This pasture was smaller than the last, a green arena, encircled almost entirely by woods. She got out and closed the gate and stood looking for some sign of Mr. Greenleaf but he had disappeared completely. She knew at once that his plan was to lose the bull in the woods. Eventually, she would see him emerge somewhere from the circle of trees and come limping toward her and when he finally reached her, he would say, "If you can find that gentleman in them woods, you're better than me."

She was going to say, "Mr. Greenleaf, if I have to walk into those woods with you and stay all afternoon, we are going to find that bull and shoot him. You are going to shoot him if I have to pull the trigger for you." When he saw she meant business he would return and shoot the bull quickly himself.

She got back into the car and drove to the center of the pasture where he would not have so far to walk to reach her when he came out of the woods. At this moment she could picture him sitting on a stump, marking lines in the ground with a stick. She decided she would wait exactly ten minutes by her watch. Then she would begin to honk. She got out of the car and walked around a little and then sat down on the front bumper to wait and rest. She was very tired and she lay her head back against the hood and closed her eyes. She did not understand why she should be so tired when it was only mid-morning. Through her closed eyes, she could feel the sun, red-hot overhead. She opened her eyes slightly but the white light forced her to close them again.

For some time she lay back against the hood, wondering drowsily why she was so tired. With her eyes closed, she didn't think of time as divided into days and nights but into past and future. She decided she was tired because she had been working continuously for fifteen years. She decided she had every right to be tired, and to rest for a few minutes before she began working again. Before any kind of judgement seat, she would be able to say: I've worked, I have not wallowed. At this very instant while she was recalling a lifetime of work, Mr. Greenleaf was loitering in the woods and Mrs. Greenleaf was probably flat on the ground, asleep over her holeful of clippings. The woman had got worse over the years and Mrs. May believed that now she was actually demented. "I'm afraid your wife has let religion warp her," she said once tactfully to Mr. Greenleaf. "Everything in moderation, you know."

"She cured a man oncet that half his gut was eat out with worms," Mr. Greenleaf said, and she had turned away, half-sickened. Poor souls, she thought now, so simple. For a few seconds she dozed.

When she sat up and looked at her watch, more than ten minutes had passed. She had not heard any shot. A new thought occurred to her: suppose Mr. Greenleaf had aroused the bull chunking stones at him and the animal had turned on him and run him up against a tree and gored him? The irony of it deepened: O. T. and E. T. would then get a shyster lawyer and sue her. It would be the fitting end to her fifteen years with the Greenleafs. She thought of it almost with pleasure as if she had hit on the perfect ending for a story she was telling her friends. Then she dropped it, for Mr. Greenleaf had a gun with him and she had insurance.

She decided to honk. She got up and reached inside the car window and gave three sustained honks and two or three shorter ones to let him know she was getting impatient. Then she went back and sat down on the bumper again.

In a few minutes something emerged from the tree line, a black heavy shadow that tossed its head several times and then bounded forward. After a second she saw it was the bull. He was crossing the pasture toward her at a slow gallop, a gay almost rocking gait as if he were overjoyed to find her again. She looked beyond him to see if Mr. Greenleaf was coming out of the woods too but he was not. "Here he is, Mr. Greenleaf!" she called and looked on the other side of the pasture to see if he could be coming out there but he was not in sight. She looked back and saw that the bull, his head lowered, was racing toward her. She remained perfectly still, not in fright, but in a freezing unbelief. She stared at the violent black streak bounding toward her as if she had no sense of distance, as if she could not decide at once what his intention was, and the bull had buried his head in her lap, like a wild tormented lover, before her expression changed. One of his horns sank until it pierced her heart and the other curved around her side and held her in an unbreakable grip. She continued to stare straight ahead but the entire scene in front of her had changed—the tree line was a dark wound in a world that was nothing but sky—and she had the look of a person whose sight has been suddenly restored but who finds the light unbearable.

Mr. Greenleaf was running toward her from the side with his gun raised and she saw him coming though she was not looking in his direction. She saw him approaching on the outside of some invisible circle, the tree line gaping behind him and nothing under his feet. He shot the bull four times through the eye. She did not hear the shots but she felt the quake in the huge body as it sank, pulling her forward on its head, so that she seemed, when Mr. Greenleaf reached her, to be bent over whispering some last discovery into the animal's ear.

A View of the Woods

The week before, Mary Fortune and the old man had spent every morning watching the machine that lifted out dirt and threw it in a pile. The construction was going on by the new lakeside on one of the lots that the old man had sold to somebody who was going to put up a fishing club. He and Mary Fortune drove down there every morning about ten o'clock and he parked his car, a battered mulberry-colored Cadillac, on the embankment that overlooked the spot where the work was going on. The red corrugated lake eased up to within fifty feet of the construction and was bordered on the other side by a black line of woods which appeared at both ends of the view to walk across the water and continue along the edge of the fields.

He sat on the bumper and Mary Fortune straddled the hood and they watched, sometimes for hours, while the machine systematically ate a square red hole in what had once been a cow pasture. It happened to be the only pasture that Pitts had succeeded in getting the bitterweed off and when the old man had sold it, Pitts had nearly had a stroke; and as far as Mr. Fortune was concerned, he could have gone on and had it.

"Any fool that would let a cow pasture interfere with progress is not on my books," he had said to Mary Fortune several times from his seat on the bumper, but the child did not have eyes for anything but the machine. She sat on the hood, looking down into the red pit, watching the big disembodied gullet gorge itself on the clay, then, with the sound of a deep sustained nausea and a slow mechanical revulsion, turn and spit it up. Her pale eyes behind her spectacles followed the repeated motion of it again and again and her face—a small replica of the old man's—never lost its look of complete absorption.

No one was particularly glad that Mary Fortune looked like her grandfather except the old man himself. He thought it added greatly to her attractiveness. He thought she was the smartest and the prettiest child he had ever seen and he let the rest of them know that if, IF that was, he left anything to anybody, it would be Mary Fortune he left it to. She was now nine, short and broad like himself, with his very light blue eyes, his wide prominent forehead, his steady penetrating scowl and his rich florid complexion; but she was like him on the inside too. She had, to a singular degree, his intelligence, his strong will, and his push and drive. Though there was seventy years' difference in their ages, the spiritual distance between them was slight. She was the only member of the family he had any respect for.

He didn't have any use for her mother, his third or fourth daughter (he could never remember which), though she considered that she took care of him. She considered—

being careful not to say it, only to look it—that she was the one putting up with him in his old age and that she was the one he should leave the place to. She had married an idiot named Pitts and had had seven children, all likewise idiots except the youngest, Mary Fortune, who was a throwback to him. Pitts was the kind who couldn't keep his hands on a nickel and Mr. Fortune had allowed them, ten years ago, to move onto his place and farm it. What Pitts made went to Pitts but the land belonged to Fortune and he was careful to keep the fact before them. When the well had gone dry, he had not allowed Pitts to have a deep well drilled but had insisted that they pipe their water from the spring. He did not intend to pay for a drilled well himself and he knew that if he let Pitts pay for it, whenever he had occasion to say to Pitts, "It's my land you're sitting on," Pitts would be able to say to him, "Well, it's my pump that's pumping the water you're drinking."

Being there ten years, the Pittses had got to feel as if they owned the place. The daughter had been born and raised on it but the old man considered that when she married Pitts she showed that she preferred Pitts to home; and when she came back, she came back like any other tenant, though he would not allow them to pay rent for the same reason he would not allow them to drill a well. Anyone over sixty years of age is in an uneasy position unless he controls the greater interest and every now and then he gave the Pittses a practical lesson by selling off a lot. Nothing infuriated Pitts more than to see him sell off a piece of the property to an outsider, because Pitts wanted to buy it himself.

Pitts was a thin, long-jawed, irascible, sullen, sulking individual and his wife was the duty-proud kind: It's my duty to stay here and take care of Papa. Who would do it if I didn't? I do it knowing full well I'll get no reward for it. I do it because it's my duty.

The old man was not taken in by this for a minute. He knew they were waiting impatiently for the day when they could put him in a hole eight feet deep and cover him up with dirt. Then, even if he did not leave the place to them, they figured they would be able to buy it. Secretly he had made his will and left everything in trust to Mary Fortune, naming his lawyer and not Pitts as executor. When he died Mary Fortune could make the rest of them jump; and he didn't doubt for a minute that she would be able to do it.

Ten years ago they had announced that they were going to name the new baby Mark Fortune Pitts, after him, if it were a boy, and he had not delayed in telling them that if they coupled his name with the name Pitts he would put them off the place. When the baby came, a girl, and he had seen that even at the age of one day she bore his unmistakable likeness, he had relented and suggested himself that they name her Mary Fortune, after his beloved mother, who had died seventy years ago, bringing him into the world.

The Fortune place was in the country on a clay road that left the paved road fifteen miles away and he would never have been able to sell off any lots if it had not been for progress, which had always been his ally. He was not one of these old people who fight improvement, who object to everything new and cringe at every change. He wanted to see a paved highway in front of his house with plenty of new-model cars on it, he wanted to see a supermarket store across the road from him, he wanted to see a gas station, a motel, a drive-in picture-show within easy distance. Progress had suddenly set all this in motion. The electric power company had built a dam on the river and flooded great areas of the surrounding country and the lake that resulted touched his land along a half-mile stretch. Every Tom, Dick and Harry, every dog and his brother, wanted a lot on the lake. There was talk of their getting a telephone line. There was talk of paving the road that ran in front of the Fortune place. There was talk of an eventual town. He thought this should be called Fortune, Georgia. He was a man of advanced vision, even if he was seventy-nine years old.

The machine that drew up the dirt had stopped the day before and today they were watching the hole being smoothed out by two huge yellow bulldozers. His property had amounted to eight hundred acres before he began selling lots. He had sold five twenty-acre lots on the back of the place and every time he sold one, Pitts's blood pressure had gone up twenty points. "The Pittses are the kind that would let a cow pasture interfere with the future," he said to Mary Fortune, "but not you and me." The fact that Mary Fortune was a Pitts too was something he ignored, in a gentlemanly fashion, as if it were an affliction the child was not responsible for. He liked to think of her as being thoroughly of his clay. He sat on the bumper and she sat on the hood with her bare feet on his shoulders. One of the bulldozers had moved under them to shave the side of the embankment they were parked on. If he had moved his feet a few inches out, the old man could have dangled them over the edge.

"If you don't watch him," Mary Fortune shouted above the noise of the machine, "he'll cut off some of your dirt!"

"Yonder's the stob," the old man yelled. "He hasn't gone beyond the stob."

"Not YET he hasn't," she roared.

The bulldozer passed beneath them and went on to the far side. "Well you watch," he said. "Keep your eyes open and if he knocks that stob, I'll stop him. The Pittses are the kind that would let a cow pasture or a mule lot or a row of beans interfere with progress," he continued. "The people like you and me with heads on their shoulders know you can't stop the marcher time for a cow. . . ."

"He's shaking the stob on the other side!" she screamed and before he could stop her, she had jumped down from the hood and was running along the edge of the embankment, her little yellow dress billowing out behind.

"Don't run so near the edge," he yelled but she had already reached the stob and was squatting down by it to see how much it had been shaken. She leaned over the embankment and shook her fist at the man on the bulldozer. He waved at her and went on about his business. More sense in her little finger than all the rest of that tribe in their heads put together, the old man said to himself, and watched with pride as she started back to him.

She had a head of thick, very fine, sand-colored hair—the exact kind he had had when he had had any—that grew straight and was cut just above her eyes and down the sides of her cheeks to the tips of her ears so that it formed a kind of door opening onto the central part of her face. Her glasses were silver-rimmed like his and she even walked the way he did, stomach forward, with a careful abrupt gait, something between a rock and a shuffle. She was walking so close to the edge of the embankment that the outside of her right foot was flush with it.

"I said don't walk so close to the edge," he called; "you fall off there and you won't live to see the day this place gets built up." He was always very careful to see that she avoided dangers. He would not allow her to sit in snakey places or put her hands on bushes that might hide hornets.

She didn't move an inch. She had a habit of his of not hearing what she didn't want to hear and since this was a little trick he had taught her himself, he had to admire the way she practiced it. He foresaw that in her own old age it would serve her well. She reached the car and climbed back onto the hood without a word and put her feet back on his shoulders where she had had them before, as if he were no more than a part of the automobile. Her attention returned to the far bulldozer.

"Remember what you won't get if you don't mind," her grandfather remarked.

He was a strict disciplinarian but he had never whipped her. There were some children, like the first six Pittses, whom he thought should be whipped once a week on principle, but there were other ways to control intelligent children and he had never laid a rough hand on Mary Fortune. Furthermore, he had never allowed her mother or her brothers and sisters so much as to slap her. The elder Pitts was a different matter.

He was a man of a nasty temper and of ugly unreasonable resentments. Time and again, Mr. Fortune's heart had pounded to see him rise slowly from his place at the table—not the head, Mr. Fortune sat there, but from his place at the side—and abruptly, for no reason, with no explanation, jerk his head at Mary Fortune and say, "Come with me," and leave the room, unfastening his belt as he went. A look that was completely foreign to the child's face would appear on it. The old man could not define the look but it infuriated him. It was a look that was part terror and part respect and part something else, something very like cooperation. This look would appear on her face and she would get up and follow Pitts out. They would get in his truck and drive down the road out of earshot, where he would beat her.

Mr. Fortune knew for a fact that he beat her because he had followed them in his car and had seen it happen. He had watched from behind a boulder about a hundred feet away while the child clung to a pine tree and Pitts, as methodically as if he were whacking a bush with a sling blade, beat her around the ankles with his belt. All she had done was jump up and down as if she were standing on a hot stove and make a whimpering noise like a dog that was being peppered. Pitts had kept at it for about three minutes and then he had turned, without a word, and got back in his truck and left her there, and she had slid down under the tree and taken both feet in her hands and rocked back and forth. The old man had crept forward to catch her. Her face was contorted into a puzzle of small red lumps and her nose and eyes were running. He sprang on her and sputtered, "Why didn't you hit him back? Where's your spirit? Do you think I'd a let him beat me?"

She had jumped up and started backing away from him with her jaw stuck out. "Nobody beat me," she said.

"Didn't I see it with my own eyes?" he exploded.

"Nobody is here and nobody beat me," she said. "Nobody's ever beat me in my life and if anybody did, I'd kill him. You can see for yourself nobody is here."

"Do you call me a liar or a blindman!" he shouted. "I saw him with my own two eyes and you never did a thing but let him do it, you never did a thing but hang onto that tree and dance up and down a little and blubber and if it had been me, I'd a swung my fist in his face and . . ."

"Nobody was here and nobody beat me and if anybody did I'd kill him!" she yelled and then turned and dashed off through the woods.

"And I'm a Poland china pig and black is white!" he had roared after her and he had sat down on a small rock under the tree, disgusted and furious. This was Pitts's revenge on him. It was as if it were *he* that Pitts was driving down the road to beat and it was as if *he* were the one submitting to it. He had thought at first that he could stop him by saying that if he beat her, he would put them off the place but when he had tried that, Pitts had said, "Put me off and you put her off too. Go right ahead. She's mine to whip and I'll whip her every day of the year if it suits me."

Any time he could make Pitts feel his hand he was determined to do it and at present he had a little scheme up his sleeve that was going to be a considerable blow to Pitts. He was thinking of it with relish when he told Mary Fortune to remember what she wouldn't get if she didn't mind, and he added, without waiting for an answer, that he might be selling another lot soon and that if he did, he might give her a bonus but not if she gave him any sass. He had frequent little verbal tilts with her but this was a sport like putting a mirror up in front of a rooster and watching him fight his reflection.

"I don't want no bonus," Mary Fortune said.

"I ain't ever seen you refuse one."

"You ain't ever seen me ask for one neither," she said.

"How much have you laid by?" he asked.

"Noner yer bidnis," she said and stamped his shoulders with her feet. "Don't be buttin into my bidnis."

"I bet you got it sewed up in your mattress," he said, "just like an old nigger woman. You ought to put it in the bank. I'm going to start you an account just as soon as I complete this deal. Won't anybody be able to check on it but me and you."

The bulldozer moved under them again and drowned out the rest of what he wanted to say. He waited and when the noise had passed, he could hold it in no longer. "I'm going to sell the lot right in front of the house for a gas station," he said. "Then we won't have to go down the road to get the car filled up, just step out the front door."

The Fortune house was set back about two hundred feet from the road and it was this two hundred feet that he intended to sell. It was the part that his daughter airily called "the lawn" though it was nothing but a field of weeds.

"You mean," Mary Fortune said after a minute, "the lawn?"

"Yes mam!" he said. "I mean the lawn," and he slapped his knee.

She did not say anything and he turned and looked up at her. There in the little rectangular opening of hair was his face looking back at him, but it was a reflection not of his present expression but of the darker one that indicated his displeasure. "That's where we play," she muttered.

"Well there's plenty of other places you can play," he said, irked by this lack of enthusiasm.

"We won't be able to see the woods across the road," she said.

The old man stared at her. "The woods across the road?" he repeated.

"We won't be able to see the view," she said.

"The view?" he repeated.

"The woods," she said; "we won't be able to see the woods from the porch."

"The woods from the porch?" he repeated.

Then she said, "My daddy grazes his calves on that lot."

The old man's wrath was delayed an instant by shock. Then it exploded in a roar. He jumped up and turned and slammed his fist on the hood of the car. "He can graze them somewheres else!"

"You fall off that embankment and you'll wish you hadn't," she said.

He moved from in front of the car around to the side, keeping his eye on her all the time. "Do you think I care where he grazes his calves! Do you think I'll let a calf interfere with my bidnis? Do you think I give a damn hoot where that fool grazes his calves?"

She sat, her red face darker than her hair, exactly reflecting his expression now. "He who calls his brother a fool is subject to hell fire," she said.

"Jedge not," he shouted, "lest ye be not jedged!" The tinge of his face was a shade more purple than hers. "You!" he said. "You let him beat you any time he wants to and don't do a thing but blubber a little and jump up and down!"

"He nor nobody else has ever touched me," she said, measuring off each word in a deadly flat tone. "Nobody's ever put a hand on me and if anybody did, I'd kill him."

"And black is white," the old man piped, "and night is day!"

The bulldozer passed below them. With their faces about a foot apart, each held the same expression until the noise had receded. Then the old man said, "Walk home by yourself. I refuse to ride a Jezebel!"

"And I refuse to ride with the Whore of Babylon," she said and slid off the other side of the car and started off through the pasture.

"A whore is a woman!" he roared. "That's how much you know!" But she did not deign to turn around and answer him back, and as he watched the small robust figure stalk across the yellow-dotted field toward the woods, his pride in her, as if it couldn't help itself, returned like the gentle little tide on the new lake—all except that part of it that had to do with her refusal to stand up to Pitts; that pulled back like an undertow. If he could have taught her to stand up to Pitts the way she stood up to him, she would have been a perfect child, as fearless and sturdy-minded as anyone could want; but it was her one failure of character. It was the one point on which she did not resemble him. He turned and looked away over the lake to the woods across it and told himself that in five years, instead of woods, there would be houses and stores and parking places, and that the credit for it could go largely to him.

He meant to teach the child spirit by example and since he had definitely made up his mind, he announced that noon at the dinner table that he was negotiating with a man named Tilman to sell the lot in front of the house for a gas station.

His daughter, sitting with her worn-out air at the foot of the table, let out a moan as if a dull knife were being turned slowly in her chest. "You mean the lawn!" she moaned and fell back in her chair and repeated in an almost inaudible voice, "He means the lawn."

The other six Pitts children began to bawl and pipe, "Where we play!" Don't let him do that, Pa!" "We won't be able to see the road!" and similar idiocies. Mary Fortune did not say anything. She had a mulish reserved look as if she were planning some business of her own. Pitts had stopped eating and was staring in front of him. His plate was full but his fists sat motionless like two dark quartz stones on either side of it. His eyes began to move from child to child around the table as if he were hunting for one particular one of them. Finally they stopped on Mary Fortune sitting next to her grandfather. "You done this to us," he muttered.

"I didn't," she said but there was no assurance in her voice. It was only a quaver, the voice of a frightened child.

Pitts got up and said, "Come with me," and turned and walked out, loosening his belt as he went, and to the old man's complete despair, she slid away from the table and followed him, almost ran after him, out the door and into the truck behind him, and they drove off.

This cowardice affected Mr. Fortune as if it were his own. It made him physically sick. "He beats an innocent child," he said to his daughter, who was apparently still prostrate at the end of the table, "and not one of you lifts a hand to stop him."

"You ain't lifted yours neither," one of the boys said in an undertone and there was a general mutter from that chorus of frogs.

"I'm an old man with a heart condition," he said. "I can't stop an ox."

"She put you up to it," his daughter murmured in a languid listless tone, her head rolling back and forth on the rim of her chair. "She puts you up to everything."

"No child never put me up to nothing!" he yelled. "You're no kind of a mother! You're a disgrace! That child is an angel! A saint!" he shouted in a voice so high that it broke and he had to scurry out of the room.

The rest of the afternoon he had to lie on his bed. His heart, whenever he knew the child had been beaten, felt as if it were slightly too large for the space that was supposed to hold it. But now he was more determined than ever to see the filling station go up in front of the house, and if it gave Pitts a stroke, so much the better. If it gave him a stroke and paralyzed him, he would be served right and he would never be able to beat her again.

Mary Fortune was never angry with him for long, or seriously, and though he did not see her the rest of that day, when he woke up the next morning, she was sitting astride his chest ordering him to make haste so that they would not miss the concrete mixer.

The workmen were laying the foundation for the fishing

club when they arrived and the concrete mixer was already in operation. It was about the size and color of a circus elephant; they stood and watched it churn for a half-hour or so. At eleven-thirty, the old man had an appointment with Tilman to discuss his transaction and they had to leave. He did not tell Mary Fortune where they were going but only that he had to see a man.

Tilman operated a combination country store, filling station, scrap-metal dump, used-car lot and dance hall five miles down the highway that connected with the dirt road that passed in front of the Fortune place. Since the dirt road would soon be paved, he wanted a good location on it for another such enterprise. He was an up-and-coming man—the kind, Mr. Fortune thought, who was never just in line with progress but always a little ahead of it so that he could be there to meet it when it arrived. Signs up and down the highway announced that Tilman's was only five miles away, only four, only three, only two, only one; then "Watch out for Tilman's, Around this bend!" and finally, "Here it is, Friends, TILMAN's!" in dazzling red letters.

Tilman's was bordered on either side by a field of old used-car bodies, a kind of ward for incurable automobiles. He also sold outdoor ornaments, such as stone cranes and chickens, urns, jardinieres, whirligigs, and farther back from the road, so as not to depress his dance-hall customers, a line of tombstones and monuments. Most of his businesses went on out-of-doors, so that his store building itself had not involved excessive expense. It was a one-room wooden structure onto which he had added, behind, a long tin hall equipped for dancing. This was divided into two sections, Colored and White, each with its private nickelodeon. He had a barbecue pit and sold barbecued sandwiches and soft drinks.

As they drove up under the shed of Tilman's place, the old man glanced at the child sitting with her feet drawn up on the seat and her chin resting on her knees. He didn't know if she would remember that it was Tilman he was going to sell the lot to or not.

"What you going in here for?" she asked suddenly, with a sniffing look as if she scented an enemy.

"Noner yer bidnis," he said. "You just sit in the car and when I come out, I'll bring you something."

"Don'tcher bring me nothing," she said darkly, "because I won't be here."

"Haw!" he said. "Now you're here, it's nothing for you to do but wait," and he got out and without paying her any further attention, he entered the dark store where Tilman was waiting for him.

When he came out in half an hour, she was not in the car. Hiding, he decided. He started walking around the store to see if she was in the back. He looked in the doors of the two sections of the dance hall and walked on around by the tombstones. Then his eye roved over the field of sinking automobiles and he realized that she could be in or behind any one of two hundred of them. He came back out in front of the store. A Negro boy, drinking a purple drink, was sitting on the ground with his back against the sweating ice cooler.

"Where did that little girl go to, boy?" he asked.

"I ain't seen nair little girl," the boy said.

The old man irritably fished in his pocket and handed him a nickel and said, "A pretty little girl in a yeller cotton dress."

"If you speakin about a stout chile look lak you," the boy said, "she gone off in a truck with a white man."

"What kind of a truck, what kind of a white man?" he yelled.

"It were a green pick-up truck," the boy said smacking his lips, "and a white man she call 'daddy.' They gone thataway some time ago."

The old man, trembling, got in his car and started home. His feelings raced back and forth between fury and mortification. She had never left him before and certainly never for Pitts. Pitts had ordered her to get in the truck and she was afraid not to. But when he reached this conclusion he was more furious than ever. What was the matter with her that she couldn't stand up to Pitts? Why was there this one flaw in her character when he had trained her so well in everything else? It was an ugly mystery.

When he reached the house and climbed the front steps, there she was sitting in the swing, looking glum-faced in front of her across the field he was going to sell. Her eyes were puffy and pink-rimmed but he didn't see any red marks on her legs. He sat down in the swing beside her. He meant to make his voice severe but instead it came out crushed, as if it belonged to a suitor trying to reinstate himself.

"What did you leave me for? You ain't ever left me before," he said.

"Because I wanted to," she said, looking straight ahead.

"You never wanted to," he said. "He made you."

"I toljer I was going and I went," she said in a slow emphatic voice, not looking at him, "and now you can go on and lemme alone." There was something very final, in the sound of this, a tone that had not come up before in their disputes. She stared across the lot where there was nothing but a profusion of pink and yellow and purple weeds, and on across the red road, to the sullen line of black pine woods fringed on top with green. Behind that line was a narrow gray-blue line of more distant woods and beyond that nothing but the sky, entirely blank except for one or two threadbare clouds. She looked into this scene as if it were a person that she preferred to him.

"It's my lot, ain't it?" he asked. "Why are you so up-in-the-air about me selling my own lot?"

"Because it's the lawn," she said. Her nose and eyes began to run horribly but she held her face rigid and licked the water off as soon as it was in reach of her tongue. "We won't be able to see across the road," she said.

The old man looked across the road to assure himself again that there was nothing over there to see. "I never have seen you act in such a way before," he said in an incredulous voice. "There's not a thing over there but the woods."

"We won't be able to see 'um," she said, "and that's the *lawn* and my daddy grazes his calves on it."

At that the old man stood up. "You act more like a Pitts than a Fortune," he said. He had never made such an ugly remark to her before and he was sorry the instant he had said it. It hurt him more than it did her. He turned and went in the house and upstairs to his room.

Several times during the afternoon, he got up from his bed and looked out the window across the "lawn" to the line of woods she said they wouldn't be able to see any more. Every time he saw the same thing: woods—not a mountain, not a waterfall, not any kind of planted bush or flower, just woods. The sunlight was woven through them at that particular time of the afternoon so that every thin pine trunk stood out in all its nakedness. A pine trunk is a pine trunk, he said to himself, and anybody that wants to see one don't have to go far in this neighborhood. Every time he got up and looked out, he was reconvinced of his wisdom in selling the lot. The dissatisfaction it caused Pitts would be permanent, but he could make it up to Mary Fortune by buying her something. With grown people, a road led either to heaven or hell, but with children there were always stops along the way where their attention could be turned with a trifle.

The third time he got up to look at the woods, it was almost six o'clock and the gaunt trunks appeared to be raised in a pool of red light that gushed from the almost hidden sun setting behind them. The old man stared for some time, as if for a prolonged instant he were caught up out of the rattle of everything that led to the future and were held there in the midst of an uncomfortable mystery that he had not apprehended before. He saw it, in his hallucination, as if someone were wounded behind the woods and the trees were bathed in blood. After a few minutes this unpleasant vision was broken by the presence of Pitts's pick-up truck grinding to a halt below the window. He returned to his bed and shut his eyes and against the closed lids hellish red trunks rose up in a black wood.

At the supper table nobody addressed a word to him, including Mary Fortune. He ate quickly and returned again to his room and spent the evening pointing out to himself the advantages for the future of having an establishment like Tilman's so near. They would not have to go any distance for gas. Anytime they needed a loaf of bread, all they would have to do would be step out their front door into Tilman's back door. They could sell milk to Tilman. Tilman was a likable fellow. Tilman would draw other business. The road would soon be paved. Travelers from all over the country would stop at Tilman's. If his daughter thought she was better than Tilman, it would be well to take her down a little. All men were created free and equal. When this phrase sounded in his head, his patriotic sense triumphed and he realized that it was his duty to sell the lot, that he must insure the future. He looked out the window at the moon shining over the woods across the road and listened for a while to the hum of crickets and treefrogs, and beneath their racket, he could hear the throb of the future town of Fortune.

He went to bed certain that just as usual, he would wake up in the morning looking into a little red mirror framed in a door of fine hair. She would have forgotten all about the sale and after breakfast they would drive into town and get the legal papers from the courthouse. On the way back he would stop at Tilman's and close the deal.

When he opened his eyes in the morning, he opened them on the empty ceiling. He pulled himself up and looked around the room but she was not there. He hung over the edge of the bed and looked beneath it but she was not there either. He got up and dressed and went outside. She was sitting in the swing on the front porch, exactly the way she had been yesterday, looking across the lawn into the woods. The old man was very much irritated. Every morning since she had been able to climb, he had waked up to find her either on his bed or underneath it. It was apparent that this morning she preferred the sight of the woods. He decided to ignore her behavior for the present and then bring it up later when she was over her pique. He sat down in the swing beside her but she continued to look at the woods. "I thought you and me'd go into town and have us a look at the boats in the new boat store," he said.

She didn't turn her head but she asked suspiciously, in a loud voice, "What else are you going for?"

"Nothing else," he said.

After a pause she said, "If that's all, I'll go," but she did not bother to look at him.

"Well put on your shoes," he said. "I ain't going to the city with a barefoot woman." She did not bother to laugh at this joke.

The weather was as indifferent as her disposition. The sky did not look as if it were going to rain or as if it were not going to rain. It was an unpleasant gray and the sun had not troubled to come out. All the way into town, she sat looking at her feet, which stuck out in front of her, encased in heavy brown school shoes. The old man had often sneaked up on her and found her alone in conversation with her feet and he thought she was speaking with them silently now. Every now and then her lips moved but she said nothing to him and let all his remarks pass as if she had not heard them. He decided it was going to cost him considerable to buy her good humor again and that he had better do it with a boat, since he wanted one too. She had been talking boats ever since the water backed up onto his place. They went first to the boat store. "Show us the yachts for po' folks!" he shouted jovially to the clerk as they entered.

"They're all for po folks!" the clerk said. "You'll be po' when you finish buying one!" He was a stout youth in a yellow shirt and blue pants and he had a ready wit. They exchanged several clever remarks in rapid-fire succession. Mr. Fortune looked at Mary Fortune to see if her face had brightened. She stood staring absently over the side of an outboard motor boat at the opposite wall.

"Ain't the lady innerested in boats?" the clerk asked.

She turned and wandered back out onto the sidewalk and got in the car again. The old man looked after her with amazement. He could not believe that a child of her intelligence could be acting this way over the mere sale of a field. "I think she must be coming down with something," he said. "We'll come back again," and he returned to the car.

"Let's go get us an ice-cream cone," he suggested, looking at her with concern.

"I don't want no ice-cream cone," she said.

His actual destination was the courthouse but he did not want to make this apparent. "How'd you like to visit the ten-cent store while I tend to a little bidnis of mine?" he asked. "You can buy yourself something with a quarter I brought along."

"I ain't got nothing to do in no ten-cent store," she said. "I don't want no quarter of yours."

If a boat was of no interest, he should not have thought a quarter would be and reproved himself for that stupidity. "Well what's the matter, sister?" he asked kindly. "Don't you feel good?"

She turned and looked him straight in the face and said with a slow concentrated ferocity, "It's the lawn. My daddy grazes his calves there. We won't be able to see the woods any more."

The old man had held his fury in as long as he could. "He beats you!" he shouted. "And you worry about where he's going to graze his calves!"

"Nobody's ever beat me in my life," she said, "and if anybody did, I'd kill him."

A man seventy-nine years of age cannot let himself be run over by a child of nine. His face set in a look that was just as determined as hers. "Are you a Fortune," he said, "or are you a Pitts? Make up your mind."

Her voice was loud and positive and belligerent. "I'm Mary—Fortune—Pitts," she said.

"Well I," he shouted, "am PURE Fortune!"

There was nothing she could say to this and she showed it. For an instant she looked completely defeated, and the old man saw with a disturbing clearness that this was the

Pitts look. What he saw was the Pitts look, pure and simple, and he felt personally stained by it, as if it had been found on his own face. He turned in disgust and backed the car out and drove straight to the courthouse.

The courthouse was a red and white blaze-faced building set in the center of a square from which most of the grass had been worn off. He parked in front of it and said, "Stay here," in an imperious tone and got out and slammed the car door.

It took him a half-hour to get the deed and have the sale paper drawn up and when he returned to the car, she was sitting on the back seat in the corner. The expression on that part of her face that he could see was foreboding and withdrawn. The sky had darkened also and there was a hot sluggish tide in the air, the kind felt when a tornado is possible.

"We better get on before we get caught in a storm," he said and added emphatically, "because I got one more place to stop at on the way home," but he might have been chauffeuring a small dead body for all the answer he got.

On the way to Tilman's he reviewed once more the many just reasons that were leading him to his present action and he could not locate a flaw in any of them. He decided that while this attitude of hers would not be permanent, he was permanently disappointed in her and that when she came around she would have to apologize; and that there would be no boat. He was coming to realize slowly that his trouble with her had always been that he had not shown enough firmness. He had been too generous. He was so occupied with these thoughts that he did not notice the signs that said how many miles to Tilman's until the last one exploded joyfully in his face: "Here it is, Friends, TILMAN's!" He pulled in under the shed.

He got out without so much as looking at Mary Fortune and entered the dark store where Tilman, leaning on the counter in front of a triple shelf of canned goods, was waiting for him.

Tilman was a man of quick action and few words. He sat habitually with his arms folded on the counter and his insignificant head weaving snake-fashion above them. He had a triangular-shaped face with the point at the bottom and the top of his skull was covered with a cap of freckles. His eyes were green and very narrow and his tongue was always exposed in his partly opened mouth. He had his checkbook handy and they got down to business at once. It did not take him long to look at the deed and sign the bill of sale. Then Mr. Fortune signed it and they grasped hands over the counter.

Mr. Fortune's sense of relief as he grasped Tilman's hand was extreme. What was done, he felt, was done and there could be no more argument, with her or with himself. He felt that he had acted on principle and that the future was assured.

Just as their hands loosened, an instant's change came over Tilman's face and he disappeared completely under the counter as if he had been snatched by the feet from below. A bottle crashed against the line of tinned goods behind where he had been. The old man whirled around. Mary Fortune was in the door, red-faced and wild-looking, with another bottle lifted to hurl. As he ducked, it broke behind him on the counter and she grabbed another from the crate. He sprang at her but she tore to the other side of the store, screaming something unintelligible and throwing everything within her reach. The old man pounced again and this time he caught her by the tail of her dress and pulled her backward out of the store. Then he got a better grip and lifted her, wheezing and whimpering but suddenly limp in his arms, the few feet to the car. He managed to get the door open and dump her inside. Then he ran around to the other side and got in himself and drove away as fast as he could.

His heart felt as if it were the size of the car and was racing forward, carrying him to some inevitable destination faster than he had ever been carried before. For the first five minutes he did not think but only sped forward as if he were being driven inside his own fury. Gradually the power of thought returned to him. Mary Fortune, rolled into a ball in the corner of the seat, was snuffling and heaving.

He had never seen a child behave in such a way in his life. Neither his own children nor anyone else's had ever displayed such temper in his presence, and he had never for an instant imagined that the child he had trained himself, the child who had been his constant companion for nine years, would embarrass him like this. The child he had never lifted a hand to!

Then he saw, with the sudden vision that sometimes comes with delayed recognition, that that had been his mistake.

She respected Pitts because, even with no just cause, he beat her; and if he—with his just cause—did not beat her now, he would have nobody to blame but himself if she turned out a hellion. He saw that the time had come, that he could no longer avoid whipping her, and as he turned off the highway onto the dirt road leading to home, he told himself that when he finished with her, she would never throw another bottle again.

He raced along the clay road until he came to the line where his own property began and then he turned off onto a side path, just wide enough for the automobile and bounced for a half a mile through the woods. He stopped the car at the exact spot where he had seen Pitts take his belt to her. It was a place where the road widened so that two cars could pass or one could turn around, an ugly red bald spot surrounded by long thin pines that appeared to be gathered there to witness anything that would take place in such a clearing. A few stones protruded from the clay.

"Get out," he said and reached across her and opened the door.

She got out without looking at him or asking what they were going to do and he got out on his side and came around the front of the car.

"Now I'm going to whip you!" he said and his voice was extra loud and hollow and had a vibrating quality that appeared to be taken up and passed through the tops of the pines. He did not want to get caught in a downpour while he was whipping her and he said, "Hurry up and get ready against that tree," and began to take off his belt.

What he had in mind to do appeared to come very slowly as if it had to penetrate a fog in her head. She did not move but gradually her confused expression began to clear. Where a few seconds before her face had been red and distorted and unorganized, it drained now of every vague line until nothing was left on it but positiveness, a look that went slowly past determination and reached certainty. "Nobody has ever beat me," she said, "and if anybody tries it, I'll kill him."

"I don't want no sass," he said and started toward her. His knees felt very unsteady, as if they might turn either backward or forward.

She moved exactly one step back and, keeping her eye on him steadily, removed her glasses and dropped them behind a small rock near the tree he had told her to get ready against. "Take off your glasses," she said.

"Don't give me orders!" he said in a high voice and slapped awkwardly at her ankles with his belt.

She was on him so quickly that he could not have recalled which blow he felt first, whether the weight of her whole solid body or the jabs of her feet or the pummeling of her fist on his chest. He flailed the belt in the air, not knowing where to hit but trying to get her off him until he could decide where to get a grip on her.

"Leggo!" he shouted. "Leggo I tell you!" But she seemed to be everywhere, coming at him from all directions at once. It was as if he were being attacked not by one child but by a pack of small demons all with stout brown school shoes and small rocklike fists. His glasses flew to the side.

"I toljer to take them off," she growled without pausing.

He caught his knee and danced on one foot and a rain of blows fell on his stomach. He felt five claws in the flesh of his upper arm where she was hanging from while her feet mechanically battered his knees and her free fist pounded him again and again in the chest. Then with horror he saw her face rise up in front of his, teeth exposed, and he roared like a bull as she bit the side of his jaw. He seemed to see his own face coming to bite him from several sides at once but he could not attend to it for he was being kicked indiscriminately, in the stomach and then in the crotch. Suddenly he threw himself on the ground and began to roll like a man on fire. She was on top of him at once, rolling with him and still kicking, and now with both fists free to batter his chest.

"I'm an old man!" he piped. "Leave me alone!" But she did not stop. She began a fresh assault on his jaw.

"Stop stop!" he wheezed. "I'm your grandfather!"

She paused, her face exactly on top of his. Pale identical eye looked into pale identical eye. "Have you had enough?" she asked.

The old man looked up into his own image. It was triumphant and hostile. "You been whipped," it said, "by me," and then it added, bearing down on each word, "and I'm PURE Pitts."

In the pause she loosened her grip and he got hold of her throat. With a sudden surge of strength, he managed to roll over and reverse their positions so that he was looking down into the face that was his own but had dared to call itself Pitts. With his hands still tight around her neck, he lifted her head and brought it down once hard against the rock that happened to be under it. Then he brought it down twice more. Then looking into the face in which the eyes, slowly rolling back, appeared to pay him not the slightest attention, he said, "There's not an ounce of Pitts in me."

He continued to stare at his conquered image until he perceived that though it was absolutely silent, there was no look of remorse on it. The eyes had rolled back down and were set in a fixed glare that did not take him in. "This ought to teach you a good lesson," he said in a voice that was edged with doubt.

He managed painfully to get up on his unsteady kicked legs and to take two steps, but the enlargement of his heart which had begun in the car was still going on. He turned his head and looked behind him for a long time at the little motionless figure with its head on the rock.

Then he fell on his back and looked up helplessly along the bare trunks into the tops of the pines and his heart expanded once more with a convulsive motion. It expanded so fast that the old man felt as if he were being pulled after it through the woods, felt as if he were running as fast as he could with the ugly pines toward the lake. He perceived that there would be a little opening there, a little place where he could escape and leave the woods behind him. He could see it in the distance already, a little opening where the white sky was reflected in the water. It grew as he ran toward it until suddenly the whole lake opened up before him, riding majestically in little corrugated folds toward his feet. He realized suddenly that he could not swim and that he had not bought the boat. On both sides of him he saw that the gaunt trees had thickened into mysterious dark files that were marching across the water and away into the distance. He looked around desperately for someone to help him but the place was deserted except for one huge yellow monster which sat to the side, as stationary as he was, gorging itself on clay.

The Enduring Chill

Asbury's train stopped so that he would get off exactly where his mother was standing waiting to meet him. Her thin spectacled face below him was bright with a wide smile that disappeared as she caught sight of him bracing himself behind the conductor. The smile vanished so suddenly, the shocked look that replaced it was so complete, that he realized for the first time that he must look as ill as he was. The sky was a chill gray and a startling white-gold sun, like some strange potentate from the east, was rising beyond the black woods that surrounded Timberboro. It cast a strange light over the single block of one-story brick and wooden shacks. Asbury felt that he was about to witness a majestic transformation, that the flat of roofs might at any moment turn into the mounting turrets of some exotic temple for a god he didn't know. The illusion lasted only a moment before his attention was drawn back to his mother.

She had given a little cry; she looked aghast. He was pleased that she should see death in his face at once. His mother, at the age of sixty, was going to be introduced to reality and he supposed that if the experience didn't kill her, it would assist her in the process of growing up. He stepped down and greeted her.

"You don't look very well," she said and gave him a long clinical stare.

"I don't feel like talking," he said at once. "I've had a bad trip."

Mrs. Fox observed that his left eye was bloodshot. He was puffy and pale and his hair had receded tragically for a boy of twenty-five. The thin reddish wedge of it left on top bore down in a point that seemed to lengthen his nose and give him an irritable expression that matched his tone of voice when he spoke to her. "It must have been cold up there," she said. "Why don't you take off your coat? It's not cold down here."

"You don't have to tell me what the temperature is!" he said in a high voice. "I'm old enough to know when I want to take my coat off!" The train glided silently away behind him, leaving a view of the twin blocks of dilapidated stores. He gazed after the aluminum speck disappearing into the woods. It seemed to him that his last connection with a larger world were vanishing forever. Then he turned and faced his mother grimly, irked that he had allowed himself, even for an instant, to see an imaginary temple in this collapsing country junction. He had become entirely accustomed to the thought of death, but he had not become accustomed to the thought of death *here*.

He had felt the end coming on for nearly four months. Alone in his freezing flat, huddled under his two blankets and his overcoat and with three thicknesses of the New York

Times between, he had had a chill one night, followed by a violent sweat that left the sheets soaking and removed all doubt from his mind about his true condition. Before this there had been a gradual slackening of his energy and vague inconsistent aches and headaches. He had been absent so many days from his part-time job in the bookstore that he had lost it. Since then he had been living, or just barely so, on his savings and these, diminishing day by day, had been all he had between him and home. Now there was nothing. He was here.

"Where's the car?" he muttered.

"It's over yonder," his mother said. "And your sister is asleep in the back because I don't like to come out this early by myself. There's no need to wake her up."

"No," he said, "let sleeping dogs lie," and he picked up his two bulging suitcases and started across the road with them.

They were too heavy for him and by the time he reached the car, his mother saw that he was exhausted. He had never come home with two suitcases before. Ever since he had first gone away to college, he had come back every time with nothing but the necessities for a two-week stay and with a wooden resigned expression that said he was prepared to endure the visit for exactly fourteen days. "You've brought more than usual," she observed, but he did not answer.

He opened the car door and hoisted the two bags in beside his sister's upturned feet, giving first the feet—in Girl Scout shoes—and then the rest of her a revolted look of recognition. She was packed into a black suit and had a white rag around her head with metal curlers sticking out from under the edges. Her eyes were closed and her mouth was open. He and she had the same features except that hers were bigger. She was eight years older than he was and was principal of the county elementary school. He shut the door softly so she wouldn't wake up and then went around and got in the front seat and closed his eyes. His mother backed the car into the road and in a few minutes he felt it swerve into the highway. Then he opened his eyes. The road stretched between two open fields of yellow bitterweed.

"Do you think Timberboro has improved?" his mother asked. This was her standard question, meant to be taken literally.

"It's still there, isn't it?" he said in an ugly voice.

"Two of the stores have new fronts," she said. Then with a sudden ferocity, she said, "You did well to come home where you can get a good doctor! I'll take you to Doctor Block this afternoon."

"I am not," he said, trying to keep his voice from shaking, "going to Doctor Block. This afternoon or ever. Don't you think if I'd wanted to go to a doctor I'd have gone up there where they have some good ones? Don't you know they have better doctors in New York?"

"He would take a personal interest in you," she said. "None of those doctors up there would take a personal interest in you."

"I don't want him taking a personal interest in me." Then after a minute, staring out across a blurred purple-looking field, he said, "What's wrong with me is way beyond Block," and his voice trailed off into a frayed sound, almost a sob.

He could not, as his friend Goetz had recommended, prepare to see it all as illusion, either what had gone before or the few weeks that were left to him. Goetz was certain that death was nothing at all. Goetz, whose whole face had always been purple-splotched with a million indignations, had returned from six months in Japan as dirty as ever but as bland as the Buddha himself. Goetz took the news of Asbury's approaching end with a calm indifference. Quoting something or other he said, "Although the Bodhisattva leads an infinite number of creatures into nirvana, in reality there are neither any Bodhisattvas to do the leading nor any creatures to be led." However, out of some feeling for his welfare, Goetz had put forth $4.50 to take him to a lecture on Vedanta. It had been a waste of his money. While Goetz had listened enthralled to the dark little man on the platform, Asbury's bored gaze had roved among the audience. It had passed over the heads of several girls in saris, past a Japanese youth, a blue-black man with a fez, and several girls who looked like secretaries. Finally, at the end of the row, it had rested on a lean spectacled figure in black, a priest. The priest's expression was of a polite but strictly reserved interest. Asbury identified his own feelings immediately in the taciturn superior expression. When the lecture was over a few students met in Goetz's flat, the priest among them, but here he was equally reserved. He listened with a marked politeness to the discussion of Asbury's approaching death, but he said little. A girl in a sari remarked that self-fulfillment was out of the question since it meant salvation and the word was meaningless. "Salvation," quoted Goetz, "is the destruction of a simple prejudice, and no one is saved."

"And what do you say to that?" Asbury asked the priest and returned his reserved smile over the heads of the others. The borders of this smile seemed to touch on some icy clarity.

"There is," the priest said, "a real probability of the New Man, assisted, of course," he added brittlely, "by the Third Person of the Trinity."

"Ridiculous!" the girl in the sari said, but the priest only brushed her with his smile, which was slightly amused now.

When he got up to leave, he silently handed Asbury a small card on which he had written his name, Ignatius Vogle, S.J., and an address. Perhaps, Asbury thought now, he should have used it for the priest appealed to him as a man of the world, someone who would have understood the unique tragedy of his death, a death whose meaning had been far beyond the twittering group around them. And how much more beyond Block. "What's wrong with me," he repeated, "is way beyond Block."

His mother knew at once what he meant: he meant he was going to have a nervous breakdown. She did not say a word. She did not say that this was precisely what she could have told him would happen. When people think they are smart—even when they are smart—there is nothing anybody else can say to make them see things straight, and with Asbury, the trouble was that in addition to being smart, he had an artistic temperament. She did not know where he had got it from because his father, who was a lawyer and businessman and farmer and politician all rolled into one, had certainly had his feet on the ground; and she had certainly always had hers on it. She had managed after he died to get the two of them through college and beyond; but she had observed that the more education they got, the less they could do. Their father had gone to a one-room schoolhouse through the eighth grade and he could do anything.

She could have told Asbury what would help him. She could have said, "If you would get out in the sunshine, or if you would work for a month in the dairy, you'd be a different person!" but she knew exactly how that suggestion would be received. He would be a nuisance in the dairy but she would let him work in there if he wanted to. She had let him work in there last year when he had come home and was writing the play. He had been writing a play about Negroes (why anybody would want to write a play about Negroes was beyond her) and he had said he wanted to work in the dairy with them and find out what their interests were. Their interests were in doing as little as they could get by with, as she could have told him if anybody could have told him anything. The Negroes had put up with him and he had learned to put the milkers on and once he had washed all the cans and she thought that once he had mixed feed. Then a cow had kicked him and he had not gone back to the barn again. She knew that if he would get in there now, or get out and fix fences, or do any kind of work—real work, not writing—that he might avoid this nervous breakdown. "Whatever happened to that play you were writing about the Negroes?" she asked.

"I am not writing plays," he said. "And get this through your head: I am not working in any dairy. I am not getting out in the sunshine. I'm ill. I have fever and chills and I'm dizzy and all I want you to do is leave me alone."

"Then if you are really ill, you should see Doctor Block."

"And I am not seeing Block," he finished and ground himself down in the seat and stared intensely in front of him.

She turned into their driveway, a red road that ran for a quarter of a mile through the two front pastures. The dry cows were on one side and the milk herd on the other. She slowed the car and then stopped altogether, her attention caught by a cow with a bad quarter. "They haven't been attending to her," she said. "Look at that bag!"

Asbury turned his head abruptly in the opposite direction, but there a small, walleyed Guernsey was watching him steadily as if she sensed some bond between them. "Good God!" he cried in an agonized voice, "can't we go on? It's six o'clock in the morning!"

"Yes yes," his mother said and started the car quickly.

"What's that cry of deadly pain?" his sister drawled from the back seat. "Oh it's you," she said. "Well well, we have the artist with us again. How utterly utterly." She had a decidedly nasal voice.

He didn't answer her or turn his head. He had learned that much. Never answer her.

"Mary George!" his mother said sharply. "Asbury is sick. Leave him alone."

"What's wrong with him?" Mary George asked.

"There's the house!" his mother said as if they were all blind but her. It rose on the crest of the hill—a white two-story farmhouse with a wide porch and pleasant columns. She always approached it with a feeling of pride and she had said more than once to Asbury, "You have a home here that half those people up there would give their eyeteeth for!"

She had been once to the terrible place he lived in New York. They had gone up five flights of dark stone steps, past open garbage cans on every landing, to arrive finally at two damp rooms and a closet with a toilet in it. "You wouldn't live like this at home," she had muttered.

"No!" he'd said with an ecstatic look, "it wouldn't be possible!"

She supposed the truth was that she simply didn't understand how it felt to be sensitive or how peculiar you were when you were an artist. His sister said he was not an artist and that he had no talent and that that was the trouble with him; but Mary George was not a happy girl herself. Asbury said she posed as an intellectual but that her I.Q. couldn't be over seventy-five, that all she was really interested in was getting a man but that no sensible man would finish a first look at her. She had tried to tell him that Mary George could be very attractive when she put her mind to it and he had said that that much strain on her mind would break her down. If she were in any way attractive, he had said, she wouldn't now be principal of a county elementary school, and Mary George had said that if Asbury had had any talent, he would by now have published something. What had he ever published, she wanted to know, and for that matter, what had he ever written?

Mrs. Fox had pointed out that he was only twenty-five years old and Mary George had said that the age most people published something at was twenty-one, which made him exactly four years overdue. Mrs. Fox was not up on things like that but she suggested that he might be writing a very *long* book. Very long book, her eye, Mary George said, he would do well if he came up with so much as a poem. Mrs. Fox hoped it wasn't going to be just a poem.

She pulled the car into the side drive and a scattering of guineas exploded into the air and sailed screaming around the house. "Home again, home again jiggity jig!" she said.

"Oh God," Asbury groaned.

"The artist arrives at the gas chamber," Mary George said in her nasal voice.

He leaned on the door and got out, and forgetting his bags he moved toward the front of the house as if he were in a daze. His sister got out and stood by the car door, squinting at his bent unsteady figure. As she watched him go up the front steps, her mouth fell slack in her astonished face. "Why," she said, "there *is* something the matter with him. He looks a hundred years old."

"Didn't I tell you so?" her mother hissed. "Now you keep your mouth shut and let him alone."

He went into the house, pausing in the hall only long enough to see his pale broken face glare at him for an instant from the pier mirror. Holding onto the banister, he pulled himself up the steep stairs, across the landing and then up the shorter second flight and into his room, a large open airy room with a faded blue rug and white curtains freshly put up for his arrival. He looked at nothing, but fell face down on his own bed. It was a narrow antique bed with a high ornamental headboard on which was carved a garlanded basket overflowing with wooden fruit.

While he was still in New York, he had written a letter to his mother which filled two notebooks. He did not mean it to be read until after his death. It was such a letter as Kafka had addressed to his father. Asbury's father had died twenty years ago and Asbury considered this a great blessing. The old man, he felt sure, had been one of the courthouse gang, a rural worthy with a dirty finger in every pie and he knew he would not have been able to stomach him. He had read some of his correspondence and had been appalled by its stupidity.

He knew, of course, that his mother would not understand the letter at once. Her literal mind would require some time to discover the significance of it, but he thought she would be able to see that he forgave her for all she had done to him. For that matter, he supposed that she would realize what she had done to him only through the letter. He didn't think she was conscious of it at all. Her self-satisfaction itself was barely conscious, but because of the letter, she might experience a painful realization and this would be the only thing of value he had to leave her.

If reading it would be painful to her, writing it had sometimes been unbearable to him—for in order to face her, he had had to face himself. "I came here to escape the slave's atmosphere of home," he had written, "to find freedom, to liberate my imagination, to take it like a hawk from its cage and set it 'whirling off into the widening gyre' (Yeats) and what did I find? It was incapable of flight. It was some bird you had domesticated, sitting huffy in its pen, refusing to come out!" The next words were underscored twice. "I have no imagination. I have no talent. I can't create. I have nothing but the desire for these things. Why didn't you kill that too? Woman, why did you pinion me?"

Writing this, he had reached the pit of despair and he thought that reading it, she would at least begin to sense his tragedy and her part in it. It was not that she had ever forced her way on him. That had never been necessary. Her way had simply been the air he breathed and when at last he had found other air, he couldn't survive in it. He felt that even if she didn't understand at once, the letter would leave her with an enduring chill and perhaps in time lead her to see herself as she was.

He had destroyed everything else he had ever written—his two lifeless novels, his half-dozen stationary plays, his prosy poems, his sketchy short stories—and kept only the two notebooks that contained the letter. They were in the black suitcase that his sister, huffing and blowing, was now dragging up the second flight of stairs. His mother was carrying the smaller bag and came on ahead. He turned over as she entered the room.

"I'll open this and get out your things," she said, "and you can go right to bed and in a few minutes I'll bring your breakfast."

He sat up and said in a fretful voice, "I don't want any breakfast and I can open my own suitcase. Leave that alone."

His sister arrived in the door, her face full of curiosity, and let the black bag fall with a thud over the doorsill. Then she began to push it across the room with her foot until she was close enough to get a good look at him. "If I looked as bad as you do," she said, "I'd go to the hospital."

Her mother cut her eyes sharply at her and she left.

Then Mrs. Fox closed the door and came to the bed and sat down on it beside him. "Now this time I want you to make a long visit and rest," she said.

"This visit," he said, "will be permanent."

"Wonderful!" she cried. "You can have a little studio in your room and in the mornings you can write plays and in the afternoons you can help in the dairy!"

He turned a white wooden face to her. "Close the blinds and let me sleep," he said.

When she was gone, he lay for some time staring at the water stains on the gray walls. Descending from the top molding, long icicle shapes had been etched by leaks and, directly over his bed on the ceiling, another leak had made a fierce bird with spread wings. It had an icicle crosswise in its beak and there were smaller icicles depending from its wings and tail. It had been there since his childhood and had always irritated him and sometimes had frightened him. He had often had the illusion that it was in motion and about to descend mysteriously and set the icicle on his head. He closed his eyes and thought: I won't have to look at it for many more days. And presently he went to sleep.

When he woke up in the afternoon, there was a pink open-mouthed face hanging over him and from two large familiar ears on either side of it the black tubes of Block's stethoscope extended down to his exposed chest. The doctor, seeing he was awake, made a face like a Chinaman, rolled his eyes almost out of his head and cried, "Say AHHHH!"

Block was irresistible to children. For miles around they vomited and went into fevers to have a visit from him. Mrs. Fox was standing behind him, smiling radiantly. "Here's Doctor Block!" she said as if she had captured this angel on the rooftop and brought him in for her little boy.

"Get him out of here," Asbury muttered. He looked at the asinine face from what seemed the bottom of a black hole.

The doctor peered closer, wiggling his ears. Block was bald and had a round face as senseless as a baby's. Nothing about him indicated intelligence except two cold clinical nickel-colored eyes that hung with a motionless curiosity over whatever he looked at. "You sho do look bad, Azzberry," he murmured. He took the stethoscope off and dropped it in his bag. "I don't know when I've seen anybody your age look as sorry as you do. What you been doing to yourself?"

There was a continuous thud in the back of Asbury's head as if his heart had got trapped in it and was fighting to get out. "I didn't send for you," he said.

Block put his hand on the glaring face and pulled the eyelid down and peered into it. "You must have been on the bum up there," he said. He began to press his hand in the small of Asbury's back. "I went up there once myself," he said, "and saw exactly how little they had and came straight on back home. Open your mouth."

Asbury opened it automatically and the drill-like gaze swung over it and bore down. He snapped it shut and in a wheezing breathless voice he said, "If I'd wanted a doctor, I'd have stayed up there where I could have got a good one!"

"Asbury!" his mother said.

"How long you been having the so' throat?" Block asked.

"She sent for you!" Asbury said. "She can answer the questions."

"Asbury!" his mother said.

Block leaned over his bag and pulled out a rubber tube. He pushed Asbury's sleeve up and tied the tube around his upper arm. Then he took out a syringe and prepared to find the vein, humming a hymn as he pressed the needle in. Asbury lay with a rigid outraged stare while the privacy of his blood was invaded by this idiot. "Slowly Lord but sure," Block sang in a murmuring voice, "Oh slowly Lord but sure." When the syringe was full, he withdrew the needle. "Blood don't lie," he said. He poured it in a bottle and stopped it up and put the bottle in his bag. "Azzberry," he started, "how long . . ."

Asbury sat up and thrust his thudding head forward and said, "I didn't send for you. I'm not answering any questions. You're not my doctor. What's wrong with me is way beyond you."

"Most things are beyond me," Block said. "I ain't found anything yet that I thoroughly understood," and he sighed and got up. His eyes seemed to glitter at Asbury as if from a great distance.

"He wouldn't act so ugly," Mrs. Fox explained, "if he weren't really sick. And *I* want you to come back every day until you get him well."

Asbury's eyes were a fierce glaring violet. "What's wrong with me is way beyond you," he repeated and lay back down and closed his eyes until Block and his mother were gone.

In the next few days, though he grew rapidly worse, his mind functioned with a terrible clarity. On the point of death, he found himself existing in a state of illumination that was totally out of keeping with the kind of talk he had to listen to from his mother. This was largely about cows with names like Daisy and Bessie Button and their intimate functions—their mastitis and their screwworms and their abortions. His mother insisted that in the middle of the day he get out and sit on the porch and "enjoy the view" and as resistance was too much of a struggle, he dragged himself out and sat there in a rigid slouch, his feet wrapped in an afghan and his hands gripped on the chair arms as if he were about to spring forward into the glaring china blue sky. The lawn extended for a quarter of an acre down to a barbed-wire fence that divided it from the front pasture. In the middle of the day the dry cows rested there under a line of sweetgum trees. On the other side of the road were two hills with a pond between and his mother could sit on the porch and watch the herd walk across the dam to the hill on the other side. The whole scene was rimmed by a wall of trees which, at the time of day he was forced to sit there, was a washed-out blue that reminded him sadly of the Negroes' faded overalls.

He listened irritably while his mother detailed the faults of the help. "Those two are not stupid," she said. "They know how to look out for themselves."

"They need to," he muttered, but there was no use to argue with her. Last year he had been writing a play about the Negro and he had wanted to be around them for a while to see how they really felt about their condition, but the two who worked for her had lost all their initiative over the years. They didn't talk. The one called Morgan was light brown, part Indian; the other, older one, Randall, was very black and fat. When they said anything to him, it was as if they were speaking to an invisible body located to the right or left of where he actually was, and after two days working side by side with them, he felt he had not established rapport. He decided to try something bolder than talk and one afternoon as he was standing near Randall, watching him adjust a milker, he had quietly taken out his cigarettes and lit one. The Negro had stopped what he was doing and watched him. He waited until Asbury had taken two draws and then he said, "She don't 'low no smoking in here."

The other one approached and stood there, grinning.

"I know it," Asbury said and after a deliberate pause, he shook the package and held it out, first to Randall, who took one, and then to Morgan, who took one. He had then lit the cigarettes for them himself and the three of them had stood there smoking. There were no sounds but the steady click of the two milking machines and the occasional slap of a cow's tail against her side. It was one of those moments of communion when the difference between black and white is absorbed into nothing.

The next day two cans of milk had been returned from the creamery because it had absorbed the odor of tobacco. He took the blame and told his mother that it was he and not the Negroes who had been smoking. "If you were doing it, they were doing it," she had said. "Don't you think I know those two?" She was incapable of thinking them innocent; but the experience had so exhilarated him that he had been determined to repeat it in some other way.

The next afternoon when he and Randall were in the milk house pouring the fresh milk into the cans, he had picked up the jelly glass the Negroes drank out of and, inspired, had poured himself a glassful of the warm milk and drained it down. Randall had stopped pouring and had remained, half-bent, over the can, watching him. "She don't 'low that," he said. "That *the* thing she don't 'low."

Asbury poured out another glassful and handed it to him.

"She don't 'low it," he repeated.

"Listen," Asbury said hoarsely, "the world is changing. There's no reason I shouldn't drink after you or you after me!"

"She don't 'low noner us to drink noner this here milk," Randall said.

Asbury continued to hold the glass out to him. "You took

the cigarette," he said. "Take the milk. It's not going to hurt my mother to lose two or three glasses of milk a day. We've got to think free if we want to live free!"

The other one had come up and was standing in the door.

"Don't want noner that milk," Randall said.

Asbury swung around and held the glass out to Morgan. "Here boy, have a drink of this," he said.

Morgan stared at him; then his face took on a decided look of cunning. "I ain't seen you drink none of it yourself," he said.

Asbury despised milk. The first warm glassful had turned his stomach. He drank half of what he was holding and handed the rest to the Negro, who took it and gazed down inside the glass as if it contained some great mystery; then he set it on the floor by the cooler.

"Don't you like milk?" Asbury asked.

"I likes it but I ain't drinking noner that."

"Why?"

"She don't 'low it," Morgan said.

"My God!' Asbury exploded, "she she she!" He had tried the same thing the next day and the next and the next but he could not get them to drink the milk. A few afternoons later when he was standing outside the milk house about to go in, he heard Morgan ask, "Howcome you let him drink all that milk every day?"

"What he do is him," Randall said. "What I do is me."

"Howcome he talks so ugly about his ma?"

"She ain't whup him enough when he was little," Randall said.

The insufferableness of life at home had overcome him and he had returned to New York two days early. So far as he was concerned he had died there, and the question now was how long he could stand to linger here. He could have hastened his end but suicide would not have been a victory. Death was coming to him legitimately, as a justification, as a gift from life. That was his greatest triumph. Then too, to the fine minds of the neighborhood, a suicide son would indicate a mother who had been a failure, and while this was the case, he felt that it was a public embarrassment he could spare her. What she would learn from the letter would be a private revelation. He had sealed the notebooks in a manila envelope and had written on it: "To be opened only after the death of Asbury Porter Fox." He had put the envelope in the desk drawer in his room and locked it and the key was in his pajama pocket until he could decide on a place to leave it.

When they sat on the porch in the morning, his mother felt that some of the time she should talk about subjects that were of interest to him. The third morning she started in on his writing. "When you get well," she said, "I think it would be nice if you wrote a book about down here. We need another good book like *Gone With the Wind.*"

He could feel the muscles in his stomach begin to tighten.

"Put the war in it," she advised. "That always makes a long book."

He put his head back gently as if he were afraid it would crack. After a moment he said, "I am not going to write any book."

"Well," she said, "if you don't feel like writing a book, you could just write poems. They're nice." She realized that what he needed was someone intellectual to talk to, but Mary George was the only intellectual she knew and he would not talk to her. She had thought of Mr. Bush, the retired Methodist minister, but she had not brought this up. Now she decided to hazard it. "I think I'll ask Dr. Bush to come to see you," she said, raising Mr. Bush's rank. "You'd enjoy him. He collects rare coins."

She was not prepared for the reaction she got. He began to shake all over and give loud spasmodic laughs. He seemed about to choke. After a minute he subsided into a cough. "If you think I need spiritual aid to die," he said, "you're quite mistaken. And certainly not from that ass Bush. My God!"

"I didn't mean that at all," she said. "He has coins dating from the time of Cleopatra."

"Well if you ask him here, I'll tell him to go to hell," he said. "Bush! That beats all!"

"I'm glad something amuses you," she said acidly.

For a time they sat there in silence. Then his mother looked up. He was sitting forward again and smiling at her. His face was brightening more and more as if he had just had an idea that was brilliant. She stared at him. "I'll tell you who I want to come," he said. For the first time since he had come home, his expression was pleasant; though there was also, she thought, a kind of crafty look about him.

"Who do you want to come?" she asked suspiciously.

"I want a priest," he announced.

"A priest?" his mother said in an uncomprehending voice.

"Preferably a Jesuit," he said, brightening more and more. "Yes, by all means a Jesuit. They have them in the city. You can call up and get me one."

"What is the matter with you?" his mother asked.

"Most of them are very well-educated," he said, "but Jesuits are foolproof. A Jesuit would be able to discuss something besides the weather." Already, remembering Ignatius Vogle, S.J., he could picture the priest. This one would be a trifle more worldly perhaps, a trifle more cynical. Protected by their ancient institution, priests could afford to be cynical, to play both ends against the middle. He would talk to a man of culture before he died—even in this desert! Furthermore, nothing would irritate his mother so much. He could not understand why he had not thought of this sooner.

"You're not a member of that church," Mrs. Fox said shortly. "It's twenty miles away. They wouldn't send one." She hoped that this would end the matter.

He sat back absorbed in the idea, determined to force her to make the call since she always did what he wanted if he kept at her. "I'm dying," he said, "and I haven't asked you to do but one thing and you refuse me that."

"You are NOT dying."

"When you realize it," he said, "it'll be too late."

There was another unpleasant silence. Presently his mother said, "Nowadays doctors don't *let* young people die. They give them some of these new medicines." She began shaking her foot with a nerve-rattling assurance. "People just don't die like they used to," she said.

"Mother," he said, "you ought to be prepared. I think even Block knows and hasn't told you yet." Block, after the first visit, had come in grimly every time, without his jokes and funny faces, and had taken his blood in silence, his nickel-colored eyes unfriendly. He was, by definition, the enemy of death and he looked now as if he knew he was battling the real thing. He had said he wouldn't prescribe until he knew what was wrong and Asbury had laughed in his face. "Mother," he said, "I AM going to die," and he tried to make each word like a hammer blow on top of her head.

She paled slightly but she did not blink. "Do you think for one minute," she said angrily, "that I intend to sit here and let you die?" Her eyes were as hard as two old mountain ranges seen in the distance. He felt the first distinct stroke of doubt.

"Do you?" she asked fiercely.

"I don't think you have anything to do with it," he said in a shaken voice.

"Humph," she said and got up and left the porch as if she could not stand to be around such stupidity an instant longer.

Forgetting the Jesuit, he went rapidly over his symptoms: his fever had increased, interspersed by chills; he barely had the energy to drag himself out on the porch; food was abhorrent to him; and Block had not been able to give her the least satisfaction. Even as he sat there, he felt the beginning of a new chill, as if death were already playfully rattling his bones. He pulled the afghan off his feet and put it around his shoulders and made his way unsteadily up the stairs to bed.

He continued to grow worse. In the next few days he became so much weaker and badgered her so constantly about the Jesuit that finally in desperation she decided to humor his foolishness. She made the call, explaining in a chilly voice that her son was ill, perhaps a little out of his head, and wished to speak to a priest. While she made the call, Asbury hung over the banisters, barefooted, with the afghan around him, and listened. When she hung up he called down to know when the priest was coming.

"Tomorrow sometime," his mother said irritably.

He could tell by the fact that she made the call that her assurance was beginning to shatter. Whenever she let Block in or out, there was much whispering in the downstairs hall. That evening, he heard her and Mary George talking in low voices in the parlor. He thought he heard his name and he got up and tiptoed into the hall and down the first three steps until he could hear the voices distinctly.

"I had to call that priest," his mother was saying. "I'm afraid this is serious. I thought it was just a nervous breakdown but now I think it's something real. Doctor Block thinks it's something real too and whatever it is is worse because he's so run-down."

"Grow up, Mamma," Mary George said, "I've told you and I tell you again: what's wrong with him is purely psychosomatic." There was nothing she was not an expert on.

"No," his mother said, "it's a real disease. The doctor says so." He thought he detected a crack in her voice.

"Block is an idiot," Mary George said. "You've got to face the facts: Asbury can't write so he gets sick. He's going to be an invalid instead of an artist. Do you know what he needs?"

"No," his mother said.

"Two or three shock treatments," Mary George said. "Get that artist business out of his head once and for all."

His mother gave a little cry and he grasped the banister.

"Mark my words," his sister continued, "all he's going to be around here for the next fifty years is a decoration."

He went back to bed. In a sense she was right. He had failed his god, Art, but he had been a faithful servant and Art was sending him Death. He had seen this from the first with a kind of mystical clarity. He went to sleep thinking of the peaceful spot in the family burying ground where he would soon lie, and after a while he saw that his body was being borne slowly toward it while his mother and Mary George watched without interest from their chairs on the porch. As the bier was carried across the dam, they could look up and see the procession reflected upside down in the pond. A lean dark figure in a Roman collar followed it. He had a mysteriously saturnine face in which there was a subtle blend of asceticism and corruption. Asbury was laid in a shallow grave on the hillside and the indistinct mourners, after standing in silence for a while, spread out over the darkening green. The Jesuit retired to a spot beneath a dead tree to smoke and meditate. The moon came up and Asbury was aware of a presence bending over him and a gentle warmth on his cold face. He knew that this was Art come to wake him and he sat up and opened his eyes. Across the hill all the lights were on in his mother's house. The black pond was speckled with little nickel-colored stars. The Jesuit had disappeared. All around him the cows were spread out grazing in the moonlight and one large white one, violently spotted, was softly licking his head as if it were a block of salt. He awoke with a shudder and discovered that his bed was soaking from a night sweat and as he sat shivering in the dark, he realized that the end was not many days distant. He gazed down into the crater of death and fell back dizzy on his pillow.

The next day his mother noted something almost ethereal about his ravaged face. He looked like one of those dying children who must have Christmas early. He sat up in the bed and directed the rearrangement of several chairs and had her remove a picture of a maiden chained to a rock for he knew it would make the Jesuit smile. He had the comfortable rocker taken away and when he finished, the room with its severe wall stains had a certain cell-like quality. He felt it would be attractive to the visitor.

All morning he waited, looking irritably up at the ceiling where the bird with the icicle in its beak seemed poised and waiting too; but the priest did not arrive until late in the afternoon. As soon as his mother opened the door, a loud unintelligible voice began to boom in the downstairs hall. Asbury's heart beat wildly. In a second there was a heavy creaking on the stairs. Then almost at once his mother, her expression constrained, came in followed by a massive old man who plowed straight across the room, picked up a chair by the side of the bed and put it under himself.

"I'm Fahther Finn—from Purrgatory," he said in a hearty voice. He had a large red face, a stiff brush of gray hair and was blind in one eye, but the good eye, blue and clear, was focussed sharply on Asbury. There was a grease spot on his vest. "So you want to talk to a priest?" he said. "Very wise. None of us knows the hour Our Blessed Lord may call us." Then he cocked his good eye up at Asbury's mother and said, "Thank you, you may leave us now."

Mrs. Fox stiffened and did not budge.

"I'd like to talk to Father Finn alone," Asbury said, feeling suddenly that here he had an ally, although he had not expected a priest like this one. His mother gave him a disgusted look and left the room. He knew she would go no farther than just outside the door.

"It's so nice to have you come," Asbury said. "This place is incredibly dreary. There's no one here an intelligent person can talk to. I wonder what you think of Joyce, Father?"

The priest lifted his chair and pushed closer. "You'll have to shout," he said. "Blind in one eye and deaf in one ear."

"What do you think of Joyce?" Asbury said louder.

"Joyce? Joyce who?" asked the priest.

"James Joyce," Asbury said and laughed.

The priest brushed his huge hand in the air as if he were bothered by gnats. "I haven't met him," he said. "Now. Do you say your morning and night prayers?"

Asbury appeared confused. "Joyce was a great writer," he murmured, forgetting to shout.

"You don't eh?" said the priest. "Well you will never learn to be good unless you pray regularly. You cannot love Jesus unless you speak to Him."

"The myth of the dying god has always fascinated me," Asbury shouted, but the priest did not appear to catch it.

"Do you have trouble with purity?" he demanded, and as Asbury paled, he went on without waiting for an answer. "We all do but you must pray to the Holy Ghost for it. Mind, heart and body. Nothing is overcome without prayer. Pray with your family. Do you pray with your family?"

"God forbid," Asbury murmured. "My mother doesn't have time to pray and my sister is an atheist," he shouted.

"A shame!" said the priest. "Then you must pray for them."

"The artist prays by creating," Asbury ventured.

"Not enough!" snapped the priest. "If you do not pray daily, you are neglecting your immortal soul. Do you know your catechism?"

"Certainly not," Asbury muttered.

"Who made you?" the priest asked in a martial tone.

"Different people believe different things about that," Asbury said.

"God made you," the priest said shortly. "Who is God?"

"God is an idea created by man," Asbury said, feeling that he was getting into stride, that two could play at this.

"God is a spirit infinitely perfect," the priest said. "You are a very ignorant boy. Why did God make you?"

"God didn't. . . ."

"God made you to know Him, to love Him, to serve Him in this world and to be happy with Him in the next!" the old priest said in a battering voice. "If you don't apply yourself to the catechism how do you expect to know how to save your immortal soul?"

Asbury saw he had made a mistake and that it was time to get rid of the old fool. "Listen," he said, "I'm not a Roman."

"A poor excuse for not saying your prayers!" the old man snorted.

Asbury slumped slightly in the bed. "I'm dying," he shouted.

"But you're not dead yet!" said the priest, "and how do you expect to meet God face to face when you've never spoken to Him? How do you expect to get what you don't ask for? God does not send the Holy Ghost to those who don't ask for Him. Ask Him to send the Holy Ghost."

"The Holy Ghost?" Asbury said.

"Are you so ignorant you've never heard of the Holy Ghost?" the priest asked.

"Certainly I've heard of the Holy Ghost" Asbury said furiously, "and the Holy Ghost is the last thing I'm looking for!"

"And He may be the last thing you get," the priest said, his one fierce eye inflamed. "Do you want your soul to suffer eternal damnation? Do you want to be deprived of God for all eternity? Do you want to suffer the most terrible pain, greater than fire, the pain of loss? Do you want to suffer the pain of loss for all eternity?"

Asbury moved his arms and legs helplessly as if he were pinned to the bed by the terrible eye.

"How can the Holy Ghost fill your soul when it's full of trash?" the priest roared. "The Holy Ghost will not come until you see yourself as you are—a lazy ignorant conceited youth!" he said, pounding his fist on the little bedside table.

Mrs. Fox burst in. "Enough of this!" she cried. "How dare you talk that way to a poor sick boy? You're upsetting him. You'll have to go."

"The poor lad doesn't even know his catechism," the priest said, rising. "I should think you would have taught him to say his daily prayers. You have neglected your duty as his mother." He turned back to the bed and said affably, "I'll give you my blessing and after this you must say your daily prayers without fail," whereupon he put his hand on Asbury's head and rumbled something in Latin. "Call me any time," he said, "and we can have another little chat," and then he followed Mrs. Fox's rigid back out. The last thing Asbury heard him say was, "He's a good lad at heart but very ignorant."

When his mother had got rid of the priest she came rapidly up the steps again to say that she had told him so, but when she saw him, pale and drawn and ravaged, sitting up in his bed, staring in front of him with large childish shocked eyes, she did not have the heart and went rapidly out again.

The next morning he was so weak that she made up her mind he must go to the hospital. "I'm not going to any hospital," he kept repeating, turning his thudding head from side to side as if he wanted to work it loose from his body. "I'm not going to any hospital as long as I'm conscious." He was thinking bitterly that once he lost consciousness, she could drag him off to the hospital and fill him full of blood and prolong his misery for days. He was convinced that the end was approaching, that it would be today, and he was tormented now thinking of his useless life. He felt as if he were a shell that had to be filled with something but he did not know what. He began to take note of everything in the room as if for the last time—the ridiculous antique furniture, the pattern in the rug, the silly picture his mother had replaced. He even looked at the fierce bird with the icicle in its beak and felt that it was there for some purpose that he could not divine.

There was something he was searching for, something that he felt he must have, some last significant culminating experience that he must make for himself before he died—make for himself out of his own intelligence. He had always relied on himself and had never been a sniveler after the ineffable.

Once when Mary George was thirteen and he was five, she had lured him with the promise of an unnamed present into a large tent full of people and had dragged him backwards up to the front where a man in a blue suit and red and white tie was standing. "Here," she said in a loud voice. "I'm already saved but you can save him. He's a real stinker and too big for his britches." He had broken her grip and shot out of there like a small cur and later when he had asked for his present, she had said, "You would have got Salvation if you had waited for it but since you acted the way you did, you get nothing!"

As the day wore on, he grew more and more frantic for fear he would die without making some last meaningful experience for himself. His mother sat anxiously by the side of the bed. She had called Block twice and could not get him. He thought even now she had not realized that he was going to die, much less than the end was only hours off.

The light in the room was beginning to have an odd quality, almost as if it were taking on presence. In a darkened form it entered and seemed to wait. Outside it appeared to move no farther than the edge of the faded treeline, which he could see a few inches over the sill of his window. Suddenly he thought of that experience of communion that he had had in the dairy with the Negroes when they had smoked together, and at once he began to tremble with excitement. They would smoke together one last time.

After a moment, turning his head on the pillow, he said, "Mother, I want to tell the Negroes good-bye."

His mother paled. For an instant her face seemed about

to fly apart. Then the line of her mouth hardened; her brows drew together. "Good-bye?" she said in a flat voice. "Where are you going?"

For a few seconds he only looked at her. Then he said, "I think you know. Get them. I don't have long."

"This is absurd," she muttered but she got up and hurried out. He heard her try to reach Block again before she went outside. He thought her clinging to Block at a time like this was touching and pathetic. He waited, preparing himself for the encounter as a religious man might prepare himself for the last sacrament. Presently he heard their steps on the stair.

"Here's Randall and Morgan," his mother said, ushering them in. "They've come to tell you hello."

The two of them came in grinning and shuffled to the side of the bed. They stood there, Randall in front and Morgan behind. "You sho do look well," Randall said. "You looks very well."

"You looks well," the other one said. "Yessuh, you looks fine."

"I ain't ever seen you looking so well before," Randall said.

"Yes, doesn't he look well?" his mother said. "I think he looks just fine."

"Yessuh," Randall said, "I speck you ain't even sick."

"Mother," Asbury said in a forced voice. "I'd like to talk to them alone."

His mother stiffened; then she marched out. She walked across the hall and into the room on the other side and sat down. Through the open doors he could see her begin to rock in little short jerks. The two Negroes looked as if their last protection had dropped away.

Asbury's head was so heavy he could not think what he had been going to do. "I'm dying," he said.

Both their grins became gelid. "You looks fine," Randall said.

"I'm going to die," Asbury repeated. Then with relief he remembered that they were going to smoke together. He reached for the package on the table and held it out to Randall, forgetting to shake out the cigarettes.

The Negro took the package and put it in his pocket. "I thank you," he said. "I certainly do prechate it."

Asbury stared as if he had forgotten again. After a second he became aware that the other Negro's face had turned infinitely sad; then he realized that it was not sad but sullen. He fumbled in the drawer of the table and pulled out an unopened package and thrust it at Morgan.

"I thanks you, Mist Asbury," Morgan said, brightening. "You certly does look well."

"I'm about to die," Asbury said irritably.

"You looks fine," Randall said.

"You be up and around in a few days," Morgan predicted. Neither of them seemed to find a suitable place to rest his gaze. Asbury looked wildly across the hall where his mother had her rocker turned so that her back faced him. It was apparent she had no intention of getting rid of them for him.

"I speck you might have a little cold," Randall said after a time.

"I takes a little turpentine and sugar when I has a cold," Morgan said.

"Shut your mouth," Randall said, turning on him.

"Shut your own mouth," Morgan said. "I know what I takes."

"He don't take what you take," Randall growled.

"Mother!" Asbury called in a shaking voice.

His mother stood up. "Mister Asbury has had company

long enough now," she called. "You all can come back to-morrow."

"We be going," Randall said. "You sho do look well."

"You sho does," Morgan said.

They filed out agreeing with each other how well he looked but Asbury's vision became blurred before they reached the hall. For an instant he saw his mother's form as if it were a shadow in the door and then it disappeared after them down the stairs. He heard her call Block again but he heard it without interest. His head was spinning. He knew now there would be no significant experience before he died. There was nothing more to do but give her the key to the drawer where the letter was, and wait for the end.

He sank into a heavy sleep from which he awoke about five o'clock to see her white face, very small, at the end of a well of darkness. He took the key out of his pajama pocket and handed it to her and mumbled that there was a letter in the desk to be opened when he was gone, but she did not seem to understand. She put the key down on the bedside table and left it there and he returned to his dream in which two large boulders were circling each other inside his head.

He awoke a little after six to hear Block's car stop below in the driveway. The sound was like a summons, bringing him rapidly and with a clear head out of his sleep. He had a sudden terrible foreboding that the fate awaiting him was going to be more shattering than any he could have reckoned on. He lay absolutely motionless, as still as an animal the instant before an earthquake.

Block and his mother talked as they came up the stairs but he did not distinguish their words. The doctor came in making faces; his mother was smiling. "Guess what you've got, Sugarpie!" she cried. Her voice broke in on him with the force of a gunshot.

"Found theter ol' bug, did ol' Block," Block said, sinking down into the chair by the bed. He raised his hands over his head in the gesture of a victorious prize fighter and let them collapse in his lap as if the effort had exhausted him. Then he removed a red bandanna handkerchief that he carried to be funny with and wiped his face thoroughly, having a different expression on it every time it appeared from behind the rag.

"I think you're just as smart as you can be!" Mrs. Fox said. "Asbury," she said, "you have undulant fever. It'll keep coming back but it won't kill you!" Her smile was as bright and intense as a lightbulb without a shade. "I'm so relieved," she said.

Asbury sat up slowly, his face expressionless; then he fell back down again.

Block leaned over him and smiled. "You ain't going to die," he said, with deep satisfaction.

Nothing about Asbury stirred except his eyes. They did not appear to move on the surface but somewhere in their blurred depths there was an almost imperceptible motion as if something were struggling feebly. Block's gaze seemed to reach down like a steel pin and hold whatever it was until the life was out of it. "Undulant fever ain't so bad, Azzberry," he murmured. "It's the same as Bang's in a cow."

The boy gave a low moan and then was quiet.

"He must have drunk some unpasteurized milk up there," his mother said softly and then the two of them tip-toed out as if they thought he were about to go to sleep.

When the sound of their footsteps had faded on the stairs, Asbury sat up again. He turned his head, almost surreptitiously, to the side where the key he had given his mother was lying on the bedside table. His hand shot out and closed over it and returned it to his pocket. He glanced across the room into the small oval-framed dresser mirror. The eyes that stared back at him were the same that had returned his gaze every day from that mirror but it seemed to him that they were paler. They looked shocked clean as if they had been prepared for some awful vision about to come down on him. He shuddered and turned his head quickly the other way and stared out the window. A blinding red-gold sun moved serenely from under a purple cloud. Below it the treeline was black against the crimson sky. It formed a brittle wall, standing as if it were the frail defense he had set up in his mind to protect him from what was coming. The boy fell back on his pillow and stared at the ceiling. His limbs that had been racked for so many weeks by fever and chill were numb now. The old life in him was exhausted. He awaited the coming of new. It was then that he felt the beginning of a chill, a chill so peculiar, so light, that it was like a warm ripple across a deeper sea of cold. His breath came short. The fierce bird which through the years of his childhood and the days of his illness had been poised over his head, waiting mysteriously, appeared all at once to be in motion. Asbury blanched and the last film of illusion was torn as if by a whirlwind from his eyes. He saw that for the rest of his days, frail, racked, but enduring, he would live in the face of a purifying terror. A feeble cry, a last impossible protest escaped him. But the Holy Ghost, emblazoned in ice instead of fire, continued, implacable, to descend.

The Comforts of Home

Thomas withdrew to the side of the window and with his head between the wall and the curtain he looked down on the driveway where the car had stopped. His mother and the little slut were getting out of it. His mother emerged slowly, stolid and awkward, and then the little slut's long slightly bowed legs slid out, the dress pulled above the knees. With a shriek of laughter she ran to meet the dog, who bounded, overjoyed, shaking with pleasure, to welcome her. Rage gathered throughout Thomas's large frame with a silent ominous intensity, like a mob assembling.

It was now up to him to pack a suitcase, go to the hotel, and stay there until the house should be cleared.

He did not know where a suitcase was, he disliked to pack, he needed his books, his typewriter was not portable, he was used to an electric blanket, he could not bear to eat in restaurants. His mother, with her daredevil charity, was about to wreck the peace of the house.

The back door slammed and the girl's laugh shot up from the kitchen, through the back hall, up the stairwell and into his room, making for him like a bolt of electricity. He jumped to the side and stood glaring about him. His words of the morning had been unequivocal: "If you bring that girl back into this house, I leave. You can choose—her or me."

She had made her choice. An intense pain gripped his throat. It was the first time in his thirty-five years . . . He felt a sudden burning moisture behind his eyes. Then he steadied himself, overcome by rage. On the contrary: she had not made any choice. She was counting on his attachment to his electric blanket. She would have to be shown.

The girl's laughter rang upward a second time and Thomas winced. He saw again her look of the night before. She had invaded his room. He had waked to find his door open and her in it. There was enough light from the hall to make her visible as she turned toward him. The face was like a comedienne's in a musical comedy—a pointed chin, wide apple cheeks and feline empty eyes. He had sprung out of his bed and snatched a straight chair and then he had backed her out the door, holding the chair in front of him like an animal trainer driving out a dangerous cat. He had driven her silently down the hall, pausing when he reached it to beat on his mother's door. The girl, with a gasp, turned and fled into the guest room.

In a moment his mother had opened her door and peered out apprehensively. Her face, greasy with whatever she put on it at night, was framed in pink rubber curlers. She looked down the hall where the girl had disappeared. Thomas stood before her, the chair still lifted in front of him as if he were about to quell another beast. "She tried to get in my room," he hissed, pushing in. "I woke up and she was trying to get in my room." He closed the door behind him and his voice rose in outrage. "I won't put up with this! I won't put up with it another day!"

His mother, backed by him to her bed, sat down on the edge of it. She had a heavy body on which sat a thin, mysteriously gaunt and incongruous head.

"I'm telling you for the last time," Thomas said, "I won't put up with this another day." There was an observable tendency in all of her actions. This was, with the best intentions in the world, to make a mockery of virtue, to pursue it with such a mindless intensity that everyone involved was made a fool of and virtue itself became ridiculous. "Not another day," he repeated.

His mother shook her head emphatically, her eyes still on the door.

Thomas put the chair on the floor in front of her and sat down on it. He leaned forward as if he were about to explain something to a defective child.

"That's just another way she's unfortunate," his mother said. "So awful, so awful. She told me the name of it but I forget what it is but it's something she can't help. Something she was born with. Thomas," she said and put her hand to her jaw, "suppose it were you?"

Exasperation blocked his windpipe. "Can't I make you see," he croaked, "that if she can't help herself you can't help her?"

His mother's eyes, intimate but untouchable, were the blue of great distances after sunset. "Nimpermaniac," she murmured.

"Nymphomaniac," he said fiercely. "She doesn't need to supply you with any fancy names. She's a moral moron.

That's all you need to know. Born without the moral faculty —like somebody else would be born without a kidney or a leg. Do you understand?"

"I keep thinking it might be you," she said, her hand still on her jaw. "If it were you, how do you think I'd feel if nobody took you in? What if you were a nimpermaniac and not a brilliant smart person and you did what you couldn't help and . . . "

Thomas felt a deep unbearable loathing for himself as if he were turning slowly into the girl.

"What did she have on?" she asked abruptly, her eyes narrowing.

"Nothing!" he roared. "Now will you get her out of here!"

"How can I turn her out in the cold?" she said. "This morning she was threatening to kill herself again."

"Send her back to jail," Thomas said.

"I would not send *you* back to jail, Thomas," she said.

He got up and snatched the chair and fled the room while he was still able to control himself.

Thomas loved his mother. He loved her because it was his nature to do so, but there were times when he could not endure her love for him. There were times when it became nothing but pure idiot mystery and he sensed about him forces, invisible currents entirely out of his control. She proceeded always from the tritest of considerations—it was the *nice thing to do*—into the most foolhardy engagements with the devil, whom, of course, she never recognized.

The devil for Thomas was only a manner of speaking, but it was a manner appropriate to the situations his mother got into. Had she been in any degree intellectual, he could have proved to her from early Christian history that no excess of virtue is justified, that a moderation of good produces likewise a moderation in evil, that if Antony of Egypt had stayed at home and attended to his sister, no devils would have plagued him.

Thomas was not cynical and so far from being opposed to virtue, he saw it as the principle of order and the only thing that makes life bearable. His own life was made bearable by the fruits of his mother's saner virtues—by the well-regulated house she kept and the excellent meals she served. But when virtue got out of hand with her, as now, a sense of devils grew upon him, and these were not mental quirks in himself or the old lady, they were denizens with personalities, present though not visible, who might any moment be expected to shriek or rattle a pot.

The girl had landed in the county jail a month ago on a bad check charge and his mother had seen her picture in the paper. At the breakfast table she had gazed at it for a long time and then had passed it over the coffee pot to him. "Imagine," she said, "only nineteen years old and in that filthy jail. And she doesn't look like a bad girl."

Thomas glanced at the picture. It showed the face of a shrewd ragamuffin. He observed that the average age for criminality was steadily lowering.

"She looks like a wholesome girl," his mother said.

"Wholesome people don't pass bad checks," Thomas said.

"You don't know what you'd do in a pinch."

"I wouldn't pass a bad check," Thomas said.

"I think," his mother said, "I'll take her a little box of candy."

If then and there he had put his foot down, nothing else would have happened. His father, had he been living, would have put his foot down at that point. Taking a box of candy was her favorite nice thing to do. When anyone within her social station moved to town, she called and took a box of candy; when any of her friend's children had babies or won a scholarship, she called and took a box of candy; when an old person broke his hip, she was at his bedside with a box of candy. He had been amused at the idea of her taking a box of candy to the jail.

He stood now in his room with the girl's laugh rocketing away in his head and cursed his amusement.

When his mother returned from the visit to the jail, she had burst into his study without knocking and had collapsed full-length on his couch, lifting her small swollen feet up on the arm of it. After a moment, she recovered herself enough to sit up and put a newspaper under them. Then she fell back again. "We don't know how the other half lives," she said.

Thomas knew that though her conversation moved from cliché to cliché there were real experiences behind them. He was less sorry for the girl's being in jail than for his mother having to see her there. He would have spared her all unpleasant sights. "Well," he said and put away his journal, "you had better forget it now. The girl has ample reason to be in jail."

"You can't imagine what all she's been through," she said, sitting up again, "listen." The poor girl, Star, had been brought up by a stepmother with three children of her own, one an almost grown boy who had taken advantage of her in such dreadful ways that she had been forced to run away and find her real mother. Once found, her real mother had sent her to various boarding schools to get rid of her. At each of these she had been forced to run away by the presence of perverts and sadists so monstrous that their acts defied description. Thomas could tell that his mother had not been spared the details that she was sparing him. Now and again when she spoke vaguely, her voice shook and he could tell that she was remembering some horror that had been put to her graphically. He had hoped that in a few days the memory of all this would wear off, but it did not. The next day she returned to the jail with Kleenex and cold-cream and a few days later, she announced that she had consulted a lawyer.

It was at these times that Thomas truly mourned the death of his father though he had not been able to endure him in life. The old man would have had none of this foolishness. Untouched by useless compassion, he would (behind her back) have pulled the necessary strings with his crony, the sheriff, and the girl would have been packed off to the state penitentiary to serve her time. He had always been engaged in some enraged action until one morning when (with an angry glance at his wife as if she alone were responsible) he had dropped dead at the breakfast table. Thomas had inherited his father's reason without his ruthlessness and his mother's love of good without her tendency to pursue it. His plan for all practical action was to wait and see what developed.

The lawyer found that the story of the repeated atrocities was for the most part untrue, but when he explained to her that the girl was a psychopathic personality, not insane enough for the asylum, not criminal enough for the jail, not stable enough for society, Thomas's mother was more deeply affected than ever. The girl readily admitted that her story was untrue on account of her being a congenital liar; she lied, she said, because she was insecure. She had passed through the hands of several psychiatrists who had put the finishing touches to her education. She knew there was no hope for her. In the presence of such an affliction as this, his mother seemed bowed down by some painful mystery that nothing would make endurable but a redoubling of effort. To his annoyance, she appeared to look on *him* with compassion, as if her hazy charity no longer made distinctions.

A few days later she burst in and said that the lawyer had got the girl paroled—to her.

Thomas rose from his Morris chair, dropping the review he had been reading. His large bland face contracted in anticipated pain. "You are not," he said, "going to bring that girl here!"

"No, no," she said, "calm yourself, Thomas." She had managed with difficulty to get the girl a job in a pet shop in town and a place to board with a crotchety old lady of her acquaintance. People were not kind. They did not put themselves in the place of someone like Star who had everything against her.

Thomas sat down again and retrieved his review. He seemed just to have escaped some danger which he did not care to make clear to himself. "Nobody can tell you anything," he said, "but in a few days that girl will have left town, having got what she could out of you. You'll never hear from her again."

Two nights later he came home and opened the parlor door and was speared by a shrill depthless laugh. His mother and the girl sat close to the fireplace where the gas logs were lit. The girl gave the immediate impression of being physically crooked. Her hair was cut like a dog's or an elf's and she was dressed in the latest fashion. She was training on him a long familiar sparkling stare that turned after a second into an intimate grin.

"Thomas!" his mother said, her voice firm with the injunction not to bolt, "this is Star you've heard so much about. Star is going to have supper with us."

The girl called herself Star Drake. The lawyer had found that her real name was Sarah Ham.

Thomas neither moved nor spoke but hung in the door in what seemed a savage perplexity. Finally he said, "How do you do, Sarah," in a tone of such loathing that he was shocked at the sound of it. He reddened, feeling it beneath him to show contempt for any creature so pathetic. He advanced into the room, determined at least on a decent politeness and sat down heavily in a straight chair.

"Thomas writes history," his mother said with a threatening look at him. "He's president of the local Historical Society this year."

The girl leaned forward and gave Thomas an even more pointed attention. "Fabulous!" she said in a throaty voice.

"Right now Thomas is writing about the first settlers in this county," his mother said.

"Fabulous!" the girl repeated.

Thomas by an effort of will managed to look as if he were alone in the room.

"Say, you know who he looks like?" Star asked, her head on one side, taking him in at an angle.

"Oh some one very distinguished!" his mother said archly.

"This cop I saw in the movie I went to last night," Star said.

"Star," his mother said, "I think you ought to be careful about the kind of movies you go to. I think you ought to see only the best ones. I don't think crime stories would be good for you."

"Oh this was a crime-does-not-pay," Star said, "and I swear this cop looked exactly like him. They were always putting something over on the guy. He would look like he couldn't stand it a minute longer or he would blow up. He was a riot. And not bad looking," she added with an appreciative leer at Thomas.

"Star," his mother said, "I think it would be grand if you developed a taste for music."

Thomas sighed. His mother rattled on and the girl, paying no attention to her, let her eyes play over him. The quality of her look was such that it might have been her hands, resting now on his knees, now on his neck. Her eyes had a mocking glitter and he knew that she was well aware he could not stand the sight of her. He needed nothing to tell him he was in the presence of the very stuff of corruption, but blameless corruption because there was no responsible faculty behind it. He was looking at the most unendurable form of innocence. Absently he asked himself what the attitude of God was to this, meaning if possible to adopt it.

His mother's behavior throughout the meal was so idiotic that he could barely stand to look at her and since he could less stand to look at Sarah Ham, he fixed on the sideboard across the room a continuous gaze of disapproval and disgust. Every remark of the girl's his mother met as if it deserved serious attention. She advanced several plans for the wholesome use of Star's spare time. Sarah Ham paid no more attention to this advice than if it came from a parrot. Once when Thomas inadvertently looked in her direction, she winked. As soon as he had swallowed the last spoonful of dessert, he rose and muttered, "I have to go, I have a meeting."

"Thomas," his mother said, "I want you to take Star home on your way. I don't want her riding in taxis by herself at night."

For a moment Thomas remained furiously silent. Then he turned and left the room. Presently he came back with a look of obscure determination on his face. The girl was ready, meekly waiting at the parlor door. She cast up at him a great look of admiration and confidence. Thomas did not offer his arm but she took it anyway and moved out of the house and down the steps, attached to what might have been a miraculously moving monument.

"Be good!" his mother called.

Sarah Ham snickered and poked him in the ribs.

While getting his coat he had decided that this would be his opportunity to tell the girl that unless she ceased to be a parasite on his mother, he would see to it, personally, that she was returned to jail. He would let her know that he understood what she was up to, that he was not an innocent and that there were certain things he would not put up with. At his desk, pen in hand, none was more articulate than Thomas. As soon as he found himself shut into the car with Sarah Ham, terror seized his tongue.

She curled her feet up under her and said, "Alone at last," and giggled.

Thomas swerved the car away from the house and drove fast toward the gate. Once on the highway, he shot forward as if he were being pursued.

"Jesus!" Sarah Ham said, swinging her feet off the seat, "where's the fire?"

Thomas did not answer. In a few seconds he could feel her edging closer. She stretched, eased nearer, and finally hung her hand limply over his shoulder. "Tomsee doesn't like me," she said, "but I think he's fabulously cute."

Thomas covered the three and a half miles into town in a little over four minutes. The light at the first intersection was red but he ignored it. The old woman lived three blocks beyond. When the car screeched to a halt at the place, he jumped out and ran around to the girl's door and opened it. She did not move from the car and Thomas was obliged to wait. After a moment one leg emerged, then her small white crooked face appeared and stared up at him. There was something about the look of it that suggested blindness but it was the blindness of those who don't know that they cannot see. Thomas was curiously sickened. The empty eyes moved over him. "Nobody likes me," she said in a sullen tone. "What if you were me and I couldn't stand to ride you three miles?"

"My mother likes you," he muttered.

"Her!" the girl said. "She's just about seventy-five years behind the times!"

Breathlessly Thomas said, "If I find you bothering her again, I'll have you put back in jail." There was a dull force behind his voice though it came out barely above a whisper.

"You and who else?" she said and drew back in the car as if now she did not intend to get out at all. Thomas reached into it, blindly grasped the front of her coat, pulled her out by it and released her. Then he lunged back to the car and sped off. The other door was still hanging open and her laugh, bodiless but real, bounded up the street as if it were about to jump in the open side of the car and ride away with him. He reached over and slammed the door and then drove toward home, too angry to attend his meeting. He intended to make his mother well-aware of his displeasure. He intended to leave no doubt in her mind. The voice of his father rasped in his head.

Numbskull, the old man said, put your foot down now. Show her who's boss before she shows you.

But when Thomas reached home, his mother, wisely, had gone to bed.

The next morning he appeared at the breakfast table, his brow lowered and the thrust of his jaw indicating that he was in a dangerous humor. When he intended to be determined, Thomas began like a bull that, before charging, backs with his head lowered and paws the ground. "All right now listen," he began, yanking out his chair and sitting down, "I have something to say to you about that girl and I don't intend to say it but once." He drew breath. "She's nothing but a little slut. She makes fun of you behind your back. She means to get everything she can out of you and you are nothing to her."

His mother looked as if she too had spent a restless night. She did not dress in the morning but wore her bathrobe and a grey turban around her head, which gave her face a disconcerting omniscient look. He might have been breakfasting with a sibyl.

"You'll have to use canned cream this morning," she said, pouring his coffee. "I forgot the other."

"All right, did you hear me?" Thomas growled.

"I'm not deaf," his mother said and put the pot back on the trivet. "I know I'm nothing but an old bag of wind to her."

"Then why do you persist in this foolhardy . . . "

"Thomas," she said, and put her hand to the side of her face, "it might be . . . "

"It is not me!" Thomas said, grasping the table leg at his knee.

She continued to hold her face, shaking her head slightly. "Think of all you have," she began. "All the comforts of home. And morals, Thomas. No bad inclinations, nothing bad you were born with."

Thomas began to breathe like some one who feels the onset of asthma. "You are not logical," he said in a limp voice. "*He* would have put his foot down."

The old lady stiffened. "You," she said, "are not like him."

Thomas opened his mouth silently.

"However," his mother said, in a tone of such subtle accusation that she might have been taking back the compliment, "I won't invite her back again since you're so dead set against her."

"I am not set against her," Thomas said. "I am set against your making a fool of yourself."

As soon as he left the table and closed the door of his study on himself, his father took up a squatting position in his mind. The old man had had the countryman's ability to converse squatting, though he was no countryman but had been born and brought up in the city and only moved to a smaller place later to exploit his talents. With steady skill he had made them think him one of them. In the midst of a conversation on the courthouse lawn, he would squat and his two or three companions would squat with him with no break in the surface of the talk. By gesture he had lived his lie; he had never deigned to tell one.

Let her run over you, he said. You ain't like me. Not enough to be a man.

Thomas began vigorously to read and presently the image faded. The girl had caused a disturbance in the depths of his being, somewhere out of the reach of his power of analysis. He felt as if he had seen a tornado pass a hundred yards away and had an intimation that it would turn again and head directly for him. He did not get his mind firmly on his work until mid-morning.

Two nights later, his mother and he were sitting in the den after their supper, each reading a section of the evening paper, when the telephone began to ring with the brassy intensity of a fire alarm. Thomas reached for it. As soon as the receiver was in his hand, a shrill female voice screamed into the room, "Come get this girl! Come get her! Drunk!

Drunk in my parlor and I won't have it! Lost her job and come back here drunk! I won't have it!"

His mother leapt up and snatched the receiver.

The ghost of Thomas's father rose before him. Call the sheriff, the old man prompted. "Call the sheriff," Thomas said in a loud voice. "Call the sheriff to go there and pick her up."

"We'll be right there," his mother was saying. "We'll come and get her right away. Tell her to get her things together."

"She ain't in no condition to get nothing together," the voice screamed. "You shouldn't have put something like her off on me! My house is repectable!"

"Tell her to call the sheriff," Thomas shouted.

His mother put the receiver down and looked at him. "I wouldn't turn a dog over to that man," she said.

Thomas sat in the chair with his arms folded and looked fixedly at the wall.

"Think of the poor girl, Thomas," his mother said, "with nothing. Nothing. And we have everything."

When they arrived, Sarah Ham was slumped spraddle-legged against the banister on the boarding house front-steps. Her tam was down on her forehead where the old woman had slammed it and her clothes were bulging out of her suitcase where the old woman had thrown them in. She was carrying on a drunken conversation with herself in a low personal tone. A streak of lipstick ran up one side of her face. She allowed herself to be guided by his mother to the car and put in the back seat without seeming to know who the rescuer was. "Nothing to talk to all day but a pack of goddamned parakeets," she said in a furious whisper.

Thomas, who had not got out of the car at all, or looked

at her after the first revolted glance, said, "I'm telling you, once and for all, the place to take her is the jail."

His mother, sitting on the back seat, holding the girl's hand, did not answer.

"All right, take her to the hotel," he said.

"I cannot take a drunk girl to a hotel, Thomas," she said. "You know that."

"Then take her to a hospital."

"She doesn't need a jail or a hotel or a hospital," his mother said, "she needs a home."

"She does not need mine," Thomas said.

"Only for tonight, Thomas," the old lady sighed. "Only for tonight."

Since then eight days had passed. The little slut was established in the guest room. Every day his mother set out to find her a job and a place to board, and failed, for the old woman had broadcast a warning. Thomas kept to his room or the den. His home was to him home, workshop, church, as personal as the shell of a turtle and as necessary. He could not believe that it could be violated in this way. His flushed face had a constant look of stunned outrage.

As soon as the girl was up in the morning, her voice throbbed out in a blues song that would rise and waver, then plunge low with insinuations of passion about to be satisfied and Thomas, at his desk, would lunge up and begin frantically stuffing his ears with Kleenex. Each time he started from one room to another, one floor to another, she would be certain to appear. Each time he was half way up or down the stairs, she would either meet him and pass, cringing coyly, or go up or down behind him, breathing small tragic spearmint-flavored sighs. She appeared to adore Thomas's repugnance to her and to draw it out of him every chance she got as if it added delectably to her martyrdom.

The old man—small, wasp-like, in his yellowed panama hat, his seersucker suit, his pink carefully-soiled shirt, his small string tie—appeared to have taken up his station in Thomas's mind and from there, usually squatting, he shot out the same rasping suggestion every time the boy paused from his forced studies. Put your foot down. Go to see the sheriff.

The sheriff was another edition of Thomas's father except that he wore a checkered shirt and a Texas type hat and was ten years younger. He was as easily dishonest, and he had genuinely admired the old man. Thomas, like his mother, would have gone far out of his way to avoid his glassy pale blue gaze. He kept hoping for another solution, for a miracle.

With Sarah Ham in the house, meals were unbearable.

"Tomsee doesn't like me," she said the third or fourth night at the supper table and cast her pouting gaze across at the large rigid figure of Thomas, whose face was set with the look of a man trapped by insufferable odors. "He doesn't want me here. Nobody wants me anywhere."

"Thomas's name is Thomas," his mother interrupted. "Not Tomsee."

"I made Tomsee up," she said. "I think it's cute. He hates me."

"Thomas does not hate you," his mother said. "We are not the kind of people who hate," she added, as if this were an imperfection that had been bred out of them generations ago.

"Oh, I know when I'm not wanted," Sarah Ham continued. "They didn't even want me in jail. If I killed myself I wonder would God want me?"

"Try it and see," Thomas muttered.

The girl screamed with laughter. Then she stopped

abruptly, her face puckered and she began to shake. "The best thing to do," she said, her teeth clattering, "is to kill myself. Then I'll be out of everybody's way. I'll go to hell and be out of God's way. And even the devil won't want me. He'll kick me out of hell, not even in hell . . . " she wailed.

Thomas rose, picked up his plate and knife and fork and carried them to the den to finish his supper. After that, he had not eaten another meal at the table but had had his mother serve him at his desk. At these meals, the old man was intensely present to him. He appeared to be tipping backwards in his chair, his thumbs beneath his galluses, while he said such things as, She never ran me away from my own table.

A few nights later, Sarah Ham slashed her wrists with a paring knife and had hysterics. From the den where he was closeted after supper, Thomas heard a shriek, then a series of screams, then his mother's scurrying footsteps through the house. He did not move. His first instant of hope that the girl had cut her throat faded as he realized she could not have done it and continue to scream the way she was doing. He returned to his journal and presently the screams subsided. In a moment his mother burst in with his coat and hat. "We have to take her to the hospital," she said. "She tried to do away with herself. I have a tourniquet on her arm. Oh Lord, Thomas," she said, "imagine being so low you'd do a thing like that!"

Thomas rose woodenly and put on his hat and coat. "We will take her to the hospital," he said, "and we will leave her there."

"And drive her to despair again?" the old lady cried. "Thomas!"

Standing in the center of his room now, realizing that he had reached the point where action was inevitable, that he must pack, that he must leave, that he must go, Thomas remained immovable.

His fury was directed not at the little slut but at his mother. Even though the doctor had found that she had barely damaged herself and had raised the girl's wrath by laughing at the tourniquet and putting only a streak of iodine on the cut, his mother could not get over the incident. Some new weight of sorrow seemed to have been thrown across her shoulders, and not only Thomas, but Sarah Ham was infuriated by this, for it appeared to be a general sorrow that would have found another object no matter what good fortune came to either of them. The experience of Sarah Ham had plunged the old lady into mourning for the world.

The morning after the attempted suicide, she had gone through the house and collected all the knives and scissors and locked them in a drawer. She emptied a bottle of rat poison down the toilet and took up the roach tablets from the kitchen floor. Then she came to Thomas's study and said in a whisper, "Where is that gun of his? I want you to lock it up."

"The gun is in my drawer," Thomas roared, "and I will not lock it up. If she shoots herself, so much the better!"

"Thomas," his mother said, "she'll hear you!"

"Let her hear me!" Thomas yelled. "Don't you know she has no intention of killing herself? Don't you know her kind never kill themselves? Don't you . . . "

His mother slipped out the door and closed it to silence him and Sarah Ham's laugh, quite close in the hall, came rattling into his room. "Tomsee'll find out. I'll kill myself and then he'll be sorry he wasn't nice to me. I'll use his own lil gun, his own lil ol' pearl-handled revol-lervuh!" she shouted and let out a loud tormented-sounding laugh in imitation of a movie monster.

Thomas ground his teeth. He pulled out his desk drawer and felt for the pistol. It was an inheritance from the old man, whose opinion it had been that every house should contain a loaded gun. He had discharged two bullets one night into the side of a prowler, but Thomas had never shot anything. He had no fear that the girl would use the gun on herself and he closed the drawer. Her kind clung tenaciously to life and were able to wrest some histrionic advantage from every moment.

Several ideas for getting rid of her had entered his head but each of these had been suggestions whose moral tone indicated that they had come from a mind akin to his father's, and Thomas had rejected them. He could not get the girl locked up again until she did something illegal. The old man would have been able with no qualms at all to get her drunk and send her out on the highway in his car, meanwhile notifying the highway patrol of her presence on the road, but Thomas considered this below his moral stature. Suggestions continued to come to him, each more outrageous than the last.

He had not the vaguest hope that the girl would get the gun and shoot herself, but that afternoon when he looked in the drawer, the gun was gone. His study locked from the inside, not the out. He cared nothing about the gun, but the thought of Sarah Ham's hands sliding among his papers infuriated him. Now even his study was contaminated. The only place left untouched by her was his bedroom.

That night she entered it.

In the morning at breakfast, he did not eat and did not sit down. He stood beside his chair and delivered his ultimatum while his mother sipped her coffee as if she were both alone in the room and in great pain. "I have stood this," he said, "for as long as I am able. Since I see plainly that you care nothing about me, about my peace or comfort or working conditions, I am about to take the only step open to me. I will give you one more day. If you bring the girl back into this house this afternoon, I leave. You can choose—her or me." He had more to say but at that point his voice cracked and he left.

At ten o'clock his mother and Sarah Ham left the house.

At four he heard the car wheels on the gravel and rushed to the window. As the car stopped, the dog stood up, alert, shaking.

He seemed unable to take the first step that would set him walking to the closet in the hall to look for the suitcase. He was like a man handed a knife and told to operate on himself if he wished to live. His huge hands clenched helplessly. His expression was a turmoil of indecision and outrage. His pale blue eyes seemed to sweat in his broiling face. He closed them for a moment and on the back of his lids, his father's image leered at him. Idiot! the old man hissed, idiot! The criminal slut stole your gun! See the sheriff! See the sheriff!

It was a moment before Thomas opened his eyes. He seemed newly stunned. He stood where he was for at least three minutes, then he turned slowly like a large vessel reversing its direction and faced the door. He stood there a moment longer, then he left, his face set to see the ordeal through.

He did not know where he would find the sheriff. The man made his own rules and kept his own hours. Thomas stopped first at the jail where his office was, but he was not in it. He went to the courthouse and was told by a clerk that the sheriff had gone to barber-shop across the street. "Yonder's the deppity," the clerk said and pointed out the window to the large figure of a man in a checkered shirt, who was leaning against the side of a police car, looking into space.

"It has to be the sheriff," Thomas said and left for the barber-shop. As little as he wanted anything to do with the sheriff, he realized that the man was at least intelligent and not simply a mound of sweating flesh.

The barber said the sheriff had just left. Thomas started back to the courthouse and as he stepped on to the sidewalk from the street, he saw a lean, slightly stooped figure gesticulating angrily at the deputy.

Thomas approached with an aggressiveness brought on by nervous agitation. He stopped abruptly three feet away and said in an over-loud voice, "Can I have a word with you?" without adding the sheriff's name, which was Farebrother.

Farebrother turned his sharp creased face just enough to take Thomas in, and the deputy did likewise, but neither spoke. The sheriff removed a very small piece of cigaret from his lip and dropped it at his feet. "I told you what to do," he said to the deputy. Then he moved off with a slight nod that indicated Thomas could follow him if he wanted to see him. The deputy slunk around the front of the police car and got inside.

Farebrother, with Thomas following, headed across the courthouse square and stopped beneath a tree that shaded a quarter of the front lawn. He waited, leaning slightly forward, and lit another cigaret.

Thomas began to blurt out his business. As he had not had time to prepare his words, he was barely coherent. By repeating the same thing over several times, he managed at length to get out what he wanted to say. When he finished, the sheriff was still leaning slightly forward, at an angle to him, his eyes on nothing in particular. He remained that way without speaking.

Thomas began again, slower and in a lamer voice, and Farebrother let him continue for some time before he said, "We had her oncet." He then allowed himself a slow, creased, all-knowing, quarter smile.

"I had nothing to do with that," Thomas said. "That was my mother."

Farebrother squatted.

"She was trying to help the girl," Thomas said. "She didn't know she couldn't be helped."

"Bit off more than she could chew, I reckon," the voice below him mused.

"She has nothing to do with this," Thomas said. "She doesn't know I'm here. The girl is dangerous with that gun."

"*He*," the sheriff said, "never let anything grow under his feet. Particularly nothing a woman planted."

"She might kill somebody with that gun," Thomas said weakly, looking down at the round top of the Texas type hat.

There was a long time of silence.

"Where's she got it?" Farebrother asked.

"I don't know. She sleeps in the guest room. It must be in there, in her suitcase probably," Thomas said.

Farebrother lapsed into silence again.

"You could come search the guest room," Thomas said in a strained voice. "I can go home and leave the latch off the front door and you can come in quietly and go upstairs and search her room."

Farebrother turned his head so that his eyes looked boldly at Thomas's knees. "You seem to know how it ought to be done," he said. "Want to swap jobs?"

Thomas said nothing because he could not think of anything to say, but he waited doggedly. Farebrother removed the cigaret butt from his lips and dropped it on the grass. Beyond him on the courthouse porch a group of loiterers who had been leaning at the left of the door moved over to the right where a patch of sunlight had settled. From one of the upper windows a crumpled piece of paper blew out and drifted down.

"I'll come along about six," Farebrother said. "Leave the latch off the door and keep out of my way—yourself and them two women too."

Thomas let out a rasping sound of relief meant to be "Thanks," and struck off across the grass like some one released. The phrase, "them two women," stuck like a burr in his brain—the subtlety of the insult to his mother hurting him more than any of Farebrother's references to his own incompetence. As he got into his car, his face suddenly flushed. Had he delivered his mother over to the sheriff—to be a butt for the man's tongue? Was he betraying her to get rid of the little slut? He saw at once that this was not the case. He was doing what he was doing for her own good, to rid her of a parasite that would ruin their peace. He started his car and drove quickly home but once he had turned in the driveway, he decided it would be better to park some distance from the house and go quietly in by the back door. He parked on the grass and on the grass walked in a circle toward the rear of the house. The sky was lined with mustard-colored streaks. The dog was asleep on the back doormat. At the approach of his master's step, he opened one yellow eye, took him in, and closed it again.

Thomas let himself into the kitchen. It was empty and the house was quiet enough for him to be aware of the loud ticking of the kitchen clock. It was a quarter to six. He tiptoed hurriedly through the hall to the front door and took the latch off it. Then he stood for a moment listening. From behind the closed parlor door, he heard his mother snoring softly and presumed that she had gone to sleep while reading. On the other side of the hall, not three feet from his study, the little slut's black coat and red pocketbook were slung on a chair. He heard water running upstairs and decided she was taking a bath.

He went into his study and sat down at his desk to wait, noting with distaste that every few moments a tremor ran through him. He sat for a minute or two doing nothing. Then he picked up a pen and began to draw squares on the back of an envelope that lay before him. He looked at his watch. It was eleven minutes to six. After a moment he idly drew the center drawer of the desk out over his lap. For a moment he stared at the gun without recognition. Then he gave a yelp and leaped up. She had put it back!

Idiot! his father hissed, idiot! Go plant it in her pocketbook. Don't just stand there. Go plant it in her pocketbook!

Thomas stood staring at the drawer.

Moron! the old man fumed. Quick while there's time! Go plant it in her pocketbook.

Thomas did not move.

Imbecile! his father cried.

Thomas picked up the gun.

Make haste, the old man ordered.

Thomas started forward, holding the gun away from him. He opened the door and looked at the chair. The black coat and red pocketbook were lying on it almost within reach.

Hurry up, you fool, his father said.

From behind the parlor door the almost inaudible snores of his mother rose and fell. They seemed to mark an order of time that had nothing to do with the instants left to Thomas. There was no other sound.

Quick, you imbecile, before she wakes up, the old man said.

The snores stopped and Thomas heard the sofa springs groan. He grabbed the red pocketbook. It had a skin-like feel to his touch and as it opened, he caught an unmistakable odor of the girl. Wincing, he thrust in the gun and then drew back. His face burned an ugly dull red.

"What is Tomsee putting in my purse?" she called and her pleased laugh bounced down the staircase. Thomas whirled.

She was at the top of the stair, coming down in the manner of a fashion model, one bare leg and then the other thrusting out the front of her kimona in a definite rhythm. "Tomsee is being naughty," she said in a throaty voice. She reached the bottom and cast a possessive leer at Thomas whose face was now more grey than red. She reached out, pulled the bag open with her finger and peered at the gun.

His mother opened the parlor door and looked out.

"Tomsee put his pistol in my bag!" the girl shrieked.

"Ridiculous," his mother said, yawning. "What would Thomas want to put his pistol in your bag for?"

Thomas stood slightly hunched, his hands hanging helplessly at the wrists as if he had just pulled them up out of a pool of blood.

"I don't know what for," the girl said, "but he sure did it," and she proceeded to walk around Thomas, her hands on her hips, her neck thrust forward and her intimate grin fixed on him fiercely. All at once her expression seemed to open as the purse had opened when Thomas touched it. She stood with her head cocked on one side in an attitude of disbelief. "Oh boy," she said slowly, "is he a case."

At that instant Thomas damned not only the girl but the entire order of the universe that made her possible.

"Thomas wouldn't put a gun in your bag," his mother said. "Thomas is a gentleman."

The girl made a chortling noise. "You can see it in there," she said and pointed to the open purse.

You *found* it in her bag, you dimwit! the old man hissed.

"I found it in her bag!" Thomas shouted. "The dirty criminal slut stole my gun!"

His mother gasped at the sound of the other presence in his voice. The old lady's sybil-like face turned pale.

"Found it my eye!" Sarah Ham shrieked and started for the pocketbook, but Thomas, as if his arm were guided by his father, caught it first and snatched the gun. The girl in a frenzy lunged at Thomas's throat and would actually have caught him around the neck had not his mother thrown herself forward to protect her.

Fire! the old man yelled.

Thomas fired. The blast was like a sound meant to bring an end to evil in the world. Thomas heard it as a sound that would shatter the laughter of sluts until all shrieks were stilled and nothing was left to disturb the peace of perfect order.

The echo died away in waves. Before the last one had faded, Farebrother opened the door and put his head inside the hall. His nose wrinkled. His expression for some few seconds was that of a man unwilling to admit surprise. His eyes were clear as glass, reflecting the scene. The old lady lay on the floor between the girl and Thomas.

The sheriff's brain worked instantly like a calculating machine. He saw the facts as if they were already in print: the fellow had intended all along to kill his mother and pin it on the girl. But Farebrother had been too quick for him. They were not yet aware of his head in the door. As he scrutinized the scene, further insights were flashed to him.

Over her body, the killer and the slut were about to collapse into each other's arms. The sheriff knew a nasty bit when he saw it. He was accustomed to enter upon scenes that were not as bad as he had hoped to find them, but this one met his expectations.

The Lame Shall Enter First

Sheppard sat on a stool at the bar that divided the kitchen in half, eating his cereal out of the individual pasteboard box it came in. He ate mechanically, his eyes on the child, who was wandering from cabinet to cabinet in the panelled kitchen, collecting the ingredients for his breakfast. He was a stocky blond boy of ten. Sheppard kept his intense blue eyes fixed on him. The boy's future was written in his face. He would be a banker. No, worse. He would operate a small loan company. All he wanted for the child was that he be good and unselfish and neither seemed likely. Sheppard was a young man whose hair was already white. It stood up like a narrow brush halo over his pink sensitive face.

The boy approached the bar with the jar of peanut butter under his arm, a plate with a quarter of a small chocolate cake on it in one hand and the ketchup bottle in the other. He did not appear to notice his father. He climbed up on the stool and began to spread peanut butter on the cake. He had very large round ears that leaned away from his head and seemed to pull his eyes slightly too far apart. His shirt was green but so faded that the cowboy charging across the front of it was only a shadow.

"Norton," Sheppard said, "I saw Rufus Johnson yesterday. Do you know what he was doing?"

The child looked at him with a kind of half attention, his eyes forward but not yet engaged. They were a paler blue than his father's as if they might have faded like the shirt; one of them listed, almost imperceptibly, toward the outer rim.

"He was in an alley," Sheppard said, "and he had his hand in a garbage can. He was trying to get something to eat out of it." He paused to let this soak in. "He was hungry," he finished, and tried to pierce the child's conscience with his gaze.

The boy picked up the piece of chocolate cake and began to gnaw it from one corner.

"Norton," Sheppard said, "do you have any idea what it means to share?"

A flicker of attention. "Some of it's yours," Norton said.

"Some of it's *his*," Sheppard said heavily. It was hopeless. Almost any fault would have been preferable to selfishness—a violent temper, even a tendency to lie.

The child turned the bottle of ketchup upside-down and began thumping ketchup onto the cake.

Sheppard's look of pain increased. "You are ten and Rufus Johnson is fourteen," he said. "Yet I'm sure your shirts would fit Rufus." Rufus Johnson was a boy he had been trying to help at the reformatory for the past year. He had been released two months ago. "When he was in the reformatory, he looked pretty good, but when I saw him yesterday, he was skin and bones. He hasn't been eating cake with peanut butter on it for breakfast."

The child paused. "It's stale," he said. "That's why I have to put stuff on it."

Sheppard turned his face to the window at the end of the bar. The side lawn, green and even, sloped fifty feet or so down to a small suburban wood. When his wife was living, they had often eaten outside, even breakfast, on the grass. He had never noticed then that the child was selfish. "Listen to me," he said, turning back to him, "look at me and listen."

The boy looked at him. At least his eyes were forward.

"I gave Rufus a key to this house when he left the reformatory—to show my confidence in him and so he would have a place he could come to and feel welcome any time. He didn't use it, but I think he'll use it now because he's seen me and he's hungry. And if he doesn't use it, I'm going out and find him and bring him here. I can't see a child eating out of garbage cans."

The boy frowned. It was dawning upon him that something of his was threatened.

Sheppard's mouth stretched in disgust. "Rufus's father died before he was born," he said. "His mother is in the state penitentiary. He was raised by his grandfather in a shack without water or electricity and the old man beat him every day. How would you like to belong to a family like that?"

"I don't know," the child said lamely.

"Well, you might think about it sometime," Sheppard said.

Sheppard was City Recreational Director. On Saturdays he worked at the reformatory as a counselor, receiving nothing for it but the satisfaction of knowing he was helping boys no one else cared about. Johnson was the most intelligent boy he had worked with and the most deprived.

Norton turned what was left of the cake over as if he no longer wanted it.

"You started that, now finish it," Sheppard said.

"Maybe he won't come," the child said and his eyes brightened slightly.

"Think of everything you have that he doesn't!" Sheppard said. "Suppose you had to root in garbage cans for food? Suppose you had a huge swollen foot and one side of you dropped lower than the other when you walked?"

The boy looked blank, obviously unable to imagine such a thing.

"You have a healthy body," Sheppard said, "a good home. You've never been taught anything but the truth. Your daddy gives you everything you need and want. You don't have a grandfather who beats you. And your mother is not in the state penitentiary."

The child pushed his plate away. Sheppard groaned aloud.

A knot of flesh appeared below the boy's suddenly distorted mouth. His face became a mass of lumps with slits for eyes. "If she was in the penitentiary," he began in a kind of racking bellow, "I could go to seeeeee her." Tears rolled down his face and the ketchup dribbled on his chin. He looked as if he had been hit in the mouth. He abandoned himself and howled.

Sheppard sat helpless and miserable, like a man lashed by some elemental force of nature. This was not a normal grief. It was all part of his selfishness. She had been dead for over a year and a child's grief should not last so long. "You're going on eleven years old," he said reproachfully.

The child began an agonizing high-pitched heaving noise.

"If you stop thinking about yourself and think what you can do for somebody else," Sheppard said, "then you'll stop missing your mother."

The boy was silent but his shoulders continued to shake. Then his face collapsed and he began to howl again.

"Don't you think I'm lonely without her too?" Sheppard said. "Don't you think I miss her at all? I do, but I'm not sitting around moping. I'm busy helping other people. When do you see me just sitting around thinking about my troubles?"

The boy slumped as if he were exhausted but fresh tears streaked his face.

"What are you going to do today?" Sheppard asked, to get his mind on something else.

The child ran his arm across his eyes. "Sell seeds," he mumbled.

Always selling something. He had four quart jars full of nickels and dimes he had saved and he took them out of his closet every few days and counted them. "What are you selling seeds for?"

"To win a prize."

"What's the prize?"

"A thousand dollars."

"And what would you do if you had a thousand dollars?"

"Keep it," the child said and wiped his nose on his shoulder.

"I feel sure you would," Sheppard said. "Listen," he said and lowered his voice to an almost pleading tone, "suppose by some chance you did win a thousand dollars. Wouldn't you like to spend it on children less fortunate than yourself? Wouldn't you like to give some swings and trapezes to the orphanage? Wouldn't you like to buy poor Rufus Johnson a new shoe?"

The boy began to back away from the bar. Then suddenly he leaned forward and hung with his mouth open over his plate. Sheppard groaned again. Everything came up, the cake, the peanut butter, the ketchup—a limp sweet batter. He hung over it gagging, more came, and he waited with his mouth open over the plate as if he expected his heart to come up next.

"It's all right," Sheppard said, "it's all right. You couldn't help it. Wipe your mouth and go lie down."

The child hung there a moment longer. Then he raised his face and looked blindly at his father.

"Go on," Sheppard said. "Go on and lie down."

The boy pulled up the end of his t-shirt and smeared his mouth with it. Then he climbed down off the stool and wandered out of the kitchen.

Sheppard sat there staring at the puddle of half-digested food. The sour odor reached him and he drew back. His gorge rose. He got up and carried the plate to the sink and turned the water on it and watched grimly as the mess ran down the drain. Johnson's sad thin hand rooted in garbage cans for food while his own child, selfish, unresponsive, greedy, had so much that he threw it up. He cut off the faucet with a thrust of his fist. Johnson had a capacity for real response and had been deprived of everything from birth; Norton was average or below and had had every advantage.

He went back to the bar to finish his breakfast. The cereal was soggy in the cardboard box but he paid no attention to what he was eating. Johnson was worth any amount of effort because he had the potential. He had seen it from the time the boy had limped in for his first interview.

Sheppard's office at the reformatory was a narrow closet with one window and a small table and two chairs in it. He had never been inside a confessional but he thought it must be the same kind of operation he had here, except that he explained, he did not absolve. His credentials were less dubious than a priest's; he had been trained for what he was doing.

When Johnson came in for his first interview, he had been reading over the boy's record—senseless destruction, windows smashed, city trash boxes set afire, tires slashed —the kind of thing he found where boys had been transplanted abruptly from the country to the city as this one had. He came to Johnson's I. Q. score. It was 140. He raised his eyes eagerly.

The boy sat slumped on the edge of his chair, his arms hanging between his thighs. The light from the window fell on his face. His eyes, steel-colored and very still, were trained narrowly forward. His thin dark hair hung in a flat forelock across the side of his forehead, not carelessly like a boy's, but fiercely like an old man's. A kind of fanatic intelligence was palpable in his face.

Sheppard smiled to diminish the distance between them.

The boy's expression did not soften. He leaned back in his chair and lifted a monstrous club foot to his knee. The foot was in a heavy black battered shoe with a sole four or five inches thick. The leather parted from it in one place and the end of an empty sock protruded like a grey tongue from a severed head. The case was clear to Sheppard instantly. His mischief was compensation for the foot.

"Well Rufus," he said, "I see by the record here that you don't have but a year to serve. What do you plan to do when you get out?"

"I don't make no plans," the boy said. His eyes shifted

indifferently to something outside the window behind Sheppard in the far distance.

"Maybe you ought to," Sheppard said and smiled.

Johnson continued to gaze beyond him.

"I want to see you make the most of your intelligence," Sheppard said. "What's important to you? Let's talk about what's important to *you*." His eyes dropped involuntarily to the foot.

"Study it and git your fill," the boy drawled.

Sheppard reddened. The black deformed mass swelled before his eyes. He ignored the remark and the leer the boy was giving him. "Rufus," he said, "you've got into a lot of senseless trouble but I think when you understand why you do these things, you'll be less inclined to do them." He smiled. They had so few friends, saw so few pleasant faces, that half his effectiveness came from nothing more than smiling at them. "There are a lot of things about yourself that I think I can explain to you," he said.

Johnson looked at him stonily. "I ain't asked for no explanation," he said. "I already know why I do what I do."

"Well good!" Sheppard said. "Suppose you tell me what's made you do the things you've done?"

A black sheen appeared in the boy's eyes. "Satan," he said. "He has me in his power."

Sheppard looked at him steadily. There was no indication on the boy's face that he had said this to be funny. The line of his thin mouth was set with pride. Sheppard's eyes hardened. He felt a momentary dull despair as if he were faced with some elemental warping of nature that had happened too long ago to be corrected now. This boy's questions about life had been answered by signs nailed on pine trees: DOES SATAN HAVE YOU IN HIS POWER? REPENT OR BURN IN HELL. JESUS SAVES. He would know the Bible with or without reading it. His despair gave way to outrage. "Rubbish!" he snorted. "We're living in the space age! You're too smart to give me an answer like that."

Johnson's mouth twisted slightly. His look was contemptuous but amused. There was a glint of challenge in his eyes.

Sheppard scrutinized his face. Where there was intelligence anything was possible. He smiled again, a smile that was like an invitation to the boy to come into a school room with all its windows thrown open to the light. "Rufus," he said, "I'm going to arrange for you to have a conference with me once a week. Maybe there's an explanation for your explanation. Maybe I can explain your devil to you."

After that he had talked to Johnson every Saturday for the rest of the year. He talked at random, the kind of talk the boy would never have heard before. He talked a little above him to give him something to reach for. He roamed from simple psychology and the dodges of the human mind to astronomy and the space capsules that were whirling around the earth faster than the speed of sound and would soon encircle the stars. Instinctively he concentrated on the stars. He wanted to give the boy something to reach for besides his neighbor's goods. He wanted to stretch his horizons. He wanted him to *see* the universe, to see that the darkest parts of it could be penetrated. He would have given anything to be able to put a telescope in Johnson's hands.

Johnson said little and what he did say, for the sake of his pride, was in dissent or senseless contradiction, with the clubfoot raised always to his knee like a weapon ready for use, but Sheppard was not deceived. He watched his eyes and every week he saw something in them crumble. From the boy's face, hard but shocked, braced against the light that was ravaging him, he could see that he was hitting dead center.

Johnson was free now to live out of garbage cans and rediscover his old ignorance. The injustice of it was infuriating. He had been sent back to the grandfather; the old man's imbecility could only be imagined. Perhaps the boy had by now run away from him. The idea of getting custody of Johnson had occurred to Sheppard before, but the fact of the grandfather had stood in the way. Nothing excited him so much as thinking what he could do for such a boy. First he would have him fitted for a new orthopedic shoe. His back was thrown out of line every time he took a step. Then he would encourage him in some particular intellectual interest. He thought of the telescope. He could buy a second-hand one and they could set it up in the attic window. He sat for almost ten minutes thinking what he could do if he had Johnson here with him. What was wasted on Norton would cause Johnson to flourish. Yesterday when he had seen him with his hand in the garbage can, he had waved and started forward. Johnson had seen him, paused a split-second, then vanished with the swiftness of a rat, but not before Sheppard had seen his expression change. Something had kindled in the boy's eyes, he was sure of it, some memory of the lost light.

He got up and threw the cereal box in the garbage. Before he left the house, he looked into Norton's room to be sure he was not still sick. The child was sitting cross-legged on his bed. He had emptied the quart jars of change into one large pile in front of him, and was sorting it out by nickels and dimes and quarters.

That afternoon Norton was alone in the house, squatting on the floor of his room arranging packages of flower seeds in rows around himself. Rain slashed against the window panes and rattled in the gutters. The room had grown dark but every few minutes it was lit by silent lightning and the seed packages showed up gaily on the floor. He squatted motionless like a large pale frog in the midst of this potential garden. All at once his eyes became alert. Without warning the rain had stopped. The silence was heavy as if the downpour had been hushed by violence. He remained motionless, only his eyes turning.

Into the silence came the distinct click of a key turning in the front door lock. The sound was a very deliberate one. It drew attention to itself and held it as if it were controlled more by a mind than by a hand. The child leapt up and got into the closet.

The footsteps began to move in the hall. They were deliberate and irregular, a light and then a heavy one, then a silence as if the visitor had paused to listen himself or to examine something. In a minute the kitchen door screeked. The footsteps crossed the kitchen to the refrigerator. The closet wall and the kitchen wall were the same. Norton stood with his ear pressed against it. The refrigerator door opened. There was a prolonged silence.

He took off his shoes and then tiptoed out of the closet and stepped over the seed packages. In the middle of the room, he stopped and remained where he was, rigid. A thin bony-faced boy in a wet black suit stood in his door, blocking his escape. His hair was flattened to his skull by the rain. He stood there like an irate drenched crow. His look went through the child like a pin and paralyzed him. Then his eyes began to move over everything in the room—the unmade bed, the dirty curtains on the one large window, a photograph of a wide-faced young woman that stood up in the clutter on top of the dresser.

The child's tongue suddenly went wild. "He's been expecting you, he's going to give you a new shoe because you have to eat out of garbage cans!" he said in a kind of mouse-like shriek.

"I eat out of garbage cans," the boy said slowly with a beady stare, "because I like to eat out of garbage cans. See?"

The child nodded.

"And I got ways of getting my own shoe. See?"

The child nodded, mesmerized.

The boy limped in and sat down on the bed. He arranged a pillow behind him and stretched his short leg out so that the big black shoe rested conspicuously on a fold of the sheet.

Norton's gaze settled on it and remained immobile. The sole was as thick as a brick.

Johnson wiggled it slightly and smiled. "If I kick somebody *once* with this," he said, "it learns them not to mess with me."

The child nodded.

"Go in the kitchen," Johnson said, "and make me a sandwich with some of that rye bread and ham and bring me a glass of milk."

Norton went off like a mechanical toy, pushed in the right direction. He made a large greasy sandwich with ham hanging out the sides of it and poured out a glass of milk. Then he returned to the room with the glass of milk in one hand and the sandwich in the other.

Johnson was leaning back regally against the pillow. "Thanks, waiter," he said and took the sandwich.

Norton stood by the side of the bed, holding the glass.

The boy tore into the sandwich and ate steadily until he finished it. Then he took the glass of milk. He held it with both hands like a child and when he lowered it for breath, there was a rim of milk around his mouth. He handed Norton the empty glass. "Go get me one of them oranges in there, waiter," he said hoarsely.

Norton went to the kitchen and returned with the orange. Johnson peeled it with his fingers and let the peeling drop in the bed. He ate it slowly, spitting the seeds out in front of him. When he finished, he wiped his hands on the sheet and gave Norton a long appraising stare. He appeared to have been softened by the service. "You're his kid all right," he said. "You got the same stupid face."

The child stood there stolidly as if he had not heard.

"He don't know his left hand from his right," Johnson said with a hoarse pleasure in his voice.

The child cast his eyes a little to the side of the boy's face and looked fixedly at the wall.

"Yaketty yaketty yak," Johnson said, "and never says a thing."

The child's upper lip lifted slightly but he didn't say anything.

"Gas," Johnson said. "Gas."

The child's face began to have a wary look of belligerence. He backed away slightly as if he were prepared to retreat instantly. "He's good," he mumbled. "He helps people."

"Good!" Johnson said savagely. He thrust his head forward. "Listen here," he hissed, "I don't care if he's good or not. He ain't *right!*"

Norton looked stunned.

The screen door in the kitchen banged and some one entered. Johnson sat forward instantly. "Is that him?" he said.

"It's the cook," Norton said. "She comes in the afternoon."

Johnson got up and limped into the hall and stood in the kitchen door and Norton followed him.

The colored girl was at the closet taking off a bright red raincoat. She was a tall light-yellow girl with a mouth like a large rose that had darkened and wilted. Her hair was dressed in tiers on top of her head and leaned to the side like the Tower of Pisa.

Johnson made a noise through his teeth. "Well look at Aunt Jemima," he said.

The girl paused and trained an insolent gaze on them. They might have been dust on the floor.

"Come on," Johnson said, "let's see what all you got besides a nigger." He opened the first door to his right in the hall and looked into a pink-tiled bathroom. "A pink can!" he murmured.

He turned a comical face to the child. "Does he sit on that?"

"It's for company," Norton said, "but he sits on it sometimes."

"He ought to empty his head in it," Johnson said.

The door was open to the next room. It was the room Sheppard had slept in since his wife died. An ascetic-looking iron bed stood on the bare floor. A heap of Little League baseball uniforms was piled in one corner. Papers were scattered over a large roll-top desk and held down in various places by his pipes. Johnson stood looking into the room silently. He wrinkled his nose. "Guess who?" he said.

The door to the next room was closed but Johnson opened it and thrust his head into the semi-darkness within. The shades were down and the air was close with a faint scent of perfume in it. There was a wide antique bed and a mammoth dresser whose mirror glinted in the half light. Johnson snapped the light switch by the door and crossed the room to the mirror and peered into it. A silver comb and brush lay on the linen runner. He picked up the comb and began to run it through his hair. He combed it straight down on his forehead. Then he swept it to the side, Hitler fashion.

"Leave her comb alone!" the child said. He stood in the door, pale and breathing heavily as if he were watching sacrilege in a holy place.

Johnson put the comb down and picked up the brush and gave his hair a swipe with it.

"She's dead," the child said.

"I ain't afraid of dead people's things," Johnson said. He opened the top drawer and slid his hand in.

"Take your big fat dirty hands off my mother's clothes!" the child said in a high suffocated voice.

"Keep your shirt on, sweetheart," Johnson murmured. He pulled up a wrinkled red polka dot blouse and dropped it back. Then he pulled out a green silk kerchief and whirled it over his head and let it float to the floor. His hand continued to plow deep into the drawer. After a moment it came up gripping a faded corset with four dangling metal supporters. "Thisyer must be her saddle," he observed.

He lifted it gingerly and shook it. Then he fastened it around his waist and jumped up and down, making the metal supporters dance. He began to snap his fingers and turn his hips from side to side. "Gonter rock, rattle and roll," he sang. "Gonter rock, rattle and roll. Can't please that woman, to save my doggone soul." He began to move around, stamping the good foot down and slinging the heavy one to the side. He danced out the door, past the stricken child and down the hall toward the kitchen.

A half hour later Sheppard came home. He dropped his raincoat on a chair in the hall and came as far as the parlor door and stopped. His face was suddenly transformed. It shone with pleasure. Johnson sat, a dark figure, in a high-backed pink upholstered chair. The wall behind him was lined with books from floor to ceiling. He was reading one. Sheppard's eyes narrowed. It was a volume of the Encyclopedia Britannica. He was so engrossed in it that he did not look up. Sheppard held his breath. This was the perfect setting for the boy. He had to keep him here. He had to manage it somehow.

"Rufus!" he said, "it's good to see you boy!" and he bounded forward with his arm outstretched.

Johnson looked up, his face blank. "Oh hello," he said. He ignored the hand as long as he was able but when Sheppard did not withdraw it, he grudgingly shook it.

Sheppard was prepared for this kind of reaction. It was part of Johnson's make-up never to show enthusiasm.

"How are things?" he said. "How's your grandfather treating you?" He sat down on the edge of the sofa.

"He dropped dead," the boy said indifferently.

"You don't mean it!" Sheppard cried. He got up and sat down on the coffee table nearer the boy.

"Naw," Johnson said, "he ain't dropped dead. I wisht he had."

"Well where is he?" Sheppard muttered.

"He's gone with a remnant to the hills," Johnson said. "Him and some others. They're going to bury some Bibles in a cave and take two of different kinds of animals and all like that. Like Noah. Only this time it's going to be fire, not flood."

Sheppard's mouth stretched wryly. "I see," he said. Then he said, "In other words the old fool has abandoned you?"

"He ain't no fool," the boy said in an indignant tone.

"Has he abandoned you or not?" Sheppard asked impatiently.

The boy shrugged.

"Where's your probation officer?"

"I ain't supposed to keep up with him," Johnson said. "He's supposed to keep up with me."

Sheppard laughed. "Wait a minute," he said. He got up and went into the hall and got his raincoat off the chair and took it to the hall closet to hang it up. He had to give himself time to think, to decide how he could ask the boy so that he would stay. He couldn't force him to stay. It would have to be voluntary. Johnson pretended not to like him. That was only to uphold his pride, but he would have to ask him in such a way that his pride could still be upheld. He opened the closet door and took out a hanger. An old grey winter coat of his wife's still hung there. He pushed it aside but it didn't move. He pulled it open roughly and winced as if he had seen the larva inside a cocoon. Norton stood in it, his face swollen and pale, with a drugged look of misery on it. Sheppard stared at him. Suddenly he was confronted with a possibility. "Get out of there," he said. He caught him by the shoulder and propelled him firmly into the parlor and over to the pink chair where Johnson was sitting with the encyclopedia in his lap. He was going to risk everything in one blow.

"Rufus," he said, "I've got a problem. I need your help."

Johnson looked up suspiciously.

"Listen," Sheppard said, "we need another boy in the house." There was a genuine desperation in his voice. "Norton here has never had to divide anything in his life. He doesn't know what it means to share. And I need somebody to teach him. How about helping me out? Stay here for a while with us, Rufus. I need your help." The excitement in his voice made it thin.

The child suddenly came to life. His face swelled with fury. "He went in her room and used her comb!" he screamed, yanking Sheppard's arm. "He put on her corset and danced with Leola, he . . ."

"Stop this!" Sheppard said sharply. "Is tattling all you're capable of? I'm not asking you for a report on Rufus's conduct. I'm asking you to make him welcome here. Do you understand?

"You see how it is?" he asked, turning to Johnson.

Norton kicked the leg of the pink chair viciously, just missing Johnson's swollen foot. Sheppard yanked him back.

"He said you weren't nothing but gas!" the child shrieked.

A sly look of pleasure crossed Johnson's face.

Sheppard was not put back. These insults were part of the boy's defensive mechanism. "What about it, Rufus?" he said. "Will you stay with us for a while?"

Johnson looked straight in front of him and said nothing. He smiled slightly and appeared to gaze upon some vision of the future that pleased him.

"I don't care," he said and turned a page of the encyclopedia. "I can stand anywhere."

"Wonderful." Sheppard said. "Wonderful."

"He said," the child said in a throaty whisper, "you didn't know your left hand from your right."

There was a silence.

Johnson wet his finger and turned another page of the encyclopedia.

"I have something to say to both of you," Sheppard said in a voice without inflection. His eyes moved from one to the other of them and he spoke slowly as if what he was saying he would say only once and it behooved them to listen. "If it made any difference to me what Rufus thinks of me," he said, "then I wouldn't be asking him here. Rufus is going to help me out and I'm going to help him out and we're both going to help you out. I'd simply be selfish if I let what Rufus thinks of me interfere with what I can do for Rufus. If I can help a person, all I want is to do it. I'm above and beyond simple pettiness."

Neither of them made a sound. Norton stared at the chair cushion. Johnson peered closer at some fine print in the encyclopedia. Sheppard was looking at the tops of their heads. He smiled. After all, he had won. The boy was staying. He reached out and ruffled Norton's hair and slapped Johnson on the shoulder. "Now you fellows sit here and get acquainted," he said gaily and started toward the door. "I'm going to see what Leola left us for supper."

When he was gone, Johnson raised his head and looked at Norton. The child looked back at him bleakly. "God, kid," Johnson said in a cracked voice, "how do you stand it?" His face was stiff with outrage. "He thinks he's Jesus Christ!"

II

Sheppard's attic was a large unfinished room with exposed beams and no electric light. They had set the telescope up on a tripod in one of the dormer windows. It pointed now toward the dark sky where a sliver of moon, as fragile as an egg shell, had just emerged from behind a cloud with a brilliant silver edge. Inside, a kerosene lantern set on a trunk cast their shadows upward and tangled them, wavering slightly, in the joists overhead. Sheppard was sitting on a packing box, looking through the telescope, and Johnson was at his elbow, waiting to get at it. Sheppard had bought it for fifteen dollars two days before at a pawn shop.

"Quit hoggin it," Johnson said.

Sheppard got up and Johnson slid onto the box and put his eye to the instrument.

Sheppard sat down on a straight chair a few feet away. His face was flushed with pleasure. This much of his dream was a reality. Within a week he had made it possible for this boy's vision to pass through a slender channel to the stars. He looked at Johnson's bent back with complete satisfaction. The boy had on one of Norton's plaid shirts and some new khaki trousers he had bought him. The shoe would be ready next week. He had taken him to the brace shop the day after he came and had him fitted for a new shoe. Johnson was as touchy about the foot as if it were a sacred object. His face had been glum while the clerk, a young man with a bright pink bald head, measured the foot with his profane hands. The shoe was going to make the greatest difference in the boy's attitude. Even a child with normal feet was in love with the world after he had got a new pair of shoes. When Norton got a new pair, he walked around for days with his eyes on his feet.

Sheppard glanced across the room at the child. He was sitting on the floor against a trunk, trussed up in a rope he had found and wound around his legs from his ankles to his knees. He appeared so far away that Sheppard might have been looking at him through the wrong end of the telescope. He had had to whip him only once since Johnson had been with them—the first night when Norton had realized that Johnson was going to sleep in his mother's bed. He did not believe in whipping children, particularly in anger. In this case, he had done both and with good results. He had had no more trouble with Norton.

The child hadn't shown any positive generosity toward Johnson but what he couldn't help, he appeared to be resigned to. In the mornings Sheppard sent the two of them to the Y swimming pool, gave them money to get their lunch at the cafeteria and instructed them to meet him in the park in the afternoon to watch his Little League baseball practice. Every afternoon they had arrived at the park, shambling, silent, their faces closed each on his own thoughts as if neither were aware of the other's existence. At least he could be thankful there were no fights.

Norton showed no interest in the telescope. "Don't you want to get up and look through the telescope, Norton?" he said. It irritated him that the child showed no intellectual curiosity whatsoever. "Rufus is going to be way ahead of you."

Norton leaned forward absently and looked at Johnson's back.

Johnson turned around from the instrument. His face had begun to fill out again. The look of outrage had retreated from his hollow cheeks and was shored up now in the caves of his eyes, like a fugitive from Sheppard's kindness. "Don't waste your valuable time, kid," he said. "You seen the moon once, you seen it."

Sheppard was amused by these sudden turns of perversity. The boy resisted whatever he suspected was meant for his improvement and contrived when he was vitally interested in something to leave the impression he was bored. Sheppard was not deceived. Secretly Johnson was learning what he wanted him to learn—that his benefactor was impervious to insult and that there were no cracks in his armor of kindness and patience where a successful shaft could be driven. "Some day you may go to the moon," he said. "In ten years men will probably be making round trips there on schedule. Why you boys may be spacemen. Astronauts!"

"Astro-nuts," Johnson said.

"Nuts or nauts," Sheppard said, "it's perfectly possible that you, Rufus Johnson, will go to the moon."

Something in the depths of Johnson's eyes stirred. All day his humor had been glum. "I ain't going to the moon and get there alive," he said, "and when I die I'm going to hell."

"It's at least possible to get to the moon," Sheppard said dryly. The best way to handle this kind of thing was with gentle ridicule. "We can see it. We know it's there. Nobody has given any reliable evidence there's a hell."

"The Bible has give the evidence," Johnson said darkly, "and if you die and go there you burn forever."

The child leaned forward.

"Whoever says it ain't a hell," Johnson said, "is contradicting Jesus. The dead are judged and the wicked are damned. They weep and gnash their teeth while they burn," he continued, "and it's everlasting darkness."

The child's mouth opened. His eyes appeared to grow hollow.

"Satan runs it," Johnson said.

Norton lurched up and took a hobbled step toward Sheppard. "Is she there?" he said in a loud voice. "Is she there burning up?" He kicked the rope off his feet. "Is she on fire?"

"Oh my God," Sheppard muttered. "No no," he said, "of course she isn't. Rufus is mistaken. Your mother isn't anywhere. She's not unhappy. She just isn't." His lot would have been easier if when his wife died he had told Norton she had gone to heaven and that some day he would see her again, but he could not allow himself to bring him up on a lie.

Norton's face began to twist. A knot formed in his chin.

"Listen," Sheppard said quickly and pulled the child to him, "your mother's spirit lives on in other people and it'll live on in you if you're good and generous like she was."

The child's pale eyes hardened in disbelief.

Sheppard's pity turned to revulsion. The boy would rather she be in hell than nowhere. "Do you understand?" he said. "She doesn't exist." He put his hand on the child's shoulder. "That's all I have to give you," he said in a softer, exasperated tone, "the truth."

Instead of howling, the boy wrenched himself away and caught Johnson by the sleeve. "Is she there, Rufus?" he said. "Is she there, burning up?"

Johnson's eyes glittered. "Well," he said, "she is if she was evil. Was she a whore?"

"Your mother was not a whore," Sheppard said sharply. He had the sensation of driving a car without brakes. "Now let's have no more of this foolishness. We were talking about the moon."

"Did she believe in Jesus?" Johnson asked.

Norton looked blank. After a second he said, "Yes," as if he saw that this was necessary. "She did," he said. "All the time."

"She did not," Sheppard muttered.

"She did all the time," Norton said. "I heard her say she did all the time."

"She's saved," Johnson said.

The child still looked puzzled. "Where?" he said. "Where is she at?"

"On high," Johnson said.

"Where's that?" Norton gasped.

"It's in the sky somewhere," Johnson said, "but you got to be dead to get there. You can't go in no space ship." There was a narrow gleam in his eyes now like a beam holding steady on its target.

"Man's going to the moon," Sheppard said grimly, "is very much like the first fish crawling out of the water onto land billions and billions of years ago. He didn't have an earth suit. He had to grow his adjustments inside. He developed lungs."

"When I'm dead will I go to hell or where she is?" Norton asked.

"Right now you'd go where she is," Johnson said, "but if you live long enough, you'll go to hell."

Sheppard rose abruptly and picked up the lantern. "Close the window, Rufus," he said. "It's time we went to bed."

On the way down the attic stairs he heard Johnson say in a loud whisper behind him, "I'll tell you all about it tomorrow, kid, when Himself has cleared out."

The next day when the boys came to the ball park, he watched them as they came from behind the bleachers and around the edge of the field. Johnson's hand was on Norton's shoulder, his head bent toward the younger boy's ear, and on the child's face there was a look of complete confidence, of dawning light. Sheppard's grimace hardened. This would be Johnson's way of trying to annoy him. But he would not be annoyed. Norton was not bright enough to be damaged much. He gazed at the child's dull absorbed little face. Why try to make him superior? Heaven and hell were for the mediocre, and he was that if he was anything.

The two boys came into the bleachers and sat down about ten feet away, facing him, but neither gave him any sign of recognition. He cast a glance behind him where the Little Leaguers were spread out in the field. Then he started for the bleachers. The hiss of Johnson's voice stopped as he approached.

"What have you fellows been doing today?" he asked genially.

"He's been telling me . . ." Norton started.

Johnson pushed the child in the ribs with his elbow. "We ain't been doing nothing," he said. His face appeared to be covered with a blank glaze but through it a look of complicity was blazoned forth insolently.

Sheppard felt his face grow warm, but he said nothing. A child in a Little League uniform had followed him and was nudging him in the back of the leg with a bat. He turned and put his arm around the boy's neck and went with him back to the game.

That night when he went to the attic to join the boys at the telescope, he found Norton there alone. He was sitting on the packing box, hunched over, looking intently through the instrument. Johnson was not there.

"Where's Rufus?" Sheppard asked.

"I said where's Rufus?" he said louder.

"Gone somewhere," the child said without turning around.

"Gone where?" Sheppard asked.

"He just said he was going somewhere. He said he was fed up looking at stars."

"I see," Sheppard said glumly. He turned and went back down the stairs. He searched the house without finding Johnson. Then he went to the living room and sat down. Yesterday he had been convinced of his success with the boy. Today he faced the possibility that he was failing with him. He had been over-lenient, too concerned to have Johnson like him. He felt a twinge of guilt. What difference did it make if Johnson liked him or not? What was that to him?

When the boy came in, they would have a few things understood. As long as you stay here there'll be no going out at night by yourself, do you understand?

I don't have to stay here. It ain't nothing to me staying here.

Oh my God, he thought. He could not bring it to that. He would have to be firm but not make an issue of it. He picked up the evening paper. Kindness and patience were always called for but he had not been firm enough. He sat holding the paper but not reading it. The boy would not respect him unless he showed firmness. The doorbell rang and he went to answer it. He opened it and stepped back, with a pained disappointed face.

A large dour policeman stood on the stoop, holding Johnson by the elbow. At the curb a patrolcar waited. Johnson looked very white. His jaw was thrust forward as if to keep from trembling.

"We brought him here first because he raised such a fit," the policeman said, "but now that you've seen him, we're going to take him to the station and ask him a few questions."

"What happened?" Sheppard muttered.

"A house around the corner from here," the policeman said. "A real smash job, dishes broken all over the floor, furniture turned upside-down . . ."

"I didn't have a thing to do with it!" Johnson said. "I was walking along minding my own bidnis when this cop came up and grabbed me."

Sheppard looked at the boy grimly. He made no effort to soften his expression.

Johnson flushed. "I was just walking along," he muttered, but with no conviction in his voice.

"Come on, bud," the policeman said.

"You ain't going to let him take me, are you?" Johnson

said. "You believe me, don't you?" There was an appeal in his voice that Sheppard had not heard there before.

This was crucial. The boy would have to learn that he could not be protected when he was guilty. "You'll have to go with him, Rufus," he said.

"You're going to let him take me and I tell you I ain't done a thing?" Johnson said shrilly.

Sheppard's face became harder as his sense of injury grew. The boy had failed him even before he had had a chance to give him the shoe. They were to have got it tomorrow. All his regret turned suddenly on the shoe; his irritation at the sight of Johnson doubled.

"You made out like you had all this confidence in me," the boy mumbled.

"I did have," Sheppard said. His face was wooden.

Johnson turned away with the policeman but before he moved, a gleam of pure hatred flashed toward Sheppard from the pits of his eyes.

Sheppard stood in the door and watched them get into the patrolcar and drive away. He summoned his compassion. He would go to the station tomorrow and see what he could do about getting him out of trouble. The night in jail would not hurt him and the experience would teach him that he could not treat with impunity someone who had shown him nothing but kindness. Then they would go get the shoe and perhaps after a night in jail it would mean even more to the boy.

The next morning at eight o'clock the police sergeant called and told him he could come pick Johnson up. "We booked a nigger on that charge," he said. "Your boy didn't have nothing to do with it."

Sheppard was at the station in ten minutes, his face

hot with shame. Johnson sat slouched on a bench in a drab outer office, reading a police magazine. There was no else in the room. Sheppard sat down beside him and put his hand tentatively on his shoulder.

The boy glanced up—his lip curled—and back to the magazine.

Sheppard felt physically sick. The ugliness of what he had done bore in upon him with a sudden dull intensity. He had failed him at just the point where he might have turned him once and for all in the right direction. "Rufus," he said, "I apologize. I was wrong and you were right. I misjudged you."

The boy continued to read.

"I'm sorry."

The boy wet his finger and turned a page.

Sheppard braced himself. "I was a fool, Rufus," he said.

Johnson's mouth slid slightly to the side. He shrugged without raising his head from the magazine.

"Will you forget it, this time?" Sheppard said. "It won't happen again."

The boy looked up. His eyes were bright and unfriendly. "I'll forget it," he said, "but you better remember it." He got up and stalked toward the door. In the middle of the room, he turned and jerked his arm at Sheppard and Sheppard jumped up and followed him as if the boy had yanked an invisible leash.

"Your shoe," he said eagerly, "today is the day to get your shoe!" Thank God for the shoe!

But when they went to the brace shop, they found that the shoe had been made two sizes too small and a new one would not be ready for another ten days. Johnson's temper improved at once. The clerk had obviously made a mistake in the measurements but the boy insisted the foot had grown.

He left the shop with a pleased expression, as if, in expanding, the foot had acted on some inspiration of its own. Sheppard's face was haggard.

After this he redoubled his efforts. Since Johnson had lost interest in the telescope, he bought a microscope and a box of prepared slides. If he couldn't impress the boy with immensity, he would try the infinitesimal. For two nights Johnson appeared absorbed in the new instrument, then he abruptly lost interest in it, but he seemed content to sit in the living room in the evening and read the encyclopedia. He devoured the encyclopedia as he devoured his dinner, steadily and without dint to his appetite. Each subject appeared to enter his head, be ravaged, and thrown out. Nothing pleased Sheppard more than to see the boy slouched on the sofa, his mouth shut, reading. After they had spent two or three evenings like this, he began to recover his vision. His confidence returned. He knew that some day he would be proud of Johnson.

On Thursday night Sheppard attended a city council meeting. He dropped the boys off at a movie on his way and picked them up on his way back. When they reached home, an automobile with a single red eye above its windshield was waiting in front of the house. Sheppard's lights as he turned into the driveway illuminated two dour faces in the car.

"The cops!" Johnson said. "Some nigger has broke in somewhere and they've come for me again."

"We'll see about that," Sheppard muttered. He stopped the car in the driveway and switched off the lights. "You boys go in the house and go to bed," he said. "I'll handle this."

He got out and strode toward the squad car. He thrust his head in the window. The two policemen were looking at him with silent knowledgeable faces. "A house on the corner of Shelton and Mills," the one in the driver's seat said. "It looks like a train run through it."

"He was in the picture show down town," Sheppard said. "My boy was with him. He had nothing to do with the other one and he had nothing to do with this one. I'll be responsible."

"If I was you," the one nearest him said, "I wouldn't be responsible for any little bastard like him."

"I said I'd be responsible," Sheppard repeated coldly. "You people made a mistake the last time. Don't make another."

The policemen looked at each other. "It ain't our funeral," the one in the driver's seat said, and turned the key in the ignition.

Sheppard went in the house and sat down in the living room in the dark. He did not suspect Johnson and he did not want the boy to think he did. If Johnson thought he suspected him again, he would lose everything. But he wanted to know if his alibi was airtight. He thought of going to Norton's room and asking him if Johnson had left the movie. But that would be worse. Johnson would know what he was doing and would be incensed. He decided to ask Johnson himself. He would be direct. He went over in his mind what he was going to say and then he got up and went to the boy's door.

It was open as if he had been expected but Johnson was in bed. Just enough light came in from the hall for Sheppard to see his shape under the sheet. He came in and stood at the foot of the bed. "They've gone," he said. "I told them you had nothing to do with it and that I'd be responsible."

There was a muttered "Yeah," from the pillow.

Sheppard hesitated. "Rufus," he said, "you didn't leave the movie for anything at all, did you?"

"You make out like you got all this confidence in me!" a sudden outraged voice cried, "and you ain't got any! You don't trust me no more now than you did then!" The voice, disembodied, seemed to come more surely from the depths of Johnson than when his face was visible. It was a cry of reproach, edged slightly with contempt.

"I do have confidence in you," Sheppard said intensely. "I have every confidence in you. I believe in you and I trust you completely."

"You got your eye on me all the time," the voice said sullenly. "When you get through asking me a bunch of questions, you're going across the hall and ask Norton a bunch of them."

"I have no intention of asking Norton anything and never did," Sheppard said gently. "And I don't suspect you at all. You could hardly have got from the picture show down town and out here to break in a house and back to the picture show in the time you had."

"That's why you believe me!" the boy cried, "—because you think I couldn't have done it."

"No, no!" Sheppard said. "I believe you because I believe you've got the brains and the guts not to get in trouble again. I believe you know yourself well enough now to know that you don't have to do such things. I believe that you can make anything of yourself that you set your mind to."

Johnson sat up. A faint light shone on his forehead but the rest of his face was invisible. "And I could have broke in there if I'd wanted to in the time I had," he said.

"But I know you didn't," Sheppard said. "There's not the least trace of doubt in my mind."

There was a silence. Johnson lay back down. Then the

voice, low and hoarse, as if it were being forced out with difficulty, said, "You don't want to steal and smash up things when you've got everything you want already."

Sheppard caught his breath. The boy was thanking him! He was thanking him! There was gratitude in his voice. There was appreciation. He stood there, smiling foolishly in the dark, trying to hold the moment in suspension. Involuntarily he took a step toward the pillow and stretched out his hand and touched Johnson's forehead. It was cold and dry like rusty iron.

"I understand. Good night, son," he said and turned quickly and left the room. He closed the door behind him and stood there, overcome with emotion.

Across the hall Norton's door was open. The child lay on the bed on his side, looking into the light from the hall.

After this, the road with Johnson would be smooth.

Norton sat up and beckoned to him.

He saw the child but after the first instant, he did not let his eyes focus directly on him. He could not go in and talk to Norton without breaking Johnson's trust. He hesitated, but remained where he was a moment as if he saw nothing. Tomorrow was the day they were to go back for the shoe. It would be a climax to the good feeling between them. He turned quickly and went back into his own room.

The child sat for some time looking at the spot where his father had stood. Finally his gaze became aimless and he lay back down.

The next day Johnson was glum and silent as if he were ashamed that he had revealed himself. His eyes had a hooded look. He seemed to have retired within himself and there to be going through some crisis of determination. Sheppard could not get to the brace shop quickly enough. He left Norton at home because he did not want his attention divided. He wanted to be free to observe Johnson's reaction minutely. The boy did not seem pleased or even interested in the prospect of the shoe, but when it became an actuality, certainly then he would be moved.

The brace shop was a small concrete warehouse lined and stacked with the equipment of affliction. Wheel chairs and walkers covered most of the floor. The walls were hung with every kind of crutch and brace. Artificial limbs were stacked on the shelves, legs and arms and hands, claws and hooks, straps and human harnesses and unidentifiable instruments for unnamed deformities. In a small clearing in the middle of the room there was a row of yellow plastic-cushioned chairs and a shoe fitting stool. Johnson slouched down in one of the chairs and set his foot up on the stool and sat with his eyes on it moodily. What was roughly the toe had broken open again and he had patched it with a piece of canvas; another place he had patched with what appeared to be the tongue of the original shoe. The two sides were laced with twine.

There was a excited flush on Sheppard's face; his heart was beating unnaturally fast.

The clerk appeared from the back of the shop with the new shoe under his arm. "Got her right this time!" he said. He straddled the shoe-fitting stool and held the shoe up, smiling as if he had produced it by magic.

It was a black slick shapeless object, shining hideously. It looked like a blunt weapon, highly polished.

Johnson gazed at it darkly.

"With this shoe," the clerk said, "you won't know you're walking. You'll think you're riding!" He bent his bright pink bald head and began gingerly to unlace the twine. He removed the old shoe as if he were skinning an animal still half alive. His expression was strained. The unsheathed mass of foot in the dirty sock made Sheppard feel queasy. He turned his eyes away until the new shoe was on. The clerk laced it up rapidly. "Now stand up and walk around," he said, "and see if that ain't power glide." He winked at Sheppard. "In that shoe," he said, "he won't know he don't have a normal foot."

Sheppard's face was bright with pleasure.

Johnson stood up and walked a few yards away. He walked stiffly with almost no dip in his short side. He stood for a moment, rigid, with his back to them.

"Wonderful!" Sheppard said. "Wonderful." It was as if he had given the boy a new spine.

Johnson turned around. His mouth was set in a thin icy line. He came back to the seat and removed the shoe. He put his foot in the old one and began lacing it up.

"You want to take it home and see if it suits you first?" the clerk murmured.

"No," Johnson said. "I ain't going to wear it at all."

"What's wrong with it?" Sheppard said, his voice rising.

"I don't need no new shoe," Johnson said. "And when I do, I got ways of getting my own." His face was stony but there was a glint of triumph in his eyes.

"Boy," the clerk said, "is your trouble in your foot or in your head?"

"Go soak your skull," Johnson said. "Your brains are on fire."

The clerk rose glumly but with dignity and asked Sheppard what he wanted done with the shoe, which he dangled dispiritedly by the lace.

Sheppard's face was a dark angry red. He was staring straight in front of him at a leather corset with an artificial arm attached.

The clerk asked him again.

"Wrap it up," Sheppard muttered. He turned his eyes to Johnson. "He's not mature enough for it yet," he said. "I had thought he was less of a child."

The boy leered. "You been wrong before," he said.

That night they sat in the living room and read as usual. Sheppard kept himself glumly entrenched behind the Sunday New York *Times*. He wanted to recover his good humor, but every time he thought of the rejected shoe, he felt a new charge of irritation. He did not trust himself even to look at Johnson. He realized that the boy had refused the shoe because he was insecure. Johnson had been frightened by his own gratitude. He didn't know what to make of the new self he was becoming conscious of. He understood that something he had been was threatened and he was facing himself and his possibilities for the first time. He was questioning his identity. Grudgingly, Sheppard felt a slight return of sympathy for the boy. In a few minutes, he lowered his paper and looked at him.

Johnson was sitting on the sofa, gazing over the top of the encyclopedia. His expression was trancelike. He might have been listening to something far away. Sheppard watched him intently but the boy continued to listen, and did not turn his head. The poor kid is lost, Sheppard thought. Here he had sat all evening, sullenly reading the paper, and had not said a word to break the tension. "Rufus," he said.

Johnson continued to sit, stock-still, listening.

"Rufus," Sheppard said in a slow hypnotic voice, "you can be anything in the world you want to be. You can be a scientist or an architect or an engineer or whatever you set your mind to, and whatever you set your mind to be, you can be the best of its kind." He imagined his voice penetrating to the boy in the black caverns of his psyche. Johnson leaned forward but his eyes did not turn. On the street a car door closed. There was a silence. Then a sudden blast from the door bell.

Sheppard jumped up and went to the door and opened it. The same policeman who had come before stood there. The patrolcar waited at the curb.

"Lemme see that boy," he said.

Sheppard scowled and stood aside. "He's been here all evening," he said. "I can vouch for it."

The policeman walked into the living room. Johnson appeared engrossed in his book. After a second he looked up with an annoyed expression, like a great man interrupted at his work.

"What was that you were looking at in that kitchen window over on Winter Avenue about a half hour ago, bud?" the policeman asked.

"Stop persecuting this boy!" Sheppard said. "I'll vouch for the fact he was here. I was here with him."

"You heard him," Johnson said. "I been here all the time."

"It ain't everybody makes tracks like you," the policeman said and eyed the clubfoot.

"They couldn't be his tracks," Sheppard growled, infuriated. "He's been here all the time. You're wasting your own time and you're wasting ours." He felt the *ours* seal his solidarity with the boy. "I'm sick of this," he said. "You people are too damn lazy to go out and find whoever is doing these things. You come here automatically."

The policeman ignored this and continued looking through Johnson. His eyes were small and alert in his fleshy face. Finally he turned toward the door. "We'll get him sooner or later," he said, "with his head in a window and his tail out."

Sheppard followed him to the door and slammed it behind him. His spirits were soaring. This was exactly what he had needed. He returned with an expectant face.

Johnson had put the book down and was sitting there, looking at him slyly. "Thanks," he said.

Sheppard stopped. The boy's expression was predatory. He was openly leering.

"You ain't such a bad liar yourself," he said.

"Liar?" Sheppard murmured. Could the boy have left and come back? He felt himself sicken. Then a rush of anger sent him forward. "Did you leave?" he said furiously. "I didn't see you leave."

The boy only smiled.

"You went up in the attic to see Norton," Sheppard said.

"Naw," Johnson said, "that kid is crazy. He don't want to do nothing but look through that stinking telescope."

"I don't want to hear about Norton," Sheppard said harshly. "Where were you?"

"I was sitting on that pink can by my ownself," Johnson said. "There wasn't no witnesses."

Sheppard took out his handkerchief and wiped his forehead. He managed to smile.

Johnson rolled his eyes. "You don't believe in me," he said. His voice was cracked the way it had been in the dark room two nights before. "You make out like you got all this confidence in me but you ain't got any. When things get hot, you'll fade like the rest of them." The crack became exaggerated, comic. The mockery in it was blatant. "You don't believe in me. You ain't got no confidence," he wailed. "And you ain't any smarter than that cop. All that about tracks—that was a trap. There wasn't any tracks. That whole place is concreted in the back and my feet were dry."

Sheppard slowly put the handkerchief back in his

pocket. He dropped down on the sofa and gazed at the rug beneath his feet. The boy's clubfoot was set within the circle of his vision. The pieced-together shoe appeared to grin at him with Johnson's own face. He caught hold of the edge of the sofa cushion and his knuckles turned white. A chill of hatred shook him. He hated the shoe, hated the foot, hated the boy. His face paled. Hatred choked him. He was aghast at himself.

He caught the boy's shoulder and gripped it fiercely as if to keep himself from falling. "Listen," he said, "you looked in that window to embarrass me. That was all you wanted—to shake my resolve to help you, but my resolve isn't shaken. I'm stronger than you are. I'm stronger than you are and I'm going to save you. The good will triumph."

"Not when it ain't true," the boy said. "Not when it ain't right."

"My resolve isn't shaken," Sheppard repeated. "I'm going to save you."

Johnson's look became sly again. "You ain't going to save me," he said. "You're going to tell me to leave this house. I did those other two jobs too—the first one as well as the one I done when I was supposed to be in the picture show."

"I'm not going to tell you to leave," Sheppard said. His voice was toneless, mechanical. "I'm going to save you."

Johnson thrust his head forward. "Save yourself," he hissed. "Nobody can save me but Jesus."

Sheppard laughed curtly. "You don't deceive me," he said. "I flushed that out of your head in the reformatory. I saved you from that, at least."

The muscles in Johnson's face stiffened. A look of such repulsion hardened on his face that Sheppard drew back. The boy's eyes were like distorting mirrors in which he saw himself made hideous and grotesque. "I'll show you," Johnson whispered. He rose abruptly and started headlong for the door as if he could not get out of Sheppard's sight quick enough, but it was the door to the back hall he went through, not the front door. Sheppard turned on the sofa and looked behind him where the boy had disappeared. He heard the door to his room slam. He was not leaving. The intensity had gone out of Sheppard's eyes. They looked flat and lifeless as if the shock of the boy's revelation were only now reaching the center of his consciousness. "If he would only leave," he murmured. "If he would only leave now of his own accord."

The next morning Johnson appeared at the breakfast table in the grandfather's suit he had come in. Sheppard pretended not to notice but one look told him what he already knew, that he was trapped, that there could be nothing now but a battle of nerves and that Johnson would win it. He wished he had never laid eyes on the boy. The failure of his compassion numbed him. He got out of the house as soon as he could and all day he dreaded to go home in the evening. He had a faint hope that the boy might be gone when he returned. The grandfather's suit might have meant he was leaving. The hope grew in the afternoon. When he came home and opened the front door, his heart was pounding.

He stopped in the hall and looked silently into the living room. His expectant expression faded. His face seemed suddenly as old as his white hair. The two boys were sitting close together on the sofa, reading the same book. Norton's cheek rested against the sleeve of Johnson's black suit. Johnson's finger moved under the lines they were reading. The elder brother and the younger. Sheppard looked woodenly at this scene for almost a minute. Then he walked into the room and took off his coat and dropped it on a chair. Neither boy noticed him. He went on to the kitchen.

Leola left the supper on the stove every afternoon before she left and he put it on the table. His head ached and his nerves were taut. He sat down on the kitchen stool and remained there, sunk in his depression. He wondered if he could infuriate Johnson enough to make him leave of his own accord. Last night what had enraged him was the Jesus business. It might enrage Johnson, but it depressed him. Why not simply tell the boy to go? Admit defeat. The thought of facing Johnson again sickened him. The boy looked at him as if he were the guilty one, as if he were a moral leper. He knew without conceit that he was a good man, that he had nothing to reproach himself with. His feelings about Johnson now were involuntary. He would like to feel compassion for him. He would like to be able to help him. He longed for the time when there would be no one but himself and Norton in the house, when the child's simple selfishness would be all he had to contend with, and his own loneliness.

He got up and took three serving dishes off the shelf and took them to the stove. Absently he began pouring the butterbeans and the hash into the dishes. When the food was on the table, he called them in.

They brought the book with them. Norton pushed his place setting around to the same side of the table as Johnson's and moved his chair next to Johnson's chair. They sat down and put the book between them. It was a black book with red edges.

"What's that you're reading?" Sheppard asked, sitting down.

"The Holy Bible," Johnson said.

God give me strength, Sheppard said under his breath.

"We lifted it from a ten cent store," Johnson said.

"We?" Sheppard muttered. He turned and glared at Norton. The child's face was bright and there was an excited sheen to his eyes. The change that had come over the boy struck him for the first time. He looked alert. He had on a blue plaid shirt and his eyes were a brighter blue than he had ever seen them before. There was a strange new life in him, the sign of new and more rugged vices. "So now you steal?" he said, glowering. "You haven't learned to be generous but you have learned to steal."

"No he ain't," Johnson said. "I was the one lifted it. He only watched. He can't sully himself. It don't make any difference about me. I'm going to hell anyway."

Sheppard held his tongue.

"Unless," Johnson said, "I repent."

"Repent, Rufus," Norton said in a pleading voice. "Repent, hear? You don't want to go to hell."

"Stop talking this nonsense," Sheppard said, looking sharply at the child.

"If I do repent, I'll be a preacher," Johnson said. "If you're going to do it, it's no sense in doing it half way."

"What are you going to be, Norton," Sheppard asked in a brittle voice, "a preacher too?"

There was a glitter of wild pleasure in the child's eyes. "A space man!" he shouted.

"Wonderful," Sheppard said bitterly.

"Those space ships ain't going to do you any good unless you believe in Jesus," Johnson said. He wet his finger and began to leaf through the pages of the Bible. "I'll read you where it says so," he said.

Sheppard leaned forward and said in a low furious voice, "Put that Bible up, Rufus, and eat your dinner."

Johnson continued searching for the passage.

"Put that Bible up!" Sheppard shouted.

The boy stopped and looked up. His expression was startled but pleased.

"That book is something for you to hide behind," Sheppard said. "It's for cowards, people who are afraid to stand on their own feet and figure things out for themselves."

Johnson's eyes snapped. He backed his chair a little way from the table. "Satan has you in his power," he said. "Not only me. You too."

Sheppard reached across the table to grab the book but Johnson snatched it and put it in his lap.

Sheppard laughed. "You don't believe in that book and you know you don't believe in it!"

"I believe it!" Johnson said. "You don't know what I believe and what I don't."

Sheppard shook his head. "You don't believe it. You're too intelligent."

"I ain't too intelligent," the boy muttered. "You don't know nothing about me. Even if I didn't believe it, it would still be true."

"You don't believe it!" Sheppard said. His face was a taunt.

"I believe it!" Johnson said breathlessly. "I'll show you I believe it!" He opened the book in his lap and tore out a page of it and thrust it into his mouth. He fixed his eyes on Sheppard. His jaws worked furiously and the paper crackled as he chewed it.

"Stop this," Sheppard said in a dry, burnt-out voice. "Stop it."

The boy raised the Bible and tore out a page with his teeth and began grinding it in his mouth, his eyes burning.

Sheppard reached across the table and knocked the book out of his hand. "Leave the table," he said coldly.

Johnson swallowed what was in his mouth. His eyes widened as if a vision of splendor were opening up before him. "I've eaten it!" he breathed. "I've eaten it like Ezekiel and it was honey to my mouth!"

"Leave this table," Sheppard said. His hands were clenched beside his plate.

"I've eaten it!" the boy cried. Wonder transformed his face. "I've eaten it like Ezekiel and I don't want none of your food after it nor no more ever."

"Go then," Sheppard said softly. "Go. Go."

The boy rose and picked up the Bible and started toward the hall with it. At the door he paused, a small black figure on the threshold of some dark apocalypse. "The devil has you in his power," he said in a jubilant voice and disappeared.

After supper Sheppard sat in the living room alone. Johnson had left the house but he could not believe that the boy had simply gone. The first feeling of release had passed. He felt dull and cold as at the onset of an illness and dread had settled in him like a fog. Just to leave would be too anticlimactic an end for Johnson's taste; he would return and try to prove something. He might come back a week later and set fire to the place. Nothing seemed too outrageous now.

He picked up the paper and tried to read. In a moment he threw it down and got up and went into the hall and listened. He might be hiding in the attic. He went to the attic door and opened it.

The lantern was lit, casting a dim light on the stairs. He didn't hear anything. "Norton," he called, "are you up there?" There was no answer. He mounted the narrow stairs to see.

Amid the strange vine-like shadows cast by the lantern, Norton sat with his eye to the telescope. "Norton," Sheppard said, "do you know where Rufus went?"

The child's back was to him. He was sitting hunched, intent, his large ears directly above his shoulders. Suddenly he waved his hand and crouched closer to the telescope as if he could not get near enough to what he saw.

"Norton!" Sheppard said in a loud voice.

The child didn't move.

"Norton!" Sheppard shouted.

Norton started. He turned around. There was an unnatural brightness about his eyes. After a moment he seemed to see that it was Sheppard. "I've found her!" he said breathlessly.

"Found who?" Sheppard said.

"Mamma!"

Sheppard steadied himself in the door way. The jungle of shadows around the child thickened.

"Come and look!" he cried. He wiped his sweaty face on the tail of his plaid shirt and then put his eye back to the telescope. His back became fixed in a rigid intensity. All at once he waved again.

"Norton," Sheppard said, "you don't see anything in the telescope but star clusters. Now you've had enough of that for one night. You'd better go to bed. Do you know where Rufus is?"

"She's there!" he cried, not turning around from the telescope. "She waved at me!"

"I want you in bed in fifteen minutes," Sheppard said. After a moment he said, "Do you hear me, Norton?"

The child began to wave frantically.

"I mean what I say," Sheppard said. "I'm going to call in fifteen minutes and see if you're in bed."

He went down the steps again and returned to the parlor. He went to the front door and cast a cursory glance out. The sky was crowded with the stars he had been fool enough to think Johnson could reach. Somewhere in the small wood behind the house, a bull frog sounded a low hollow note. He went back to his chair and sat a few minutes. He decided to go to bed. He put his hands on the arms of the chair and leaned forward and heard, like the first shrill note of a disaster warning, the siren of a police car, moving slowly into the neighborhood and nearer until it subsided with a moan outside the house.

He felt a cold weight on his shoulders as if an icy cloak had been thrown about him. He went to the door and opened it.

Two policemen were coming up the walk with a dark snarling Johnson between them, handcuffed to each. A reporter jogged alongside and another policeman waited in the patrol car.

"Here's your boy," the dourest of the policemen said. "Didn't I tell you we'd get him?"

Johnson jerked his arm down savagely. "I was waitin for you!" he said. "You wouldn't have got me if I hadn't of wanted to get caught. It was my idea." He was addressing the policemen but leering at Sheppard.

Sheppard looked at him coldly.

"Why did you want to get caught?" the reporter asked, running around to get beside Johnson. "Why did you deliberately want to get caught?"

The question and the sight of Sheppard seemed to throw the boy into a fury. "To show up that big tin Jesus!" he hissed and kicked his leg out at Sheppard. "He thinks he's God. I'd rather be in the reformatory than in his house, I'd rather be in the pen! The Devil has him in his power. He don't know his left hand from his right, he don't have as much sense as his crazy kid!" He paused and then swept on to his fantastic conclusion. "He made suggestions to me!"

Sheppard's face blanched. He caught hold of the door facing.

"Suggestions?" the reporter said eagerly, "what kind of suggestions?"

"Immor'l suggestions!" Johnson said. "What kind of suggestions do you think? But I ain't having none of it, I'm a Christian, I'm . . ."

Sheppard's face was tight with pain. "He knows that's not true," he said in a shaken voice. "He knows he's lying. I did everything I knew how for him. I did more for him than I did for my own child. I hoped to save him and I failed, but it was an honorable failure. I have nothing to reproach myself with. I made no suggestions to him."

"Do you remember the suggestions?" the reporter asked. "Can you tell us exactly what he said?"

"He's a dirty atheist," Johnson said. "He said there wasn't no hell."

"Well, they seen each other now," one of the policemen said with a knowing sigh. "Let's us go."

"Wait," Sheppard said. He came down one step and fixed his eyes on Johnson's eyes in a last desperate effort to save himself. "Tell the truth, Rufus," he said. "You don't want to perpetrate this lie. You're not evil, you're mortally confused. You don't have to make up for that foot, you don't have to . . ."

Johnson hurled himself forward. "Listen at him!" he screamed. "I lie and steal because I'm good at it! My foot don't have a thing to do with it! The lame shall enter first! The halt'll be gathered together. When I get ready to be saved, Jesus'll save me, not that lying stinking atheist, not that . . ."

"That'll be enough out of you," the policeman said and yanked him back. "We just wanted you to see we got him," he said to Sheppard, and the two of them turned around and dragged Johnson away, half turned and screaming back at Sheppard.

"The lame'll carry off the prey!" he screeched, but his voice was muffled inside the car. The reporter scrambled into the front seat with the driver and slammed the door and the siren wailed into the darkness.

Sheppard remained there, bent slightly like a man who has been shot but continues to stand. After a minute he turned and went back in the house and sat down in the chair he had left. He closed his eyes on a picture of Johnson in a circle of reporters at the police station, elaborating his lies. "I have nothing to reproach myself with," he murmured. His every action had been selfless, his one aim had been to save Johnson for some decent kind of service, he had not spared himself, he had sacrificed his reputation, he had done more for Johnson than he had done for his own child. Foulness hung about him like an odor in the air, so close that it seemed to come from his own breath. "I have nothing to reproach myself with," he repeated. His voice sounded dry and harsh. "I did more for him than I did for my own child." He was swept with a sudden panic. He heard the boy's jubilant voice. Satan has you in his power.

"I have nothing to reproach myself with," he began again. "I did more for him than I did for my own child." He heard his voice as if it were the voice of his accuser. He repeated the sentence silently.

Slowly his face drained of color. It became almost grey beneath the white halo of his hair. The sentence echoed in his mind, each syllable like a dull blow. His mouth twisted and he closed his eyes against the revelation. Norton's face rose before him, empty, forlorn, his left eye listing almost imperceptibly toward the outer rim as if it could not bear a full view of grief. His heart constricted with a repulsion for himself so clear and intense that he gasped for breath. He had stuffed his own emptiness with good works like a glutton. He had ignored his own child to feed his vision of himself. He saw the clear-eyed Devil, the sounder of hearts, leering at him from the eyes of Johnson. His image of himself shrivelled until everything was black before him. He sat there paralyzed, aghast.

He saw Norton at the telescope, all back and ears, saw his arm shoot up and wave frantically. A rush of agonizing love for the child rushed over him like a transfusion of life. The little boy's face appeared to him transformed; the image of his salvation; all light. He groaned with joy. He would make everything up to him. He would never let him suffer again. He would be mother and father. He jumped up and ran to his room, to kiss him, to tell him that he loved him, that he would never fail him again.

The light was on in Norton's room but the bed was empty. He turned and dashed up the attic stairs and at the top reeled back like a man on the edge of a pit. The tripod had fallen and the telescope lay on the floor. A few feet over it, the child hung in the jungle of shadows, just below the beam from which he had launched his flight into space.

Revelation

The doctor's waiting room, which was very small, was almost full when the Turpins entered and Mrs. Turpin, who was very large, made it look even smaller by her presence. She stood looming at the head of the magazine table set in the center of it, a living demonstration that the room was inadequate and ridiculous. Her little bright black eyes took in all the patients as she sized up the seating situation. There was one vacant chair and a place on the sofa occupied by a blond child in a dirty blue romper who should have been told to move over and make room for the lady. He was five or six, but Mrs. Turpin saw at once that no one was going to tell him to move over. He was slumped down in the seat, his arms idle at his sides and his eyes idle in his head; his nose ran unchecked.

Mrs. Turpin put a firm hand on Claud's shoulder and said in a voice that included anyone who wanted to listen,

"Claud, you sit in that chair there," and gave him a push down into the vacant one. Claud was florid and bald and sturdy, somewhat shorter than Mrs. Turpin, but he sat down as if he were accustomed to doing what she told him to.

Mrs. Turpin remained standing. The only man in the room besides Claud was a lean stringy old fellow with a rusty hand spread out on each knee, whose eyes were closed as if he were asleep or dead or pretending to be so as not to get up and offer her his seat. Her gaze settled agreeably on a well-dressed grey-haired lady whose eyes met hers and whose expression said: if that child belonged to me, he would have some manners and move over—there's plenty of room there for you and him too.

Claud looked up with a sigh and made as if to rise.

"Sit down," Mrs. Turpin said. "You know you're not supposed to stand on that leg. He has an ulcer on his leg," she explained.

Claud lifted his foot onto the magazine table and rolled his trouser leg up to reveal a purple swelling on a plump marble-white calf.

"My!" the pleasant lady said. "How did you do that?"

"A cow kicked him," Mrs. Turpin said.

"Goodness!" said the lady.

Claud rolled his trouser leg down.

"Maybe the little boy would move over," the lady suggested, but the child did not stir.

"Somebody will be leaving in a minute," Mrs. Turpin said. She could not understand why a doctor—with as much money as they made charging five dollars a day to just stick their head in the hospital door and look at you—couldn't afford a decent-sized waiting room. This one was hardly bigger than a garage. The table was cluttered with limp-looking magazines and at one end of it there was a big green glass ash tray full of cigaret butts and cotton wads with little blood spots on them. If she had had anything to do with the running of the place, that would have been emptied every so often. There were no chairs against the wall at the head of the room. It had a rectangular-shaped panel in it that permitted a view of the office where the nurse came and went and the secretary listened to the radio. A plastic fern in a gold pot sat in the opening and trailed its fronds down almost to the floor. The radio was softly playing gospel music.

Just then the inner door opened and a nurse with the highest stack of yellow hair Mrs. Turpin had ever seen put her face in the crack and called for the next patient. The woman sitting beside Claud grasped the two arms of her chair and hoisted herself up; she pulled her dress free from her legs and lumbered through the door where the nurse had disappeared.

Mrs. Turpin eased into the vacant chair, which held her tight as a corset. "I wish I could reduce," she said, and rolled her eyes and gave a comic sigh.

"Oh, *you* aren't fat," the stylish lady said.

"Ooooo I am too," Mrs. Turpin said. "Claud he eats all he wants to and never weighs over one hundred and seventy-five pounds, but me I just look at something good to eat and I gain some weight," and her stomach and shoulders shook with laughter. "You can eat all you want to, can't you, Claud?" she asked, turning to him.

Claud only grinned.

"Well, as long as you have such a good disposition," the stylish lady said, "I don't think it makes a bit of difference what size you are. You just can't beat a good disposition."

Next to her was a fat girl of eighteen or nineteen, scowling into a thick blue book which Mrs. Turpin saw was entitled *Human Development*. The girl raised her head and directed her scowl at Mrs. Turpin as if she did not like her looks. She appeared annoyed that anyone should speak while she tried to read. The poor girl's face was blue with acne and Mrs. Turpin thought how pitiful it was to have a face like that at that age. She gave the girl a friendly smile but the girl only scowled the harder. Mrs. Turpin herself was fat but she had always had good skin, and, though she was forty-seven years old, there was not a wrinkle in her face except around her eyes from laughing too much.

Next to the ugly girl was the child, still in exactly the same position, and next to him was a thin leathery old woman in a cotton print dress. She and Claud had three sacks of chicken feed in their pump house that was in the same print. She had seen from the first that the child belonged with the old woman. She could tell by the way they sat—kind of vacant and white-trashy, as if they would sit there until Doomsday if nobody called and told them to get up. And at right angles but next to the well-dressed pleasant lady was a lank-faced woman who was certainly the child's mother. She had on a yellow sweat shirt and wine-colored slacks, both gritty-looking, and the rims of her lips were stained with snuff. Her dirty yellow hair was tied behind with a little piece of red paper ribbon. Worse than niggers any day, Mrs. Turpin thought.

The gospel hymn playing was, "When I looked up and He looked down," and Mrs. Turpin, who knew it, supplied the last line mentally, "And wona these days I know I'll we-eara crown."

Without appearing to, Mrs. Turpin always noticed people's feet. The well-dressed lady had on red and grey suede shoes to match her dress. Mrs. Turpin had on her good black patent leather pumps. The ugly girl had on Girl Scout shoes and heavy socks. The old woman had on tennis shoes and the white-trashy mother had on what appeared to be bedroom slippers, black straw with gold braid threaded through them—exactly what you would have expected her to have on.

Sometimes at night when she couldn't go to sleep, Mrs. Turpin would occupy herself with the question of who she would have chosen to be if she couldn't have been herself. If Jesus had said to her before he made her, "There's only two places available for you. You can either be a nigger or white-trash," what would she have said? "Please, Jesus, please," she would have said, "just let me wait until there's another place available," and he would have said, "No, you have to go right now and I have only those two places so make up your mind." She would have wiggled and squirmed and begged and pleaded but it would have been no use and finally she would have said, "All right, make me a nigger then—but that don't mean a trashy one." And he would have made her a neat clean respectable Negro woman, herself but black.

Next to the child's mother was a red-headed youngish woman, reading one of the magazines and working a piece of chewing gum, hell for leather, as Claud would say. Mrs. Turpin could not see the woman's feet. She was not white-trash, just common. Sometimes Mrs. Turpin occupied herself at night naming the classes of people. On the bottom of the heap were most colored people, not the kind she would have been if she had been one, but most of them; then next to them—not above, just away from—were the white-trash; then above them were the home-owners, and above them the home-and-land owners, to which she and Claud belonged. Above she and Claud were people with a lot of money and much bigger houses and much more land. But here the complexity of it would begin to bear in on her, for some of the people with a lot of money were common and ought to be below she and Claud and some of the people who had good blood had lost their money and had to rent and then there were colored people who owned their homes and land as well. There was a colored dentist in town who had two red Lincolns and a swimming pool and a farm with registered white-face cattle on it. Usually by the time she had fallen asleep all the classes of people were moiling and roiling around in her head, and she would dream they were all crammed in together in a box car, being ridden off to be put in a gas oven.

"That's a beautiful clock," she said and nodded to her right. It was a big wall clock, the face encased in a brass sunburst.

"Yes, it's very pretty," the stylish lady said agreeably. "And right on the dot too," she added, glancing at her watch.

The ugly girl beside her cast an eye upward at the clock, smirked, then looked directly at Mrs. Turpin and smirked again. Then she returned her eyes to her book. She was obviously the lady's daughter because, although they didn't look anything alike as to disposition, they both had the same shape of face and the same blue eyes. On the lady they sparkled pleasantly but in the girl's seared face they appeared alternately to smolder and to blaze.

What if Jesus had said, "All right, you can be white-trash or a nigger or ugly"!

Mrs. Turpin felt an awful pity for the girl, though she thought it was one thing to be ugly and another to act ugly.

The woman with the snuff-stained lips turned around in her chair and looked up at the clock. Then she turned back and appeared to look a little to the side of Mrs. Turpin. There was a cast in one of her eyes. "You want to know wher you can get you one of themther clocks?" she asked in a loud voice.

"No, I already have a nice clock," Mrs. Turpin said. Once somebody like her got a leg in the conversation, she would be all over it.

"You can get you one with green stamps," the woman said. "That's most likely wher he got hisn. Save you up enough, you can get you most anythang. I got me some joo'ry."

Ought to have got you a wash rag and some soap, Mrs. Turpin thought.

"I get contour sheets with mine," the pleasant lady said.

The daughter slammed her book shut. She looked straight in front of her, directly through Mrs. Turpin and on through the yellow curtain and the plate glass window which made the wall behind her. The girl's eyes seemed lit all of a sudden with a peculiar light, an unnatural light like night road signs give. Mrs. Turpin turned her head to see if there was anything going on outside that she should see, but she could not see anything. Figures passing cast only a pale shadow through the curtain. There was no reason the girl should single her out for her ugly looks.

"Miss Finley," the nurse said, cracking the door. The gum-chewing woman got up and passed in front of her and Claud and went into the office. She had on red high-heeled shoes.

Directly across the table, the ugly girl's eyes were fixed on Mrs. Turpin as if she had some very special reason for disliking her.

"This is wonderful weather, isn't it?" the girl's mother said.

"It's good weather for cotton if you can get the niggers to pick it," Mrs. Turpin said, "but niggers don't want to pick cotton any more. You can't get the white folks to pick it and now you can't get the niggers—because they got to be right up there with the white folks."

"They gonna *try* anyways," the white-trash woman said, leaning forward.

"Do you have one of those cotton-picking machines?" the pleasant lady asked.

"No," Mrs. Turpin said, "they leave half the cotton in the field. We don't have much cotton anyway. If you want to make it farming now, you have to have a little of everything. We got a couple of acres of cotton and a few hogs and chickens and just enough white-face that Claud can look after them himself."

"One thang I don't want," the white-trash woman said, wiping her mouth with the back of her hand. "Hogs. Nasty stinking things, a-gruntin and a-rootin all over the place."

Mrs. Turpin gave her the merest edge of her attention. "Our hogs are not dirty and they don't stink," she said. "They're cleaner than some children I've seen. Their feet never touch the ground. We have a pig-parlor—that's where you raise them on concrete," she explained to the pleasant lady, "and Claud scoots them down with the hose every afternoon and washes off the floor." Cleaner by far than that child right there, she thought. Poor nasty little thing. He had not moved except to put the thumb of his dirty hand into his mouth.

The woman turned her face away from Mrs. Turpin. "I know I wouldn't scoot down no hog with no hose," she said to the wall.

You wouldn't have no hog to scoot down, Mrs. Turpin said to herself.

"A-gruntin and a-rootin and a-groanin," the woman muttered.

"We got a little of everything," Mrs. Turpin said to the pleasant lady. "It's no use in having more than you can handle yourself with help like it is. We found enough niggers to pick our cotton this year but Claud he has to go after them and take them home again in the evening. They can't walk that half a mile. No they can't. I tell you," she said and laughed merrily, "I sure am tired of buttering up niggers, but you got to love em if you want em to work for you. When they come in the morning, I run out and I say, 'Hi yawl this morning?' and when Claud drives them off to the field I just wave to beat the band and they just wave back." And she waved her hand rapidly to illustrate.

"Like you read out of the same book," the lady said, showing she understood perfectly.

"Child, yes," Mrs. Turpin said. "And when they come in from the field, I run out with a bucket of icewater. That's the way it's going to be from now on," she said. "You may as well face it."

"One thang I know," the white-trash woman said. "Two thangs I ain't going to do: love no niggers or scoot down no hog with no hose." And she let out a bark of contempt.

The look that Mrs. Turpin and the pleasant lady exchanged indicated they both understood that you had to *have* certain things before you could *know* certain things. But every time Mrs. Turpin exchanged a look with the lady, she was aware that the ugly girl's peculiar eyes were still on her, and she had trouble bringing her attention back to the conversation.

"When you got something," she said, "you got to look after it." And when you ain't got a thing but breath and britches, she added to herself, you can afford to come to town every morning and just sit on the Court House coping and spit.

A grotesque revolving shadow passed across the curtain behind her and was thrown palely on the opposite wall. Then a bicycle clattered down against the outside of the building. The door opened and a colored boy glided in with a tray from the drug store. It had two large red and white paper cups on it with tops on them. He was a tall, very black boy in discolored white pants and a green nylon shirt. He was chewing gum slowly, as if to music. He set the tray down in the office opening next to the fern and stuck his head through to look for the secretary. She was not in there. He rested his arms on the ledge and waited, his narrow bottom stuck out, swaying slowly to the left and right. He raised a hand over his head and scratched the base of his skull.

"You see that button there, boy?" Mrs. Turpin said. "You can punch that and she'll come. She's probably in the back somewhere."

"Is thas right?" the boy said agreeably, as if he had never seen the button before. He leaned to the right and put his finger on it. "She sometime out," he said and twisted around to face his audience, his elbows behind him on the counter. The nurse appeared and he twisted back again. She handed him a dollar and he rooted in his pocket and made the change and counted it out to her. She gave him fifteen cents for a tip and he went out with the empty tray. The heavy door swung to slowly and closed at length with the sound of suction. For a moment no one spoke.

"They ought to send all them niggers back to Africa," the white-trash woman said. "That's wher they come from in the first place."

"Oh, I couldn't do without my good colored friends," the pleasant lady said.

"There's a heap of things worse than a nigger," Mrs.

Turpin agreed. "It's all kinds of them just like it's all kinds of us."

"Yes, and it takes all kinds to make the world go round," the lady said in her musical voice.

As she said it, the raw-complexioned girl snapped her teeth together. Her lower lip turned downwards and inside out, revealing the pale pink inside of her mouth. After a second it rolled back up. It was the ugliest face Mrs. Turpin had ever seen anyone make and for a moment she was certain that the girl had made it at her. She was looking at her as if she had known and disliked her all her life—all of Mrs. Turpin's life, it seemed too, not just all the girl's life. Why, girl, I don't even know you, Mrs. Turpin said silently.

She forced her attention back to the discussion. "It wouldn't be practical to send them back to Africa," she said. "They wouldn't want to go. They got it too good here."

"Wouldn't be what they wanted—if I had anythang to do with it," the woman said.

"It wouldn't be a way in the world you could get all the niggers back over there," Mrs. Turpin said. "They'd be hiding out and lying down and turning sick on you and wailing and hollering and raring and pitching. It wouldn't be a way in the world to get them over there."

"They got over here," the trashy woman said. "Get back like they got over."

"It wasn't so many of them then," Mrs. Turpin explained.

The woman looked at Mrs. Turpin as if here was an idiot indeed but Mrs. Turpin was not bothered by the look, considering where it came from.

"Nooo," she said, "they're going to stay here where they can go to New York and marry white folks and improve their color. That's what they all want to do, every one of them, improve their color."

"You know what comes of that, don't you?" Claud asked.

"No, Claud, what?" Mrs. Turpin said.

Claud's eyes twinkled. "White-faced niggers," he said with never a smile.

Everybody in the office laughed except the white-trash and the ugly girl. The girl gripped the book in her lap with white fingers. The trashy woman looked around her from face to face as if she thought they were all idiots. The old woman in the feed sack dress continued to gaze expressionless across the floor at the high-top shoes of the man opposite her, the one who had been pretending to be asleep when the Turpins came in. He was laughing heartily, his hands still spread out on his knees. The child had fallen to the side and was lying now almost face down in the old woman's lap.

While they recovered from their laughter, the nasal chorus on the radio kept the room from silence.

"You go to blank blank
And I'll go to mine
But we'll all blank along
To-geth-ther,
And all along the blank
We'll hep eachother out
Smile-ling in any kind of
Weath-ther!"

Mrs. Turpin didn't catch every word but she caught enough to agree with the spirit of the song and it turned her thoughts sober. To help anybody out that needed it was her philosophy of life. She never spared herself when she found somebody in need, whether they were white or black, trash or decent. And of all she had to be thankful for, she was most thankful that this was so. If Jesus had said, "You can be high society and have all the money you want and be thin and svelte-like, but you can't be a good woman with it," she would have had to say, "Well don't make me that then. Make me a good woman and it don't matter what else, how fat or how ugly or how poor!" Her heart rose. He had not made her a nigger or white-trash or ugly! He had made her herself and given her a little of everything. Jesus, thank you! she said. Thank you thank you thank you! Whenever she counted her blessings she felt as buoyant as if she weighed one hundred and twenty-five pounds instead of one hundred and eighty.

"What's wrong with your little boy?" the pleasant lady asked the white-trashy woman.

"He has a ulcer," the woman said proudly. "He ain't give me a minute's peace since he was born. Him and her are just alike," she said, nodding at the old woman, who was running her leathery fingers through the child's pale hair. "Look like I can't get nothing down them two but Co' Cola and candy."

That's all you try to get down em, Mrs. Turpin said to herself. Too lazy to light the fire. There was nothing you could tell her about people like them that she didn't know already. And it was not just that they didn't have anything. Because if you gave them everything, in two weeks it would all be broken or filthy or they would have chopped it up for lightwood. She knew all this from her own experience. Help them you must, but help them you couldn't.

All at once the ugly girl turned her lips inside out again. Her eyes were fixed like two drills on Mrs. Turpin. This time there was no mistaking that there was something urgent behind them.

Girl, Mrs. Turpin exclaimed silently, I haven't done a thing to you! The girl might be confusing her with somebody else. There was no need to sit by and let herself be intimidated. "You must be in college," she said boldly, looking directly at the girl. "I see you reading a book there."

The girl continued to stare and pointedly did not answer.

Her mother blushed at this rudeness. "The lady asked you a question, Mary Grace," she said under her breath.

"I have ears," Mary Grace said.

The poor mother blushed again. "Mary Grace goes to Wellesley College," she explained. She twisted one of the buttons on her dress. "In Massachusetts," she added with a grimace. "And in the summer she just keeps right on studying. Just reads all the time, a real book worm. She's done real well at Wellesley; she's taking English and Math and History and Psychology and Social Studies," she rattled on, "and I think it's too much. I think she ought to get out and have fun."

The girl looked as if she would like to hurl them all through the plate glass window.

"Way up north," Mrs. Turpin murmured and thought, well, it hasn't done much for her manners.

"I'd almost rather to have him sick," the white-trash woman said, wrenching the attention back to herself. "He's so mean when he ain't. Look like some children just take natural to meanness. It's some gets bad when they get sick but he was the opposite. Took sick and turned good. He don't give me no trouble now. It's me waitin to see the doctor," she said.

If I was going to send anybody back to Africa, Mrs. Turpin thought, it would be your kind, woman. "Yes, indeed," she said aloud, but looking up at the ceiling, "it's a heap of things worse than a nigger." And dirtier than a hog, she added to herself.

"I think people with bad dispositions are more to be pitied than anyone on earth," the pleasant lady said in a voice that was decidedly thin.

"I thank the Lord he has blessed me with a good one," Mrs. Turpin said. "The day has never dawned that I couldn't find something to laugh at."

"Not since she married me anyways," Claud said with a comical straight face.

Everybody laughed except the girl and the white-trash.

Mrs. Turpin's stomach shook. "He's such a caution," she said, "that I can't help but laugh at him."

The girl made a loud ugly noise through her teeth.

Her mother's mouth grew thin and tight. "I think the worst thing in the world," she said, "is an ungrateful person. To have everything and not appreciate it. I know a girl," she said, "who has parents who would give her anything, a little brother who loves her dearly, who is getting a good education, who wears the best clothes, but who can never say a kind word to anyone, who never smiles, who just criticizes and complains all day long."

"Is she too old to paddle?" Claud asked.

The girl's face was almost purple.

"Yes," the lady said, "I'm afraid there's nothing to do but leave her to her folly. Some day she'll wake up and it'll be too late."

"It never hurt anyone to smile," Mrs. Turpin said. "It just makes you feel better all over."

"Of course," the lady said sadly, "but there are just some people you can't tell anything to. They can't take criticism."

"If it's one thing I am," Mrs. Turpin said with feeling, "it's grateful. When I think who all I could have been besides myself and what all I got, a little of everything, and a good disposition besides, I just feel like shouting, 'Thank you, Jesus, for making everything the way it is!' It could have been different!" For one thing, somebody else could have got Claud. At the thought of this, she was flooded with gratitude and a terrible pang of joy ran through her. "Oh thank you, Jesus, Jesus, thank you!" she cried aloud.

The book struck her directly over her left eye. It struck almost at the same instant that she realized the girl was about to hurl it. Before she could utter a sound, the raw face came crashing across the table toward her, howling. The girl's fingers sank like clamps into the soft flesh of her neck. She heard the mother cry out and Claud shout, "Whoa!" There was an instant when she was certain that she was about to be in an earthquake.

All at once her vision narrowed and she saw everything as if it were happening in a small room far away, or as if she were looking at it through the wrong end of a telescope. Claud's face crumpled and fell out of sight. The nurse ran in, then out, then in again. Then the gangling figure of the doctor rushed out of the inner door. Magazines flew this way and that as the table turned over. The girl fell with a thud and Mrs. Turpin's vision suddenly reversed itself and she saw everything large instead of small. The eyes of the white-trashy woman were staring hugely at the floor. There the girl, held down on one side by the nurse and on the other by her mother, was wrenching and turning in their grasp. The doctor was kneeling astride her, trying to hold her arm down. He managed after a second to sink a long needle into it.

Mrs. Turpin felt entirely hollow except for her heart which swung from side to side as if it were agitated in a great empty drum of flesh.

"Somebody that's not busy call for the ambulance," the

doctor said in the off-hand voice young doctors adopt for terrible occasions.

Mrs. Turpin could not have moved a finger. The old man who had been sitting next to her skipped nimbly into the office and made the call, for the secretary still seemed to be gone.

"Claud!" Mrs. Turpin called.

He was not in his chair. She knew she must jump up and find him but she felt like some one trying to catch a train in a dream, when everything moves in slow motion and the faster you try to run the slower you go.

"Here I am," a suffocated voice, very unlike Claud's, said.

He was doubled up in the corner on the floor, pale as paper, holding his leg. She wanted to get up and go to him but she could not move. Instead, her gaze was drawn slowly downward to the churning face on the floor, which she could see over the doctor's shoulder.

The girl's eyes stopped rolling and focused on her. They seemed a much lighter blue than before, as if a door that had been tightly closed behind them was now open to admit light and air.

Mrs. Turpin's head cleared and her power of motion returned. She leaned forward until she was looking directly into the fierce brilliant eyes. There was no doubt in her mind that the girl did know her, knew her in some intense and personal way, beyond time and place and condition. "What you got to say to me?" she asked hoarsely and held her breath, waiting, as for a revelation.

The girl raised her head. Her gaze locked with Mrs. Turpin's. "Go back to hell where you came from, you old wart hog," she whispered. Her voice was low but clear. Her eyes burned for a moment as if she saw with pleasure that her message had struck its target.

Mrs. Turpin sank back in her chair.

After a moment the girl's eyes closed and she turned her head wearily to the side.

The doctor rose and handed the nurse the empty syringe. He leaned over and put both hands for a moment on the mother's shoulders, which were shaking. She was sitting on the floor, her lips pressed together, holding Mary Grace's hand in her lap. The girl's fingers were gripped like a baby's around her thumb. "Go on to the hospital," he said. "I'll call and make the arrangements."

"Now let's see that neck," he said in a jovial voice to Mrs. Turpin. He began to inspect her neck with his first two fingers. Two little moon-shaped lines like pink fish bones were indented over her windpipe. There was the beginning of an angry red swelling above her eye. His fingers passed over this also.

"Lea' me be," she said thickly and shook him off. "See about Claud. She kicked him."

"I'll see about him in a minute," he said and felt her pulse. He was a thin grey-haired man, given to pleasantries. "Go home and have yourself a vacation the rest of the day," he said and patted her on the shoulder.

Quit your pattin me, Mrs. Turpin growled to herself.

"And put an ice pack over that eye," he said. Then he went and squatted down beside Claud and looked at his leg. After a moment he pulled him up and Claud limped after him into the office.

Until the ambulance came, the only sounds in the room were the tremulous moans of the girl's mother, who continued to sit on the floor. The white-trash woman did not take her eyes off the girl. Mrs. Turpin looked straight ahead at nothing. Presently the ambulance drew up, a long dark shadow, behind the curtain. The attendants came in and set the stretcher down beside the girl and lifted her expertly onto it and carried her out. The nurse helped the mother gather up her things. The shadow of the ambulance moved silently away and the nurse came back in the office.

"That ther girl is going to be a lunatic, ain't she?" the white-trash woman asked the nurse, but the nurse kept on to the back and never answered her.

"Yes, she's going to be a lunatic," the white-trash woman said to the rest of them.

"Po' critter," the old woman murmured. The child's face was still in her lap. His eyes looked idly out over her knees. He had not moved during the disturbance except to draw one leg up under him.

"I thank Gawd," the white-trash woman said fervently, "I ain't a lunatic."

Claud came limping out and the Turpins went home.

As their pick-up truck turned into their own dirt road and made the crest of the hill, Mrs. Turpin gripped the window ledge and looked out suspiciously. The land sloped gracefully down through a field dotted with lavender weeds and at the start of the rise their small yellow frame house, with its little flower beds spread out around it like a fancy apron, sat primly in its accustomed place between two giant hickory trees. She would not have been startled to see a burnt wound between two blackened chimneys.

Neither of them felt like eating so they put on their house clothes and lowered the shade in the bedroom and lay down, Claud with his leg on a pillow and herself with a damp washcloth over her eye. The instant she was flat on her back, the image of a razor-backed hog with warts on its face and horns coming out behind its ears snorted into her head. She moaned, a low quiet moan.

"I am not," she said tearfully, "a wart hog. From hell." But the denial had no force. The girl's eyes and her words, even the tone of her voice, low but clear, directed only to her, brooked no repudiation. She had been singled out for the message, though there was trash in the room to whom it might justly have been applied. The full force of this fact struck her only now. There was a woman there who was neglecting her own child but she had been overlooked. The message had been given to Ruby Turpin, a respectable, hard-working, church-going woman. The tears dried. Her eyes began to burn instead with wrath.

She rose on her elbow and the washcloth fell into her hand. Claud was lying on his back, snoring. She wanted to tell him what the girl had said. At the same time, she did not wish to put the image of herself as a wart hog from hell into his mind.

"Hey, Claud," she muttered and pushed his shoulder.

Claud opened one pale baby blue eye.

She looked into it warily. He did not think about anything. He just went his way.

"Wha, whasit?" he said and closed the eye again.

"Nothing," she said. "Does your leg pain you?"

"Hurts like hell," Claud said.

"It'll quit terreckly," she said and lay back down. In a moment Claud was snoring again. For the rest of the afternoon they lay there. Claud slept. She scowled at the ceiling. Occasionally she raised her fist and made a small stabbing motion over her chest as if she was defending her innocence to invisible guests who were like the comforters of Job, reasonable-seeming but wrong.

About five-thirty Claud stirred. "Got to go after those niggers," he sighed, not moving.

She was looking straight up as if there were unintelligible handwriting on the ceiling. The protuberance over her eye had turned a greenish-blue. "Listen here," she said.

"What?"

"Kiss me."

Claud leaned over and kissed her loudly on the mouth. He pinched her side and their hands interlocked. Her expression of ferocious concentration did not change. Claud got up, groaning and growling, and limped off. She continued to study the ceiling.

She did not get up until she heard the pick-up truck coming back with the Negroes. Then she rose and thrust her feet in her brown oxfords, which she did not bother to lace, and stumped out onto the back porch and got her red plastic bucket. She emptied a tray of ice cubes into in and filled it half full of water and went out into the back yard. Every afternoon after Claud brought the hands in, one of the boys helped him put out hay and the rest waited in the back of the truck until he was ready to take them home. The truck was parked in the shade under one of the hickory trees.

"Hi yawl this evening?" Mrs. Turpin asked grimly, appearing with the bucket and the dipper. There were three women and a boy in the truck.

"Us doin nicely," the oldest woman said. "Hi you doin?" and her gaze stuck immediately on the dark lump on Mrs. Turpin's forehead. "You done fell down, ain't you?" she asked in a solicitous voice. The old woman was dark and almost toothless. She had on an old felt hat of Claud's set back on her head. The other two women were younger and lighter and they both had new bright green sun hats. One of them had hers on her head; the other had taken hers off and the boy was grinning beneath it.

Mrs. Turpin set the bucket down on the floor of the truck. "Yawl hep yourselves," she said. She looked around to make sure Claud had gone. "No. I didn't fall down," she said, folding her arms. "It was something worse than that."

"Ain't nothing bad happen to you!" the old woman said. She said it as if they all knew that Mrs. Turpin was protected in some special way by Divine Providence. "You just had you a little fall."

"We were in town at the doctor's office for where the cow kicked Mr. Turpin," Mrs. Turpin said in a flat tone that indicated they could leave off their foolishness. "And there was this girl there. A big fat girl with her face all broke out. I could look at that girl and tell she was peculiar but I couldn't tell how. And me and her mama were just talking and going along and all of a sudden WHAM! She throws this big book she was reading at me and . . ."

"Naw!" the old woman cried out.

"And then she jumps over the table and commences to choke me."

"Naw!" they all exclaimed, "naw!"

"Hi come she do that?" the old woman asked. "What ail her?"

Mrs. Turpin only glared in front of her.

"Somethin ail her," the old woman said.

"They carried her off in an ambulance," Mrs. Turpin continued, "but before she went she was rolling on the floor and they were trying to hold her down to give her a shot and she said something to me." She paused. "You know what she said to me?"

"What she say?" they asked.

"She said," Mrs. Turpin began, and stopped, her face

very dark and heavy. The sun was getting whiter and whiter, blanching the sky overhead so that the leaves of the hickory tree were black in the face of it. She could not bring forth the words. "Something real ugly," she muttered.

"She sho shouldn't said nothin ugly to you," the old woman said. "You so sweet. You the sweetest lady I know."

"She pretty too," the one with the hat on said.

"And stout," the other one said. "I never knowed no sweeter white lady."

"That's the truth befo' Jesus," the old woman said. "Amen! You des as sweet and pretty as you can be."

Mrs. Turpin knew just exactly how much Negro flattery was worth and it added to her rage. "She said," she began again and finished this time with a fierce rush of breath, "that I was an old wart hog from hell."

There was an astounded silence.

"Where she at?" the youngest woman cried in a piercing voice.

"Lemme see her. I'll kill her!"

"I'll kill her with you!" the other one cried.

"She b'long in the sylum," the old woman said emphatically. "You the sweetest white lady I know."

"She pretty too," the other two said. "Stout as she can be and sweet. Jesus satisfied with her!"

"Deed he is," the old woman declared.

Idiots! Mrs. Turpin growled to herself. You could never say anything intelligent to a nigger. You could talk at them but not with them. "Yawl ain't drunk your water," she said shortly. "Leave the bucket in the truck when you're finished with it. I got more to do than just stand around and pass the time of day," and she moved off and into the house.

She stood for a moment in the middle of the kitchen. The dark protuberance over her eye looked like a miniature tornado cloud which might any moment sweep across the horizon of her brow. Her lower lip protruded dangerously. She squared her massive shoulders. Then she marched into the front of the house and out the side door and started down the road to the pig parlor. She had the look of a woman going single-handed, weaponless, into battle.

The sun was a deep yellow now like a harvest moon and was riding westward very fast over the far tree line as if it meant to reach the hogs before she did. The road was rutted and she kicked several good-sized stones out of her path as she strode along. The pig parlor was on a little knoll at the end of a lane that ran off from the side of the barn. It was a square of concrete as large as a small room, with a board fence about four feet high around it. The concrete floor sloped slightly so that the hog wash could drain off into a trench where it was carried to the field for fertilizer. Claud was standing on the outside, on the edge of the concrete, hanging onto the top board, hosing down the floor inside. The hose was connected to the faucet of a water trough nearby.

Mrs. Turpin climbed up beside him and glowered down at the hogs inside. There were seven long-snouted bristly shoats in it—tan with liver-colored spots—and an old sow a few weeks off from farrowing. She was lying on her side grunting. The shoats were running about shaking themselves like idiot children, their little slit pig eyes searching the floor for anything left. She had read that pigs were the most intelligent animal. She doubted it. They were supposed to be smarter than dogs. There had even been a pig astronaut. He had performed his assignment perfectly but died of a heart attack afterwards because they left him in his electric suit, sitting upright throughout his examination when naturally a hog should be on all fours.

A-gruntin and a-rootin and a-groanin.

"Gimme that hose," she said, yanking it away from Claud. "Go on and carry them niggers home and then get off that leg."

"You look like you might have swallowed a mad dog," Claud observed, but he got down and limped off. He paid no attention to her humors.

Until he was out of earshot, Mrs. Turpin stood on the side of the pen, holding the hose and pointing the stream of water at the hind quarters of any shoat that looked as if it might try to lie down. When he had had time to get over the hill, she turned her head slightly and her wrathful eyes scanned the path. He was nowhere in sight. She turned back again and seemed to gather herself up. Her shoulders rose and she drew in her breath.

"What do you send me a message like that for?" she said in a low fierce voice, barely above a whisper but with the force of a shout in its concentrated fury. "How am I a hog and me both? How am I saved and from hell too?" Her free fist was knotted and with the other she gripped the hose, blindly pointing the stream of water in and out of the eye of the old sow whose outraged squeal she did not hear.

The pig parlor commanded a view of the back pasture where their twenty beef cows were gathered around the hay-bales Claud and the boy had put out. The freshly cut pasture sloped down to the highway. Across it was their cotton field and beyond that a dark green dusty wood which they owned as well. The sun was behind the wood, very red, looking over the paling of trees like a farmer inspecting his own hogs.

"Why me?" she rumbled. "It's no trash around here, black or white, that I haven't given to. And break my back to the bone every day working. And do for the church."

She appeared to be the right size woman to command the arena before her. "How am I a hog?" she demanded. "Exactly how am I like them?" and she jabbed the stream of water at the shoats. "There was plenty of trash there. It didn't have to be me.

"If you like trash better, go get yourself some trash then," she railed. "You could have made me trash. Or a nigger. If trash is what you wanted why didn't you make me trash?" She shook her fist with the hose in it and a watery snake appeared momentarily in the air. "I could quit working and take it easy and be filthy," she growled. "Lounge about the sidewalks all day drinking root beer. Dip snuff and spit in every puddle and have it all over my face. I could be nasty.

"Or you could have made me a nigger. It's too late for me to be a nigger," she said with deep sarcasm, "but I could act like one. Lay down in the middle of the road and stop traffic. Roll on the ground."

In the deepening light everything was taking on a mysterious hue. The pasture was growing a peculiar glassy green and the streak of highway had turned lavender. She braced herself for a final assault and this time her voice rolled out over the pasture. "Go on," she yelled, "call me a hog! Call me a hog again. From hell. Call me a wart hog from hell. Put that bottom rail on top. There'll still be a top and bottom!"

A garbled echo returned to her.

A final surge of fury shook her and she roared, "Who do you think you are?"

The color of everything, field and crimson sky, burned for a moment with a transparent intensity. The question carried over the pasture and across the highway and the cotton field and returned to her clearly like an answer from beyond the wood.

She opened her mouth but no sound came out of it.

A tiny truck, Claud's, appeared on the highway, heading rapidly out of sight. Its gears scraped thinly. It looked like a child's toy. At any moment a bigger truck might smash into it and scatter Claud's and the niggers' brains all over the road.

Mrs. Turpin stood there, her gaze fixed on the highway, all her muscles rigid, until in five or six minutes the truck reappeared, returning. She waited until it had had time to turn into their own road. Then like a monumental statue coming to life, she bent her head slowly and gazed, as if through the very heart of mystery, down into the pig parlor at the hogs. They had settled all in one corner around the old sow who was grunting softly. A red glow suffused them. They appeared to pant with a secret life.

Until the sun slipped finally behind the tree line, Mrs. Turpin remained there with her gaze bent to them as if she were absorbing some abysmal life-giving knowledge. At last she lifted her head. There was only a purple streak in the sky, cutting through a field of crimson and leading, like an extension of the highway, into the descending dusk. She raised her hands from the side of the pen in a gesture hieratic and profound. A visionary light settled in her eyes. She saw the streak as a vast swinging bridge extending upward from the earth through a field of living fire. Upon it a vast horde of souls were rumbling toward heaven. There were whole companies of white-trash, clean for the first time in their lives, and bands of black niggers in white robes, and battalions of freaks and lunatics shouting and clapping and leaping like frogs. And bringing up the end of the procession was a tribe of people whom she recognized at once as those who, like herself and Claud, had always had a little of everything and the God-given wit to use it right. She leaned forward to observe them closer. They were marching behind the others with great dignity, accountable as they had always been for good order and common sense and respectable behavior. They alone were on key. Yet she could see by their shocked and altered faces that even their virtues were being burned away. She lowered her hands and gripped the rail of the hog pen, her eyes small but fixed unblinkingly on what lay ahead. In a moment the vision faded but she remained where she was, immobile.

At length she got down and turned off the faucet and made her slow way on the darkening path to the house. In the woods around her the invisible cricket choruses had struck up, but what she heard were the voices of the souls climbing upward into the starry field and shouting hallelujah.

Parker's Back

Parker's wife was sitting on the front porch floor, snapping beans. Parker was sitting on the step, some distance away, watching her sullenly. She was plain, plain. The skin on her face was thin and drawn as tight as the skin on an onion and her eyes were grey and sharp like the points of two icepicks. Parker understood why he had married her—he couldn't have got her any other way—but he couldn't understand why he stayed with her now. She was pregnant and pregnant women were not his favorite kind. Nevertheless, he stayed as if she had him conjured. He was puzzled and ashamed of himself.

The house they rented sat alone save for a single tall pecan tree on a high embankment overlooking a highway. At intervals a car would shoot past below and his wife's eyes would swerve suspiciously after the sound of it and then come back to rest on the newspaper full of beans in her lap. One of the things she did not approve of was automobiles. In addition to her other bad qualities, she was forever sniffing up sin. She did not smoke or dip, drink whiskey, use bad language or paint her face, and God knew some paint would have improved it, Parker thought. Her being against color, it was the more remarkable she had married him. Sometimes he supposed that she had married him because she meant to save him. At other times he had a suspicion that she actually liked everything she said she didn't. He could account for her one way or another; it was himself he could not understand.

She turned her head in his direction and said, "It's no reason you can't work for a man. It don't have to be a woman."

"Aw shut your mouth for a change," Parker muttered.

If he had been certain she was jealous of the woman he worked for he would have been pleased but more likely she was concerned with the sin that would result if he and the woman took a liking to each other. He had told her that the woman was a hefty young blonde; in fact she was nearly seventy years old and too dried up to have an interest in anything except getting as much work out of him as she could. Not that an old woman didn't sometimes get an interest in a young man, particularly if he was as attractive as Parker felt he was, but this old woman looked at him the same way she looked at her old tractor—as if she had to put up with it because it was all she had. The tractor had broken down the second day Parker was on it and she had set him at once to cutting bushes, saying out of the side of her mouth to the nigger, "Everything he touches, he breaks." She also asked him to wear his shirt when he worked; Parker had removed it even though the day was not sultry; he put it back on reluctantly.

This ugly woman Parker married was his first wife. He had had other women but he had planned never to get himself tied up legally. He had first seen her one morning when his truck broke down on the highway. He had managed to pull it off the road into a neatly swept yard on which sat a peeling two-room house. He got out and opened the hood of the truck and began to study the motor. Parker had an extra sense that told him when there was a woman nearby watching him. After he had leaned over the motor a few minutes, his neck began to prickle. He cast his eye over the empty yard and porch of the house. A woman he could not see was either nearby beyond a clump of honeysuckle or in the house, watching him out the window.

Suddenly Parker began to jump up and down and fling his hand about as if he had mashed it in the machinery. He doubled over and held his hand close to his chest. "God dammit!" he hollered, "Jesus Christ in hell! Jesus God Almighty damm! God dammit to hell!" he went on, flinging out the same few oaths over and over as loud as he could.

Without warning a terrible bristly claw slammed the side of his face and he fell backwards on the hood of the truck. "You don't talk no filth here!" a voice close to him shrilled.

Parker's vision was so blurred that for an instant he thought he had been attacked by some creature from above, a giant hawk-eyed angel wielding a hoary weapon. As his sight cleared, he saw before him a tall raw-boned girl with a broom.

"I hurt my hand," he said. "I HURT my hand." He was so incensed that he forgot that he hadn't hurt his hand. "My hand may be broke," he growled although his voice was still unsteady.

"Lemme see it," the girl demanded.

Parker stuck out his hand and she came closer and looked at it. There was no mark on the palm and she took the hand and turned it over. Her own hand was dry and hot and rough and Parker felt himself jolted back to life by her touch. He looked more closely at her. I don't want nothing to do with this one, he thought.

The girl's sharp eyes peered at the back of the stubby reddish hand she held. There emblazoned in red and blue was a tattooed eagle perched on a cannon. Parker's sleeve was rolled to the elbow. Above the eagle a serpent was coiled about a shield and in the spaces between the eagle and the serpent there were hearts, some with arrows through them. Above the serpent there was a spread hand of cards. Every space on the skin of Parker's arm, from wrist to elbow, was covered in some loud design. The girl gazed at this with an almost stupefied smile of shock, as if she had accidentally grasped a poisonous snake; she dropped the hand.

"I got most of my other ones in foreign parts," Parker said. "These here I mostly got in the United States. I got my first one when I was only fifteen year old."

"Don't tell me," the girl said, "I don't like it. I ain't got any use for it."

"You ought to see the ones you can't see," Parker said and winked.

Two circles of red appeared like apples on the girl's cheeks and softened her appearance. Parker was intrigued. He did not for a minute think that she didn't like the tattoos. He had never yet met a woman who was not attracted to them.

Parker was fourteen when he saw a man in a fair, tattooed from head to foot. Except for his loins which were girded with a panther hide, the man's skin was patterned in what seemed from Parker's distance—he was near the back of the tent, standing on a bench—a single intricate design of brilliant color. The man, who was small and sturdy, moved about on the platform, flexing his muscles so that the arabesque of men and beasts and flowers on his skin appeared to have a subtle motion of its own. Parker was filled with emotion, lifted up as some people are when the flag passes. He was a boy whose mouth habitually hung open. He was heavy and earnest, as ordinary as a loaf of bread. When the show was over, he had remained standing on the bench, staring where the tattooed man had been, until the tent was almost empty.

Parker had never before felt the least motion of wonder in himself. Until he saw the man at the fair, it did not enter his head that there was anything out of the ordinary about the fact that he existed. Even then it did not enter his head, but a peculiar unease settled in him. It was as if a blind boy had been turned so gently in a different direction that he did not know his destination had been changed.

He had his first tattoo some time after—the eagle perched on the cannon. It was done by a local artist. It hurt very little, just enough to make it appear to Parker to be worth doing. This was peculiar too for before he had thought that only what did not hurt was worth doing. The next year he quit school because he was sixteen and could. He went to the trade school for a while, then he quit the trade school and worked for six months in a garage. The only reason he worked at all was to pay for more tattoos. His mother worked in a laundry and could support him, but she would not pay for any tattoo except her name on a heart, which he had put on, grumbling. However, her name was Betty Jean and nobody had to know it was his mother. He found out that the tattoos were attractive to the kind of girls he liked but who had never liked him before. He began to drink beer and get in fights. His mother wept over what was becoming of him. One night she dragged him off to a revival with her, not telling him where they were going. When he saw the big lighted church, he jerked out of her grasp and ran. The next day he lied about his age and joined the navy.

Parker was large for the tight sailor's pants but the silly white cap, sitting low on his forehead, made his face by contrast look thoughtful and almost intense. After a month or two in the navy, his mouth ceased to hang open. His features hardened into the features of a man. He stayed in the navy five years and seemed a natural part of the grey mechanical ship, except for his eyes, which were the same pale slate-color as the ocean and reflected the immense spaces around him as if they were a microcosm of the mysterious sea. In port Parker wandered about comparing the run-down places he was in to Birmingham, Alabama. Everywhere he went he picked up more tattoos.

He had stopped having lifeless ones like anchors and crossed rifles. He had a tiger and a panther on each shoulder, a cobra coiled about a torch on his chest, hawks on his thighs, Elizabeth II and Philip over where his stomach and liver were respectively. He did not care much what the subject was so long as it was colorful; on his abdomen he had a few obscenities but only because that seemed the proper place for them. Parker would be satisfied with each tattoo about a month, then something about it that had attracted him would wear off. Whenever a decent-sized mirror was available, he would get in front of it and study his overall look. The effect was not of one intricate arabesque of colors but of something haphazard and botched. A huge dissatisfaction would come over him and he would go off and find another tattooist and have another space filled up. The front of Parker was almost completely covered but there were no tattoos on his back. He had no desire for one anywhere he could not readily see it himself. As the space on the front of him for tattoos decreased, his dissatisfaction grew and became general.

After one of his furloughs, he didn't go back to the navy but remained away without official leave, drunk, in a rooming house in a city he did not know. His dissatisfaction, from being chronic and latent, had suddenly become acute and raged in him. It was as if the panther and the lion and the serpents and the eagles and the hawks had penetrated his skin and lived inside him in a raging warfare. The navy caught up with him, put him in the brig for nine months and then gave him a dishonorable discharge.

After that Parker decided that country air was the only kind fit to breathe. He rented the shack on the embankment and bought the old truck and took various jobs which he kept as long as it suited him. At the time he met his future wife, he was buying apples by the bushel and selling them for the same price by the pound to isolated homesteaders on back country roads.

"All that there," the woman said, pointing to his arm, "is no better than what a fool Indian would do. It's a heap of vanity." She seemed to have found the word she wanted. "Vanity of vanities," she said.

Well what the hell do I care what she thinks of it? Parker asked himself, but he was plainly bewildered. "I reckon you like one of these better than another anyway," he said, dallying until he thought of something that would impress her. He thrust the arm back at her. "Which you like best?"

"None of them," she said, "but the chicken is not as bad as the rest."

"What chicken?" Parker almost yelled.

She pointed to the eagle.

"That's an eagle," Parker said. "What fool would waste their time having a chicken put on themself?"

"What fool would have any of it?" the girl said and turned away. She went slowly back to the house and left him there to get going. Parker remained for almost five minutes, looking agape at the dark door she had entered.

The next day he returned with a bushel of apples. He was not one to be outdone by anything that looked like her. He liked women with meat on them, so you didn't feel their muscles, much less their old bones. When he arrived, she was sitting on the top step and the yard was full of children, all as thin and poor as herself; Parker remembered it was Saturday. He hated to be making up to a woman when there were children around, but it was fortunate he had brought the bushel of apples off the truck. As the children approached him to see what he carried, he gave each child an apple and told it to get lost; in that way he cleared out the whole crowd.

The girl did nothing to acknowledge his presence. He might have been a stray pig or goat that had wandered into the yard and she too tired to take up the broom and send it off. He set the bushel of apples down next to her on the step. He sat down on a lower step.

"Hep yourself," he said, nodding at the basket; then he lapsed into silence.

She took an apple quickly as if the basket might disappear if she didn't make haste. Hungry people made Parker nervous. He had always had plenty to eat himself. He grew very uncomfortable. He reasoned he had nothing to say so why should he say it? He could not think now why he had come or why he didn't go before he wasted another bushel of apples on the crowd of children. He supposed they were her brothers and sisters.

She chewed the apple slowly but with a kind of relish of concentration, bent slightly but looking out ahead. The view from the porch stretched off across a long incline studded with iron weed and across the highway to a vast vista of hills and one small mountain. Long views depressed Parker. You look out into space like that and you begin to feel as if someone were after you, the navy or the government or religion.

"Who them children belong to, you?" he said at length.

"I ain't married yet," she said. "They belong to momma." She said it as if it were only a matter of time before she would be married.

Who in God's name would marry her? Parker thought.

A large barefooted woman with a wide gap-toothed face appeared in the door behind Parker. She had apparently been there for several minutes.

"Good evening," Parker said.

The woman crossed the porch and picked up what was left of the bushel of apples. "We thank you," she said and returned with it into the house.

"That your old woman?" Parker muttered.

The girl nodded. Parker knew a lot of sharp things he could have said like "You got my sympathy," but he was gloomily silent. He just sat there, looking at the view. He thought he must be coming down with something.

"If I pick up some peaches tomorrow I'll bring you some," he said.

"I'll be much obliged to you," the girl said.

Parker had no intention of taking any basket of peaches back there but the next day he found himself doing it. He and the girl had almost nothing to say to each other. One thing he did say was, "I ain't got any tattoo on my back."

"What you got on it?" the girl said.

"My shirt," Parker said. "Haw."

"Haw, haw," the girl said politely.

Parker thought he was losing his mind. He could not believe for a minute that he was attracted to a woman like this. She showed not the least interest in anything but what he brought until he appeared the third time with two cantaloups. "What's your name?" she asked.

"O. E. Parker," he said.

"What does the O.E. stand for?"

"You can just call me O.E.," Parker said. "Or Parker. Don't nobody call me by my name."

"What's it stand for?" she persisted.

"Never mind," Parker said. "What's yours?"

"I'll tell you when you tell me what them letters are the short of," she said. There was just a hint of flirtatiousness in her tone and it went rapidly to Parker's head. He had never revealed the name to any man or woman, only to the files of the navy and the government, and it was on his baptismal record which he got at the age of a month; his mother was a Methodist. When the name leaked out of the navy files, Parker narrowly missed killing the man who used it.

"You'll go blab it around," he said.

"I'll swear I'll never tell nobody," she said. "On God's holy word I swear it."

Parker sat for a few minutes in silence. Then he reached for the girl's neck, drew her ear close to his mouth and revealed the name in a low voice.

"Obadiah," she whispered. Her face slowly brightened as if the name came as a sign to her. "Obadiah," she said.

The name still stank in Parker's estimation.

"Obadiah Elihue," she said in a reverent voice.

"If you call me that aloud, I'll bust your head open," Parker said. "What's yours?"

"Sarah Ruth Cates," she said.

"Glad to meet you, Sarah Ruth," Parker said.

Sarah Ruth's father was a Straight Gospel preacher but he was away, spreading it in Florida. Her mother did not seem to mind his attention to the girl so long as he brought a basket of something with him when he came. As for Sarah Ruth herself, it was plain to Parker after he had visited three times that she was crazy about him. She liked him even though she insisted that pictures on the skin were vanity of vanities and even after hearing him curse, and even after she had asked him if he was saved and he had replied that he didn't see it was anything in particular to save him from. After that, inspired, Parker had said, "I'd be saved enough if you was to kiss me."

She scowled. "That ain't being saved," she said.

Not long after that she agreed to take a ride in his truck. Parker parked it on a deserted road and suggested to her that they lie down together in the back of it.

"Not until after we're married," she said—just like that.

"Oh that ain't necessary," Parker said and as he reached for her, she thrust him away with such force that the door of the truck came off and he found himself flat on his back on the ground. He made up his mind then and there to have nothing further to do with her.

They were married in the County Ordinary's office because Sarah Ruth thought churches were idolatrous. Parker had no opinion about that one way or the other. The Ordinary's office was lined with cardboard file boxes and record books with dusty yellow slips of paper hanging on out of them. The Ordinary was an old woman with red hair who had held office for forty years and looked as dusty as her books. She married them from behind the iron-grill of a stand-up desk and when she finished, she said with a flourish, "Three dollars and fifty cents and till death do you part!" and yanked some forms out of a machine.

Marriage did not change Sarah Ruth a jot and it made Parker gloomier than ever. Every morning he decided he had had enough and would not return that night; every night he returned. Whenever Parker couldn't stand the way he felt, he would have another tattoo, but the only surface left on him now was his back. To see a tattoo on his own back he would have to get two mirrors and stand between them in just the correct position and this seemed to Parker a good way to make an idiot of himself. Sarah Ruth who, if she had had better sense, could have enjoyed a tattoo on his back, would not even look at the ones he had elsewhere. When he attempted to point out especial details of them, she would shut her eyes tight and turn her back as well. Except in total darkness, she preferred Parker dressed and with his sleeves rolled down.

"At the judgement seat of God, Jesus is going to say to you, 'What you been doing all your life besides have pictures drawn all over you?' " she said.

"You don't fool me none," Parker said, "you're just afraid that hefty girl I work for'll like me so much she'll say, 'Come on, Mr. Parker, let's you and me . . .' "

"You're tempting sin," she said, "and at the judgement seat of God you'll have to answer for that too. You ought to go back to selling the fruits of the earth."

Parker did nothing much when he was at home but

listen to what the judgement seat of God would be like for him if he didn't change his ways. When he could, he broke in with tales of the hefty girl he worked for. " 'Mr. Parker,' " he said she said, 'I hired you for your brains.' " (She had added, "So why don't you use them?")

"And you should have seen her face the first time she saw me without my shirt," he said. " 'Mr. Parker,' she said, 'you're a walking panner-rammer!' " This had, in fact, been her remark but it had been delivered out of one side of her mouth.

Dissatisfaction began to grow so great in Parker that there was no containing it outside of a tattoo. It had to be his back. There was no help for it. A dim half-formed inspiration began to work in his mind. He visualized having a tattoo put there that Sarah Ruth would not be able to resist—a religious subject. He thought of an open book with HOLY BIBLE tattooed under it and an actual verse printed on the page. This seemed just the thing for a while; then he began to hear her say, "Ain't I already got a real Bible? What you think I want to read the same verse over and over for when I can read it all?" He needed something better even than the Bible! He thought about it so much that he began to lose sleep. He was already losing flesh—Sarah Ruth just threw food in the pot and let it boil. Not knowing for certain why he continued to stay with a woman who was both ugly and pregnant and no cook made him generally nervous and irritable, and he developed a little tic in the side of his face.

Once or twice he found himself turning around abruptly as if someone were trailing him. He had had a granddaddy who had ended in the state mental hospital, although not until he was seventy-five, but as urgent as it might be for him to get a tattoo, it was just as urgent that he get exactly the right one to bring Sarah Ruth to heel. As he continued to worry over it, his eyes took on a hollow preoccupied expression. The old woman he worked for told him that if he couldn't keep his mind on what he was doing, she knew where she could find a fourteen-year-old colored boy who could. Parker was too preoccupied even to be offended. At any time previous, he would have left her then and there, saying drily, "Well, you go ahead on and get him then."

Two or three mornings later he was baling hay with the old woman's sorry baler and her broken down tractor in a large field, cleared save for one enormous old tree standing in the middle of it. The old woman was the kind who would not cut down a large old tree because it was a large old tree. She had pointed it out to Parker as if he didn't have eyes and told him to be careful not to hit it as the machine picked up hay near it. Parker began at the outside of the field and made circles inward toward it. He had to get off the tractor every now and then and untangle the baling cord or kick a rock out of the way. The old woman had told him to carry the rocks to the edge of the field, which he did when she was there watching. When he thought he could make it, he ran over them. As he circled the field his mind was on a suitable design for his back. The sun, the size of a golf ball, began to switch regularly from in front to behind him, but he appeared to see it both places as if he had eyes in the back of his head. All at once he saw the tree reaching out to grasp him. A ferocious thud propelled him into the air, and he heard himself yelling in an unbelievably loud voice, "GOD ABOVE!"

He landed on his back while the tractor crashed upside-down into the tree and burst into flame. The first thing Parker saw were his shoes, quickly being eaten by the fire; one was caught under the tractor, the other was some distance away, burning by itself. He was not in them. He could feel the hot breath of the burning tree on his face. He scrambled backwards, still sitting, his eyes cavernous, and if he had known how to cross himself he would have done it.

His truck was on a dirt road at the edge of the field. He moved toward it, still sitting, still backwards, but faster and faster; halfway to it he got up and began a kind of forward-bent run from which he collapsed on his knees twice. His legs felt like two old rusted rain gutters. He reached the truck finally and took off in it, zigzagging up the road. He drove past his house on the embankment and straight for the city, fifty miles distant.

Parker did not allow himself to think on the way to the city. He only knew that there had been a great change in his life, a leap forward into a worse unknown, and that there was nothing he could do about it. It was for all intents accomplished.

The artist had two large cluttered rooms over a chiropodist's office on a back street. Parker, still barefooted, burst silently in on him at a little after three in the afternoon. The artist, who was about Parker's own age—twenty-eight—but thin and bald, was behind a small drawing table, tracing a design in green ink. He looked up with an annoyed glance and did not seem to recognize Parker in the hollow-eyed creature before him.

"Let me see the book you got with all the pictures of God in it," Parker said breathlessly. "The religious one."

The artist continued to look at him with his intellectual, superior stare. "I don't put tattoos on drunks," he said.

"You know me!" Parker cried indignantly. "I'm O. E. Parker! You done work for me before and I always paid!"

The artist looked at him another moment as if he were

not altogether sure. "You've fallen off some," he said. "You must have been in jail."

"Married," Parker said.

"Oh," said the artist. With the aid of mirrors the artist had tattooed on the top of his head a miniature owl, perfect in every detail. It was about the size of a half-dollar and served him as a show piece. There were cheaper artists in town but Parker had never wanted anything but the best. The artist went over to a cabinet at the back of the room and began to look over some art books. "Who are you interested in?" he said, "saints, angels, Christs or what?"

"God," Parker said.

"Father, Son or Spirit?"

"Just God," Parker said impatiently. "Christ. I don't care. Just so it's God."

The artist returned with a book. He moved some papers off another table and put the book down on it and told Parker to sit down and see what he liked. "The up-t-date ones are in the back," he said.

Parker sat down with the book and wet his thumb. He began to go through it, beginning at the back where the up-to-date pictures were. Some of them he recognized—The Good Shepherd, Forbid Them Not, The Smiling Jesus, Jesus the Physician's Friend, but he kept turning rapidly backwards and the pictures became less and less reassuring. One showed a gaunt green dead face streaked with blood. One was yellow with sagging purple eyes. Parker's heart began to beat faster and faster until it appeared to be roaring inside him like a great generator. He flipped the pages quickly, feeling that when he reached the one ordained, a sign would come. He continued to flip through until he had almost reached the front of the book. On one of the pages a pair of eyes glanced at him swiftly. Parker sped on, then stopped. His heart too appeared to cut off; there was absolute silence. It said as plainly as if silence were a language itself, GO BACK.

Parker returned to the picture—the haloed head of a flat stern Byzantine Christ with all-demanding eyes. He sat there trembling; his heart began slowly to beat again as if it were being brought to life by a subtle power.

"You found what you want?" the artist asked.

Parker's throat was too dry to speak. He got up and thrust the book at the artist, opened at the picture.

"That'll cost you plenty," the artist said. "You don't want all those little blocks though, just the outline and some better features."

"Just like it is," Parker said, "just like it is or nothing."

"It's your funeral," the artist said, "but I don't do that kind of work for nothing."

"How much?" Parker asked.

"It'll take maybe two days work."

"How much?" Parker said.

"On time or cash?" the artist asked. Parker's other jobs had been on time, but he had paid.

"Ten down and ten for every day it takes," the artist said.

Parker drew ten dollar bills out of his wallet; he had three left in.

"You come back in the morning," the artist said, putting the money in his own pocket. "First I'll have to trace that out of the book."

"No no!" Parker said. "Trace it now or gimme my money back," and his eyes blared as if he were ready for a fight.

The artist agreed. Any one stupid enough to want a Christ on his back, he reasoned, would be just as likely as not to change his mind the next minute, but once the work was begun he could hardly do so.

While he worked on the tracing, he told Parker to go wash his back at the sink with the special soap he used there. Parker did it and returned to pace back and forth across the room, nervously flexing his shoulders. He wanted to go look at the picture again but at the same time he did not want to. The artist got up finally and had Parker lie down on the table. He swabbed his back with ethyl chloride and then began to outline the head on it with his iodine pencil. Another hour passed before he took up his electric instrument. Parker felt no particular pain. In Japan he had had a tattoo of the Buddha done on his upper arm with ivory needles; in Burma, a little brown root of a man had made a peacock on each of his knees using thin pointed sticks, two feet long; amateurs had worked on him with pins and soot. Parker was usually so relaxed and easy under the hand of the artist that he often went to sleep, but this time he remained awake, every muscle taut.

At midnight the artist said he was ready to quit. He propped one mirror, four feet square, on a table by the wall and took a smaller mirror off the lavatory wall and put it in Parker's hands. Parker stood with his back to the one on the table and moved the other until he saw a flashing burst of color reflected from his back. It was almost completely covered with little red and blue and ivory and saffron squares; from them he made out the lineaments of the face—a mouth, the beginning of heavy brows, a straight nose, but the face was empty; the eyes had not yet been put in. The impression for the moment was almost as if the artist had tricked him and done the Physician's Friend.

"It don't have eyes," Parker cried out.

"That'll come," the artist said, "in due time. We have another day to go on it yet."

Parker spent the night on a cot at the Haven of Light Christian Mission. He found these the best places to stay in the city because they were free and included a meal of sorts. He got the last available cot and because he was still barefooted, he accepted a pair of second-hand shoes which, in his confusion, he put on to go to bed; he was still shocked from all that had happened to him. All night he lay awake in the long dormitory of cots with lumpy figures on them. The only light was from a phosphorescent cross glowing at the end of the room. The tree reached out to grasp him again, then burst into flame; the shoe burned quietly by itself; the eyes in the book said to him distinctly GO BACK and at the same time did not utter a sound. He wished that he were not in this city, not in this Haven of Light Mission, not in a bed by himself. He longed miserably for Sarah Ruth. Her sharp tongue and icepick eyes were the only comfort he could bring to mind. He decided he was losing it. Her eyes appeared soft and dilatory compared with the eyes in the book, for even though he could not summon up the exact look of those eyes, he could still feel their penetration. He felt as though, under their gaze, he was as transparent as the wing of a fly.

The tattooist had told him not to come until ten in the morning, but when he arrived at that hour, Parker was sitting in the dark hallway on the floor, waiting for him. He had decided upon getting up that, once the tattoo was on him, he would not look at it, that all his sensations of the day and night before were those of a crazy man and that he would return to doing things according to his own sound judgement.

The artist began where he left off. "One thing I want

to know," he said presently as he worked over Parker's back, "why do you want this on you? Have you gone and got religion? Are you saved?" he asked in a mocking voice.

Parker's throat felt salty and dry. "Naw," he said, "I ain't got no use for none of that. A man can't save his self from whatever it is he don't deserve none of my sympathy." These words seemed to leave his mouth like wraiths and to evaporate at once as if he had never uttered them.

"Then why . . ."

"I married this woman that's saved," Parker said. "I never should have done it. I ought to leave her. She's done gone and got pregnant."

"That's too bad," the artist said. "Then it's her making you have this tattoo."

"Naw," Parker said, "she don't know nothing about it. It's a surprise for her."

"You think she'll like it and lay off you a while?"

"She can't hep herself," Parker said. "She can't say she don't like the looks of God." He decided he had told the artist enough of his business. Artists were all right in their place but he didn't like them poking their noses into the affairs of regular people. "I didn't get no sleep last night," he said. "I think I'll get some now."

That closed the mouth of the artist but it did not bring him any sleep. He lay there, imagining how Sarah Ruth would be struck speechless by the face on his back and every now and then this would be interrupted by a vision of the tree of fire and his empty shoe burning beneath it.

The artist worked steadily until nearly four o'clock, not stopping to have lunch, hardly pausing with the electric instrument except to wipe the dripping dye off Parker's back as he went along. Finally he finished. "You can get up and look at it now," he said.

Parker sat up but he remained on the edge of the table.

The artist was pleased with his work and wanted Parker to look at it at once. Instead Parker continued to sit on the edge of the table, bent forward slightly but with a vacant look. "What ails you?" the artist said. "Go look at it."

"Ain't nothing ail me," Parker said in a sudden belligerent voice. "That tattoo ain't going nowhere. It'll be there when I get there." He reached for his shirt and began gingerly to put it on.

The artist took him roughly by the arm and propelled him between the two mirrors. "Now *look*," he said, angry at having his work ignored.

Parker looked, turned white and moved away. The eyes in the reflected face continued to look at him—still, straight, all-demanding, enclosed in silence.

"It was your idea, remember," the artist said. "I would have advised something else."

Parker said nothing. He put on his shirt and went out the door while the artist shouted, "I'll expect all of my money!"

Parker headed toward a package shop on the corner. He bought a pint of whiskey and took it into a nearby alley and drank it all in five minutes. Then he moved on to a pool hall nearby which he frequented when he came to the city. It was a well-lighted barn-like place with a bar up one side and gambling machines on the other and pool tables in the back. As soon as Parker entered, a large man in a red and black checkered shirt hailed him by slapping him on the back and yelling, "Yeyyyyyy boy! O. E. Parker!"

Parker was not yet ready to be struck on the back. "Lay off," he said, "I got a fresh tattoo there."

"What you got this time?" the man asked and then

yelled to a few at the machines. "O.E.'s got him another tattoo."

"Nothing special this time," Parker said and slunk over to a machine that was not being used.

"Come on," the big man said, "let's have a look at O.E.'s tattoo," and while Parker squirmed in their hands, they pulled up his shirt. Parker felt all the hands drop away instantly and his shirt fell again like a veil over the face. There was a silence in the pool room which seemed to Parker to grow from the circle around him until it extended to the foundations under the building and upward through the beams in the roof.

Finally some one said, "Christ!" Then they all broke into noise at once. Parker turned around, an uncertain grin on his face.

"Leave it to O.E.!" the man in the checkered shirt said. "That boy's a real card!"

"Maybe he's gone and got religion," some one yelled.

"Not on your life," Parker said.

"O.E.'s got religion and is witnessing for Jesus, ain't you, O.E.?" a little man with a piece of cigar in his mouth said wryly. "An o-riginal way to do it if I ever saw one."

"Leave it to Parker to think of a new one!" the fat man said.

"Yyeeeeeeyyyyyyy boy!" someone yelled and they all began to whistle and curse in compliment until Parker said, "Aaa shut up."

"What'd you do it for?" somebody asked.

"For laughs," Parker said. "What's it to you?"

"Why ain't you laughing then?" somebody yelled. Parker lunged into the midst of them and like a whirlwind on a summer's day there began a fight that raged amid overturned tables and swinging fists until two of them grabbed him and ran to the door with him and threw him out. Then a calm descended on the pool hall as nerve shattering as if the long barn-like room were the ship from which Jonah had been cast into the sea.

Parker sat for a long time on the ground in the alley behind the pool hall, examining his soul. He saw it as a spider web of facts and lies that was not at all important to him but which appeared to be necessary in spite of his opinion. The eyes that were now forever on his back were eyes to be obeyed. He was as certain of it as he had ever been of anything. Throughout his life, grumbling and sometimes cursing, often afraid, once in rapture, Parker had obeyed whatever instinct of this kind had come to him—in rapture when his spirit had lifted at the sight of the tattooed man at the fair, afraid when he had joined the navy, grumbling when he had married Sarah Ruth.

The thought of her brought him slowly to his feet. She would know what he had to do. She would clear up the rest of it, and she would at least be pleased. It seemed to him that, all along, that was what he wanted, to please her. His truck was still parked in front of the building where the artist had his place, but it was not far away. He got in it and drove out of the city and into the country night. His head was almost clear of liquor and he observed that his dissatisfaction was gone, but he felt not quite like himself. It was as if he were himself but a stranger to himself, driving into a new country though everything he saw was familiar to him, even at night.

He arrived finally at the house on the embankment, pulled the truck under the pecan tree and got out. He made as much noise as possible to assert that he was still in charge here, that his leaving her for a night without word meant nothing except it was the way he did things. He slammed the car door, stamped up the two steps and across the porch and rattled the door knob. It did not respond to his touch. "Sarah Ruth!" he yelled, "let me in."

There was no lock on the door and she had evidently placed the back of a chair against the knob. He began to beat on the door and rattle the knob at the same time.

He heard the bed springs screak and bent down and put his head to the keyhole, but it was stopped up with paper. "Let me in!" he hollered, bamming on the door again. "What you got me locked out for?"

A sharp voice close to the door said, "Who's there?"

"Me," Parker said, "O.E."

He waited a moment.

"Me," he said impatiently, "O.E."

Still no sound from inside.

He tried once more. "O.E.," he said, bamming the door two or three more times. "O. E. Parker. You know me."

There was a silence. Then the voice said slowly, "I don't know no O.E."

"Quit fooling," Parker pleaded. "You ain't got any business doing me this way. It's me, old O.E., I'm back. You ain't afraid of me."

"Who's there?" the same unfeeling voice said.

Parker turned his head as if he expected someone behind him to give him the answer. The sky had lightened slightly and there were two or three streaks of yellow floating above the horizon. Then as he stood there, a tree of light burst over the skyline.

Parker fell back against the door as if he had been pinned there by a lance.

"Who's there?" the voice from inside said and there was a quality about it now that seemed final. The knob rattled and the voice said peremptorily, "Who's there, I ast you?"

Parker bent down and put his mouth near the stuffed keyhole. "Obadiah," he whispered and all at once he felt the light pouring through him, turning his spider web soul into a perfect arabesque of colors, a garden of trees and birds and beasts.

"Obadiah Elihue!" he whispered.

The door opened and he stumbled in. Sarah Ruth loomed there, hands on her hips. She began at once, "That was no hefty blonde woman you was working for and you'll have to pay her every penny on her tractor you busted up. She don't keep insurance on it. She came here and her and me had us a long talk and I . . ."

Trembling, Parker set about lighting the kerosene lamp.

"What's the matter with you, wasting that keresene this near daylight?" she demanded. "I ain't got to look at you."

A yellow glow enveloped them. Parker put the match down and began to unbutton his shirt.

"And you ain't going to have none of me this near morning," she said.

"Shut your mouth," he said quietly. "Look at this and then I don't want to hear no more out of you." He removed the shirt and turned his back to her.

"Another picture," Sarah Ruth growled. "I might have known you was off after putting some more trash on yourself."

Parker's knees went hollow under him. He wheeled around and cried, "Look at it! Don't just say that! *Look* at it!"

"I done looked," she said.

"Don't you know who it is?" he cried in anguish.

"No, who is it?" Sarah Ruth said. "It ain't anybody I know."

"It's him," Parker said.

"Him who?"

"God!" Parker cried.

"God? God don't look like that!"

"What do you know how he looks?" Parker moaned. "You ain't seen him."

"He don't *look*," Sarah Ruth said. "He's a spirit. No man shall see his face."

"Aw listen," Parker groaned, "this is just a picture of him."

"Idolatry!" Sarah Ruth screamed. "Idolatry! Enflaming yourself with idols under every green tree! I can put up with lies and vanity but I don't want no idolator in this house!" and she grabbed up the broom and began to thrash him across the shoulders with it.

Parker was too stunned to resist. He sat there and let her beat him until she had nearly knocked him senseless and large welts had formed on the face of the tattooed Christ. Then he staggered up and made for the door.

She stamped the broom two or three times on the floor and went to the window and shook it out to get the taint of him off it. Still gripping it, she looked toward the pecan tree and her eyes hardened still more. There he was—who called himself Obadiah Elihue—leaning against the tree, crying like a baby.

Judgement Day

Tanner was conserving all his strength for the trip home. He meant to walk as far as he could get and trust to the Almighty to get him the rest of the way. That morning and the morning before, he had allowed his daughter to dress him and had conserved that much more energy. Now he sat in the chair by the window—his blue shirt buttoned at the collar, his coat on the back of the chair, and his hat on his head—waiting for her to leave. He couldn't escape until she got out of the way. The window looked out on a brick wall and down into an alley full of New York air, the kind fit for cats and garbage. A few snow flakes drifted past the window but they were too thin and scattered for his failing vision.

The daughter was in the kitchen washing dishes. She dawdled over everything, talking to herself. When he had first come, he had answered her, but that had not been wanted. She glowered at him as if, old fool that he was, he should still have had sense enough not to answer a woman talking to herself. She questioned herself in one voice and answered herself in another. With the energy he had conserved yesterday letting her dress him, he had written a note and pinned it in his pocket. IF FOUND DEAD SHIP EXPRESS COLLECT TO COLEMAN PARRUM, CORINTH, GEORGIA. Under this he had continued: COLEMAN SELL MY BELONGINGS AND PAY THE FREIGHT ON ME & THE UNDERTAKER. ANYTHING LEFT OVER YOU CAN KEEP. YOURS TRULY T. C. TANNER. P.S. STAY WHERE YOU ARE. DON'T LET THEM TALK YOU INTO COMING UP HERE. ITS NO KIND OF PLACE. It had taken him the better part of thirty minutes to write the paper; the script was wavery but decipherable with patience. He controlled one hand by holding the other on top of it. By the time he had got it written, she was back in the apartment from getting her groceries.

Today he was ready. All he had to do was push one foot in front of the other until he got to the door and down the steps. Once down the steps, he would get out of the neighborhood. Once out of it, he would hail a taxi cab and go to the freight yards. Some bum would help him onto a car. Once he got in the freight car, he would lie down and rest. During the night the train would start South, and the next day or the morning after, dead or alive, he would be home. Dead or alive. It was being there that mattered; the dead or alive did not.

If he had had good sense he would have gone the day after he arrived; better sense and he would not have arrived. He had not got desperate until two days ago when he had heard his daughter and son-in-law taking leave of each other after breakfast. They were standing in the front door, she seeing him off for a three-day trip. He drove a long distance moving van. She must have handed him his leather headgear. "You ought to get you a hat," she said, "a real one."

"And sit all day in it," the son-in-law said, "like him in there. Yah! All he does is sit all day with that hat on. Sits all day with that damn black hat on his head. Inside!"

"Well you don't even have you a hat," she said. "Nothing but that leather cap with flaps. People that are somebody wear hats. Other kinds wear those leather caps like you got on."

"People that are somebody!" he cried. "People that are somebody! That kills me! That really kills me!" The son-in-law had a stupid muscular face and a yankee voice to go with it.

"My daddy is here to stay," his daughter said. "He ain't going to last long. He was somebody when he was somebody. He never worked for nobody in his life but himself and had people—other people—working for him."

"Yah? Niggers is what he had working for him," the son-in-law said. "That's all. I've worked a nigger or two myself."

"Those were just nawthun niggers you worked," she said, her voice suddenly going lower so that Tanner had to lean forward to catch the words. "It takes brains to work a real nigger. You got to know how to handle them."

"Yah so I don't have brains," the son-in-law said.

One of the sudden, very occasional, feelings of warmth for the daughter came over Tanner. Every now and then she said something that might make you think she had a little sense stored away somewhere for safe keeping.

"You got them," she said. "You don't always use them."

"He has a stroke when he sees a nigger in the building," the son-in-law said, "and she tells me . . ."

"Shut up talking so loud," she said. "That's not why he had the stroke."

There was a silence. "Where you going to bury him?" the son-in-law asked, taking a different tack.

"Bury who?"

"Him in there."

"Right here in New York," she said. "Where do you think? We got a lot. I'm not taking that trip down there again with nobody."

"Yah. Well I just wanted to make sure," he said.

When she returned to the room, Tanner had both hands gripped on the chair arms. His eyes were trained on her like the eyes of an angry corpse. "You promised you'd bury me there," he said. "Your promise ain't any good. Your promise ain't any good. Your promise ain't any good." His voice was so dry it was barely audible. He began to shake, his hands, his head, his feet. "Bury me here and burn in hell!" he cried and fell back into his chair.

The daughter shuddered to attention. "You ain't dead yet!" She threw out a ponderous sigh. "You got a long time to be worrying about that." She turned and began to pick up parts of the newspaper scattered on the floor. She had grey hair that hung to her shoulders and a round face, beginning to wear. "I do every last living thing for you," she muttered, "and this is the way you carry on." She stuck the papers under her arm and said, "And don't throw hell at me. I don't believe in it. That's a lot of hardshell Baptist hooey." Then she went into the kitchen.

He kept his mouth stretched taut, his top plate gripped between his tongue and the roof of his mouth. Still the tears flooded down his cheeks; he wiped each one furtively on his shoulder.

Her voice rose from the kitchen. "As bad as having a child. He wanted to come and now he's here, he don't like it."

He had not wanted to come.

"Pretended he didn't but I could tell. I said if you don't want to come I can't make you. If you don't want to live like decent people there's nothing I can do about it."

"As for me," her higher voice said, "when I die that ain't the time I'm going to start getting choosey. They can lay me in the nearest spot. When I pass from this world I'll be considerate of them that stay in it. I won't be thinking of just myself."

"Certainly not," the other voice said, "You never been that selfish. You're the kind that looks out for other people."

"Well I try," she said, "I try."

He laid his head on the back of the chair for a moment and the hat tilted down over his eyes. He had raised three boys and her. The three boys were gone, two in the war and one to the devil and there was nobody left who felt a duty toward him but her, married and childless, in New York City like Mrs. Big and ready when she came back and found him living the way he was to take him back with her. She had put her face in the door of the shack and had stared, expressionless, for a second. Then all at once she had screamed and jumped back.

"What's that on the floor?"

"Coleman," he said.

The old Negro was curled up on a pallet asleep at the foot of Tanner's bed, a stinking skin full of bones, arranged in what seemed vaguely human form. When Coleman was young, he had looked like a bear; now that he was old he looked like a monkey. With Tanner it was the opposite; when he was young he had looked like a monkey but when he got old, he looked like a bear.

The daughter stepped back onto the porch. There were the bottoms of two cane chairs tilted against the clapboard but she declined to take a seat. She stepped out about ten feet from the house as if it took that much space to clear the odor. Then she had spoken her piece.

"If you don't have any pride I have and I know my duty and I was raised to do it. My mother raised me to do it if you didn't. She was from plain people but not the kind that likes to settle in with niggers."

At that point the old Negro roused up and slid out the door, a doubled-up shadow which Tanner just caught sight of gliding away.

She had shamed him. He shouted so they both could hear. "Who you think cooks? Who you think cuts my firewood and empties my slops? He's paroled to me. That no-good scoundrel has been on my hands for thirty years. He ain't a bad nigger."

She was unimpressed. "Whose shack is this anyway?" she had asked. "Yours or his?"

"Him and me built it," he said. "You go on back up there. I wouldn't come with you for no million dollars or no sack of salt."

"It looks like him and you built it. Whose land is it on?"

"Some people that live in Florida," he said evasively. He had known then that it was land up for sale but he thought it was too sorry for anyone to buy. That same afternoon he had found out different. He had found out in time to go back with her. If he had found out a day later, he might still be there, squatting on the doctor's land.

When he saw the brown porpoise-shaped figure striding across the field that afternoon, he had known at once what had happened; no one had to tell him. If that nigger had owned the whole world except for one runty rutted peafield and he acquired it, he would walk across it that way, beating the weeds aside, his thick neck swelled, his stomach a throne for his gold watch and chain. Doctor Foley. He was only part black. The rest was Indian and white.

He was everything to the niggers—druggist and undertaker and general counsel and real estate man and sometimes he got the evil eye off them and sometimes he put it on. Be prepared, he said to himself, watching him approach, to take something off him, nigger though he be. Be prepared, because you ain't got a thing to hold up to him but the skin you come in, and that's no more use to you now than what a snake would shed. You don't have a chance with the government against you.

He was sitting on the porch in the piece of straight chair tilted against the shack. "Good evening, Foley," he said and nodded as the doctor came up and stopped short at the edge of the clearing, as if he had only just that minute seen him though it was plain he had sighted him as he crossed the field.

"I be out here to look at my property," the doctor said. "Good evening." His voice was quick and high.

Ain't been your property long, he said to himself. "I seen you coming," he said.

"I acquired this here recently," the doctor said and proceeded without looking at him again to walk around to one side of the shack. In a moment he came back and stopped in front of him. Then he stepped boldly to the door of the shack and put his head in. Coleman was in there that time too, asleep. He looked for a moment and then turned aside. "I know that nigger," he said. "Coleman Parrum—how long does it take him to sleep off that stump liquor you all make?"

Tanner took hold of the knobs on the chair bottom and held them hard. "This shack ain't in your property. Only on it, by my mistake," he said.

The Doctor removed his cigar momentarily from his mouth. "It ain't my mis-take," he said and smiled.

He had only sat there, looking ahead.

"It don't pay to make this kind of mis-take," the doctor said.

"I never found nothing that paid yet," he muttered.

"Everything pays," the Negro said, "if you knows how to make it," and he remained there smiling, looking the squatter up and down. Then he turned and went around the other side of the shack. There was a silence. He was looking for the still.

Then would have been the time to kill him. There was a gun inside the shack and he could have done it as easy as not, but, from childhood, he had been weakened for that kind of violence by the fear of hell. He had never killed one, he had always handled them with his wits and with luck. He was known to have a way with niggers. There was an art to handling them. The secret of handling a nigger was to show him his brains didn't have a chance against yours; then he would jump on your back and know he had a good thing there for life. He had had Coleman on his back for thirty years.

Tanner had first seen Coleman when he was working six of them at a saw mill in the middle of a pine forest fifteen miles from nowhere. They were as sorry a crew as he had worked, the kind that on Monday they didn't show up. What was in the air had reached them. They thought there was a new Lincoln elected who was going to abolish work. He managed them with a very sharp penknife. He had had something wrong with his kidney then that made his hands shake and he had taken to whittling to force that waste motion out of sight. He did not intend them to see that his hands shook of their own accord and he did not intend to see it himself or to countenance it. The knife had moved constantly, violently, in his quaking hands and here and there small crude figures—that he never looked at again and could not have said what they were if he had—dropped to the ground. The Negroes picked them up and took them home; there was not much time between them and darkest Africa. The knife glittered constantly in his hands. More than once he had stopped short and said in an off-hand voice to some half-reclining, head-averted Negro, "Nigger, this knife is in my hand now but if you don't quit wasting my time and money, it'll be in your gut shortly." And the Negro would begin to rise—slowly, but he would be in the act—before the sentence was completed.

A large black loose-jointed Negro, twice his own size, had begun hanging around the edge of the saw mill, watching the others work and when he was not watching, sleeping, in full view of them, sprawled like a gigantic bear on his back. "Who is that?" he had asked. "If he wants to work, tell him to come here. If he don't, tell him to go. No idlers are going to hang around here."

None of them knew who he was. They knew he didn't want to work. They knew nothing else, not where he had come from, nor why, though he was probably brother to one, cousin to all of them. He had ignored him for a day; against the six of them he was one yellow-faced scrawny white man with shaky hands. He was willing to wait for trouble, but not forever. The next day the stranger came again. After the six Tanner worked had seen the idler there for half the morning, they quit and began to eat, a full thirty minutes before noon. He had not risked ordering them up. He had gone to the source of the trouble.

The stranger was leaning against a tree on the edge of the clearing, watching with half-closed eyes. The insolence on his face barely covered the wariness behind it. His look said, this ain't much of a white man so why he come on so big, what he fixing to do?

He had meant to say, "Nigger, this knife is in my hand now but if you ain't out of my sight . . ." but as he drew closer he changed his mind. The Negro's eyes were small and bloodshot. Tanner supposed there was a knife on him somewhere that he would as soon use as not. His own penknife moved, directed solely by some intruding intelligence that worked in his hands. He had no idea what he was carving, but when he reached the Negro, he had already made two holes the size of half dollars in the piece of bark.

The Negro's gaze fell on his hands and was held. His jaw slackened. His eyes did not move from the knife tearing recklessly around the bark. He watched as if he saw an invisible power working on the wood.

He looked himself then and, astonished, saw the connected rims of a pair of spectacles.

He held them away from him and looked through the holes past a pile of shavings and on into the woods to the edge of the pen where they kept their mules.

"You can't see so good, can you, boy?" he said and began scraping the ground with his foot to turn up a piece of wire. He picked up a small piece of haywire; in a minute he found another, shorter piece and picked that up. He began to attach these to the bark. He was in no hurry now that he knew what he was doing. When the spectacles were finished, he handed them to the Negro. "Put these on," he said. "I hate to see anybody can't see good."

There was an instant when the Negro might have done one thing or another, might have taken the glasses and crushed them in his hand or grabbed the knife and turned it on him. He saw the exact instant in the muddy liquor-swollen eyes when the pleasure of having a knife in this white man's gut was balanced against something else, he could not tell what.

The Negro reached for the glasses. He attached the bows carefully behind his ears and looked forth. He peered this way and that with exaggerated solemnity. And then he looked directly at Tanner and grinned, or grimaced, Tanner could not tell which, but he had an instant's sensation of seeing before him a negative image of himself, as if clownishness and captivity had been their common lot. The vision failed him before he could decipher it.

"Preacher," he said, "what you hanging around here for?" He picked up another piece of bark and began, without looking at it, to carve again. "This ain't Sunday."

"This here ain't Sunday?" the Negro said.

"This is Friday," he said. "That's the way it is with you preachers—drunk all week so you don't know when Sunday is. What you see through those glasses?"

"See a man."

"What kind of a man?"

"See the man make theseyer glasses."

"Is he white or black?"

"He white!" the Negro said as if only at that moment was his vision sufficiently improved to detect it. "Yessuh, he white!" he said.

"Well, you treat him like he was white," Tanner said. "What's your name?"

"Name Coleman," the Negro said.

And he had not got rid of Coleman since. You make a monkey out of one of them and he jumps on your back and stays there for life, but let one make a monkey out of you and all you can do is kill him or disappear. And he was not going to hell for killing a nigger. Behind the shack he heard the doctor kick over a bucket. He sat and waited.

In a moment the doctor appeared again, beating his way around the other side of the house, whacking at scattered clumps of Johnson grass with his cane. He stopped in the middle of the yard, about where that morning the daughter had delivered her ultimatum.

"You don't belong here," he began. "I could have you prosecuted."

Tanner remained there, dumb, staring across the field.

"Where's your still?" the doctor asked.

"If it's a still around here, it don't belong to me," he said and shut his mouth tight.

The Negro laughed softly. "Down on your luck, ain't you?" he murmured. "Didn't you used to own a little piece of land over acrost the river and lost it?"

He had continued to study the woods ahead.

"If you want to run the still for me, that's one thing," the doctor said. "If you don't, you might as well had be packing up."

"I don't have to work for you," he said. "The governmint ain't got around yet to forcing the white folks to work for the colored."

The doctor polished the stone in his ring with the ball of his thumb. "I don't like the governmint no bettern you," he said. "Where you going instead? You going to the city and get you a soot of rooms at the Biltmo' Hotel?"

Tanner said nothing.

"The day coming," the doctor said, "when the white folks IS going to be working for the colored and you mights well to git ahead of the crowd."

"That day ain't coming for me," Tanner said shortly.

"Done come for you," the doctor said. "Ain't come for the rest of them."

Tanner's gaze drove on past the farthest blue edge of the treeline into the pale empty afternoon sky. "I got a daughter in the north," he said. "I don't have to work for you."

The doctor took his watch from his watch pocket and looked at it and put it back. He gazed for a moment at the back of his hands. He appeared to have measured and to know secretly the time it would take everything to change finally upsidedown. "She don't want no old daddy like you," he said. "Maybe she say she do, but that ain't likely. Even if you rich," he said, "they don't want you. They got they own ideas. The black ones they rares and they pitches. I made mine," he said, "and I ain't done none of that." He looked again at Tanner. "I be back here next week," he said, "and if you still here, I know you going to work for me." He remained there a moment, rocking on his heels, waiting for some answer. Finally he turned and started beating his way back through the overgrown path.

Tanner had continued to look across the field as if his spirit had been sucked out of him into the woods and nothing was left on the chair but a shell. If he had known it was a question of this—sitting here looking out of this window all day in this no-place, or just running a still for a nigger, he would have run the still for the nigger. He would have been a nigger's white nigger any day. Behind him he heard the daughter come in from the kitchen. His heart accelerated but after a second he heard her plump herself down on the sofa. She was not yet ready to go. He did not turn and look at her.

She sat there silently a few moments. Then she began. "The trouble with you is," she said, "you sit in front of that window all the time where there's nothing to look out at. You need some inspiration and an out-let. If you would let me pull your chair around to look at the TV, you would quit thinking about morbid stuff, death and hell and judgement. My Lord."

"The Judgement is coming," he muttered. "The sheep'll be separated from the goats. Them that kept their promises from them that didn't. Them that did the best they could with what they had from them that didn't. Them that honored their father and their mother from them that cursed them. Them that . . ."

She heaved a mammoth sigh that all but drowned him out. "What's the use in me wasting my good breath?" she asked. She rose and went back in the kitchen and began knocking things about.

She was so high and mighty! At home he had been living in a shack but there was at least air around it. He could put his feet on the ground. Here she didn't even live in a house. She lived in a pigeon-hutch of a building, with all stripes of foreigner, all of them twisted in the tongue. It was no place for a sane man. The first morning here she had taken him sightseeing and he had seen in fifteen minutes exactly how it was. He had not been out of the apartment since. He never wanted to set foot again on the underground railroad or the steps that moved under you while you stood still or any elevator to the thirty-fourth floor. When he was safely back in the apartment again, he had imagined going over it with Coleman. He had to turn his head every few seconds to make sure Coleman was behind him. Keep to the inside or these people'll knock you down, keep right behind me or you'll get left, keep your hat on, you damn idiot, he had said, and Coleman had come on with his bent running shamble, panting and muttering, What we doing here? Where you get this fool idea coming here?

I come to show you it was no kind of place. Now you know you were well off where you were.

I knowed it before, Coleman said. Was you didn't know it.

When he had been here a week, he had got a postcard from Coleman that had been written for him by Hooten at the railroad station. It was written in green ink and said, "This is Coleman—X—howyou boss." Under it Hooten had written from himself, "Quit frequenting all those nitespots and come on home, you scoundrel, yours truly, W. P. Hooten." He had sent Coleman a card in return, care of Hooten, that said, "This place is alrite if you like it. Yours truly, W. T. Tanner." Since the daughter had to mail the card, he had not put on it that he was returning as soon as his pension check came. He had not intended to tell her but to leave her a note. When the check came, he would hire himself a taxi to the bus station and be on his way. And it would have made her as happy as it made him. She had found his company dour and her duty irksome. If he had sneaked out, she would have had the pleasure of having tried to do it and to top that off, the pleasure of his ingratitude.

As for him, he would have returned to squat on the doctor's land and to take his orders from a nigger who chewed ten-cent cigars. And to think less about it than formerly. Instead he had been done in by a nigger actor, or one who called himself an actor. He didn't believe the nigger was any actor.

There were two apartments on each floor of the building. He had been with the daughter three weeks when the people in the next hutch moved out. He had stood in the hall and watched the moving-out and the next day he had watched a moving-in. The hall was narrow and dark and he stood in the corner out of the way, offering only a suggestion every now and then to the movers that would have made their work easier for them if they had paid any attention. The furniture was new and cheap so he decided the people moving in might be a newly married couple and he would just wait around until they came and wish them well. After a while a large Negro in a light blue suit came lunging up the stairs, carrying two canvas suitcases, his head lowered against the strain. Behind him stepped a young tan-skinned woman with bright copper-colored hair. The Negro dropped the suitcases with a thud in front of the door of the next apartment.

"Be careful, Sweetie," the woman said. "My make-up is in there."

It broke upon him then just what was happening.

The Negro was grinning. He took a swipe at one of her hips.

"Quit it," she said, "there's an old guy watching."

They both turned and looked at him.

"Had-do," he said and nodded. Then he turned quickly into his own door.

His daughter was in the kitchen. "Who you think's rented that apartment over there?" he asked, his face alight.

She looked at him suspiciously. "Who?" she muttered.

"A nigger!" he said in a gleeful voice. "A South Alabama nigger if I ever saw one. And got him this high-yeller, high-stepping woman with red hair and they two are going to live next door to you!" He slapped his knee. "Yes siree!" he said. "Damn if they ain't!" It was the first time since coming up here that he had had occasion to laugh.

Her face squared up instantly. "All right now you listen to me," she said. "You keep away from them. Don't you go over there trying to get friendly with him. They ain't the same around here and I don't want any trouble with niggers, you hear me? If you have to live next to them, just you mind your business and they'll mind theirs. That's the way people were meant to get along in this world. Everybody can get along if they just mind their business. Live and let live." She began to wrinkle her nose like a rabbit, a stupid way she had. "Up here everybody minds their own business and everybody gets along. That's all you have to do."

"I was getting along with niggers before you were born," he said. He went back out into the hall and waited. He was willing to bet the nigger would like to talk to someone who understood him. Twice while he waited, he forgot and in his excitement, spit his tobacco juice against the baseboard. In about twenty minutes, the door of the apartment opened again and the Negro came out. He had put on a tie and a pair of horn-rimmed spectacles and Tanner noticed for the first time that he had a small almost invisible goatee. A real swell. He came on without appearing to see there was anyone else in the hall.

"Haddy, John," Tanner said and nodded, but the Negro brushed past without hearing and went rattling rapidly down the stairs.

Could be deaf and dumb, Tanner thought. He went back into the apartment and sat down but each time he heard a noise in the hall, he got up and went to the door and stuck his head out to see if it might be the Negro. Once in the middle of the afternoon, he caught the Negro's eye just as he was rounding the bend of the stairs again but before he could get out a word, the man was in his own apartment and had slammed the door. He had never known one to move that fast unless the police were after him.

He was standing in the hall early the next morning when the woman came out of her door alone, walking on high gold-painted heels. He wished to bid her good morning or simply to nod but instinct told him to beware. She didn't look like any kind of woman, black or white, he had ever seen before and he remained pressed against the wall, frightened more than anything else, and feigning invisibility.

The woman gave him a flat stare, then turned her head away and stepped wide of him as if she were skirting an open garbage can. He held his breath until she was out of sight. Then he waited patiently for the man.

The Negro came out about eight o'clock.

This time Tanner advanced squarely in his path. "Good morning, Preacher," he said. It had been his experience that if a Negro tended to be sullen, this title usually cleared up his expression.

The Negro stopped abruptly.

"I seen you move in," Tanner said. "I ain't been up here long myself. It ain't much of a place if you ask me. I reckon you wish you were back in South Alabama."

The Negro did not take a step or answer. His eyes began to move. They moved from the top of the black hat, down to the collarless blue shirt, neatly buttoned at the neck, down the faded galluses to the grey trousers and the high-top shoes and up again, very slowly, while some unfathomable dead-cold rage seemed to stiffen and shrink him.

"I thought you might know somewhere around here we could find us a pond, Preacher," Tanner said in a voice growing thinner but still with considerable hope in it.

A seething noise came out of the Negro before he spoke. "I'm not from South Alabama," he said in a breathless wheezing voice. "I'm from New York City. And I'm not no preacher! I'm an actor."

Tanner chortled. "It's a little actor in most preachers, ain't it?" he said and winked. "I reckon you just preach on the side."

"I don't preach!" the Negro cried and rushed past him as if a swarm of bees had suddenly come down on him out of nowhere. He dashed down the stairs and was gone.

Tanner stood there for some time before he went back in the apartment. The rest of the day he sat in his chair and debated whether he would have one more try at making friends with him. Every time he heard a noise on the stairs he went to the door and looked out, but the Negro did not return until late in the afternoon. Tanner was standing in the hall waiting for him when he reached the top of the stairs. "Good evening, preacher," he said, forgetting that the Negro called himself an actor.

The Negro stopped and gripped the banister rail. A tremor racked him from his head to his crotch. Then he began to come forward slowly. When he was close enough he lunged and grasped Tanner by both shoulders. "I don't take no crap," he whispered, "off no wool-hat red-neck son-of-a-bitch peckerwood old bastard like you." He caught his breath. And then his voice came out in the sound of an exasperation so profound that it rocked on the verge of a laugh. It was high and piercing and weak. "And I'm not no preacher! I'm not even no Christian. I don't believe that crap. There ain't no Jesus and there ain't no God."

The old man felt his heart inside him hard and tough as an oak knot. "And you ain't black," he said. "And I ain't white!"

The Negro slammed him against the wall. He yanked the black hat down over his eyes. Then he grabbed his shirt front and shoved him backwards to his open door and knocked him through it. From the kitchen the daughter saw him blindly hit the edge of the inside hall door and fall reeling into the living-room.

For days his tongue appeared to be frozen in his mouth. When it unthawed it was twice its normal size and he could not make her understand him. What he wanted to know was if the government check had come because he meant to buy a bus ticket with it and go home. After a few days, he made her understand. "It came," she said, "and it'll just pay the first two weeks' doctor-bill and please tell me how you're going home when you can't talk or walk or think straight and you got one eye crossed yet? Just please tell me that?"

It had come to him then slowly just what his present situation was. At least he would have to make her understand that he must be sent home to be buried. They could have him shipped back in a refrigerated car so that he would keep for the trip. He didn't want any undertaker up here messing with him. Let them get him off at once and he would come in on the early morning train and they could wire Hooten to get Coleman and Coleman would do the rest; she would not even have to go herself. After a lot of argument, he wrung the promise from her. She would ship him back.

After that he slept peacefully and improved a little. In his dreams he could feel the cold early morning air of home coming in through the cracks of the pine box. He could see Coleman waiting, red-eyed, on the station platform and Hooten standing there with his green eyeshade and black alpaca sleeves. If the old fool had stayed at home where he belonged, Hooten would be thinking, he wouldn't be arriving on the 6:03 in no box. Coleman had turned the borrowed mule and cart so that they could slide the box off the platform onto the open end of the wagon. Everything was ready and the two of them, shut-mouthed, inched the loaded coffin toward the wagon. From inside he began to scratch on the wood. They let go as if it had caught fire.

They stood looking at each other, then at the box.

"That him," Coleman said. "He in there his self."

"Naw," Hooten said, "must be a rat got in there with him."

"That him. This here one of his tricks."

"If it's a rat he might as well stay."

"That him. Git a crowbar."

Hooten went grumbling off and got the crowbar and came back and began to pry open the lid. Even before he had the upper end pried open, Coleman was jumping up and down, wheezing and panting from excitement. Tanner gave a thrust upward with both hands and sprang up in the box. "Judgement Day! Judgement Day!" he cried. "Don't you two fools know it's Judgement Day?"

Now he knew exactly what her promises were worth. He would do as well to trust to the note pinned in his coat and to any stranger who found him dead in the street or in the boxcar or wherever. There was nothing to be looked for from her except that she would do things her way. She came out of the kitchen again, holding her hat and coat and rubber boots.

"Now listen," she said, "I have to go to the store. Don't you try to get up and walk around while I'm gone. You've been to the bathroom and you shouldn't have to go again. I don't want to find you on the floor when I get back."

You won't find me atall when you get back, he said to himself. This was the last time he would see her flat dumb face. He felt guilty. She had been good to him and he had been nothing but a nuisance to her.

"Do you want you a glass of milk before I go?" she asked.

"No," he said. Then he drew breath and said, "You got a nice place here. It's a nice part of the country. I'm sorry if I've give you a lot of trouble getting sick. It was my fault trying to be friendly with that nigger." And I'm a damned liar besides, he said to himself to kill the outrageous taste such a statement made in his mouth.

For a moment she stared as if he were losing his mind. Then she seemed to think better of it. "Now don't saying something pleasant like that once in a while make you feel better?" she asked and sat down on the sofa.

His knees itched to unbend. Git on, git on, he fumed silently. Make haste and go.

"It's great to have you here," she said. "I wouldn't have you any other place. My own daddy." She gave him a big smile and hoisted her right leg up and began to pull on her boot. "I wouldn't wish a dog out on a day like this," she said, "but I got to go. You can sit here and hope I don't slip and break my neck." She stamped the booted foot on the floor and then began to tackle the other one.

He turned his eyes to the window. The snow was beginning to stick and freeze to the outside pane. When he looked at her again, she was standing there like a big doll stuffed into its hat and coat. She drew on a pair of green knitted gloves. "Okay," she said, "I'm gone. You sure you don't want anything?"

"No," he said, "go ahead on."

"Well so long then," she said.

He raised the hat enough to reveal a bald palely speckled head. The hall door closed behind her. He began to tremble with excitement. He reached behind him and drew the coat into his lap. When he got it on, he waited until he had stopped panting, then he gripped the arms of the chair and pulled himself up. His body felt like a great heavy bell whose clapper swung from side to side but made no noise. Once up, he remained standing a moment, swaying until he got his balance. A sensation of terror and defeat swept over him. He would never make it. He would never get there dead or alive. He pushed one foot forward and did not fall and his confidence returned. "The Lord is my shepherd," he muttered, "I shall not want." He began moving toward the sofa where he would have support. He reached it. He was on his way.

By the time he got to the door, she would be down the four flights of steps and out of the building. He got past the sofa and crept along by the wall, keeping his hand on it for support. Nobody was going to bury him here. He was as confident as if the woods of home lay at the bottom of the stairs. He reached the front door of the apartment and opened it and peered into the hall. This was the first time he had looked into it since the actor had knocked him down. It was dank-smelling and empty. The thin piece of linoleum stretched its moldy length to the door of the other apartment, which was closed. "Nigger actor," he said.

The head of the stairs was ten or twelve feet from where he stood and he bent his attention to getting there without creeping around the long way with a hand on the wall. He held his arms a little way out from his sides and pushed forward directly. He was half way there when all at once his legs disappeared, or felt as if they had. He looked down, bewildered, for they were still there. He fell forward and grasped the banister post with both hands. Hanging there, he gazed for what seemed the longest time he had ever looked at anything down the steep unlighted steps;

then he closed his eyes and pitched forward. He landed upsidedown in the middle of the flight.

He felt presently the tilt of the box as they took it off the train and got it on the baggage wagon. He made no noise yet. The train jarred and slid away. In a moment the baggage wagon was rumbling under him, carrying him back to the station side. He heard footsteps rattling closer and closer to him and he supposed that a crowd was gathering. Wait until they see this, he thought.

"That him," Coleman said, "one of his tricks."

"It's a damm rat in there," Hooten said.

"It's him. Git the crowbar."

In a moment a shaft of greenish light fell on him. He pushed through it and cried in a weak voice, "Judgement Day! Judgement Day! You idiots didn't know it was Judgement Day, did you?

"Coleman?" he murmured.

The Negro bending over him had a large surly mouth and sullen eyes.

"Ain't any coal man, either," he said. This must be the wrong station, Tanner thought. Those fools put me off too soon. Who is this nigger? It ain't even daylight here.

At the Negro's side was another face, a woman's—pale, topped with a pile of copper-glinting hair and twisted as if she had just stepped in a pile of dung.

"Oh," Tanner said, "it's you."

The actor leaned closer and grasped him by the front of his shirt. "Judgement day," he said in a mocking voice. "Ain't no judgement day, old man. Cept this. Maybe this here judgement day for you."

Tanner tried to catch hold of a banister-spoke to raise himself but his hand grasped air. The two faces, the black one and the pale one, appeared to be wavering. By an effort of will he kept them focussed before him while he lifted his hand, as light as a breath, and said in his jauntiest voice, "Hep me up, Preacher. I'm on my way home!"

His daughter found him when she came in from the grocery store. His hat had been pulled down over his face and his head and arms thrust between the spokes of the banister; his feet dangled over the stairwell like those of a man in the stocks. She tugged at him frantically and then flew for the police. They cut him out with a saw and said he had been dead about an hour.

She buried him in New York City, but after she had done it she could not sleep at night. Night after night she turned and tossed and very definite lines began to appear in her face, so she had him dug up and shipped the body to Corinth. Now she rests well at night and her good looks have mostly returned.